RUBIES

Samantha McKeating

Published by Samantha McKeating 2011

Acknowledgements

This book has probably been in the making all my life, and my husband has been the rock upon which it has been built. He is unfalteringly patient, and has never tired of my endless bleatings, 'there's a book inside me, I just can't get round to writing it'. He has listened to all my ideas over the last forty years and has supported all of them. He has even thrown ideas in himself. He has never 'expected' the book to be finished. He has just waited patiently until it is. All my children, who inspire me daily, have also waited. But on Christmas Day 2006, they gave me a final push which prompted me to begin writing seriously. Therefore, to Tony, James, Amy, Andrew, Joanne, Cathryn, Ian, and my beautiful grandchildren, I dedicate this, my first novel. Intense love has been the motivation for my first effort to tempt the world with a taste of my imagination and a subsequent hope that the lives of my children and their offspring will be easier than that of their parents.

Mention belongs to Mum and Dad, who strived to give my sister and I a good start in life, on absolutely nothing. It is they who gave me the strength in life to endure those events which shouldn't have to be endured. It is their patience and profound love for us which enabled us to grow in strength of mind and heart and gave us both a deep and sincere love of life and humanity.

My big sister has always had a faith in me which I believe I didn't always deserve. Dorothy knew when I was thirteen and writing letters on flimsy air-mail paper, that, in *her* words 'I had a gift'. I kept some of those letters, and maybe one day I will put all their contents together and who knows what might happen! She too, has waited for this novel, encouraging me with extreme enthusiasm each time the subject arose, and keeping the light burning always in my heart.

There is another person in my life and without her this book would never have been written. She has been my 'literary agent' since I was fifteen. She said then, that she would never give up trying to make me write, and she never did. She has waited with great patience, but has constantly kept the concept of writing foremost in my mind. Doey, you have been my stability for as long as I can remember. You knew I could do it, and you never gave up trying. I cost you a fortune in parking fees, while you sat and listened, while I ate and drank you out of house and home, re-iterating the fact that I wanted to write, but never actually doing it.

Thanks to my friend Pat, who has provided me with a lifetime of friendship. You have consistently gone along with my hair-brained ideas, even though you didn't agree with some of them and hated most of them. You always gave me support and encouragement and inspired some of my heartfelt emotions which began the pen working.

A huge big thank you to Toe, Cath, Dot and Doey for painstakingly proof reading this story and being honest with me. Without your honesty, frank opinions, support and encouragement, I would have fallen by the wayside.

Well here it is world, thanks to every single one mentioned above. I hope you all enjoy this book and continue to inspire me to write.

Email to my sister when I had finished this novel

Hi you, well it's here, it's landed. My 93,000 word novel is sitting on the

desk in front of me. I finished it today (as you know, thanks for message),

and I have just printed it off. Its 138 A4 pages long and has taken fifteen

months to complete. There have been times when I just could not summon the

enthusiasm to get off my butt and go and do it. There have been times when

I have vacuumed, washed dishes, changed beds, gone shopping, visited a

friend and even stayed late at work, JUST so I didn't have to do any more.

There have been nights when I have awoken with such a vivid idea, that I've

run down and immediately switched on the computer and rattled in a couple

of thousand words. There are times when I've sat and written 5,000 words in

one sitting, but never never never, have I not wanted to finish it. I'm

ready world to show you what I'm made of. I'm ready to stand up and be

counted for what I have to say and the way I have to say it. This novel is

a new beginning for my family and I, and I hope the name Samantha McKeating

will resound in countries across the world. Are these the thoughts of every

new aspiring writer? From small beginnings and all that. Well, we're about

to find out. I'm up to editing now. Looks like a long job!!!! Then it's off

for proof reading. Meanwhile Book number 2 is coming up the rear. I've

already mapped out the 'plot' for that one and it's on the drawing board as

we speak. The only character in that one is ...... guess you'll have to

wait and find out!!!! Love you sis, x x x

"We're losing her. We're losing her"

The anaesthetist's concerns that the frail body lying in his care would be unable to endure the operation made him shout louder than usual. He had voiced his concerns earlier. The alternative was certain death. In the adjacent operating theatre lay a woman with similar injuries. Paramedics had attempted resuscitation on arrival at the scene but both women had suffered life-threatening injuries and the race for life was on.

Two off-duty surgeons had been recalled. Medical staff struggled to ascertain next of kin and it took one dedicated member of staff two hours to locate Alan Oliver. He now paced the corridors in a state of utter disbelief that Fiona may not survive the night. Melvin Goodwin paced beside him, devastated that an accident so horrific could befall his wife and her friend.

Carrie and Fiona had been lucky to survive the accident but their families were briefed by the surgeons that they should brace themselves for the worst. Two hours passed and the men silently waited for news while other members of their families sat broken hearted in the waiting room.

* * * * * *

1

Pegu 1323 AD

The golden orb atop the southernmost pinnacle of Mya Palace was glistening in the early morning sunlight. Two large rubies mined at the dawn of mankind had been placed in the orb to ward off marauding warriors and encourage good fortune. They were believed to harness the mystical powers of ancient priests and goddesses. Princess Shariyan believed it was an omen of destiny that they watched over her today. Possessing a perfectly formed statuesque figure, pert silky breasts, a tiny waist, and slender legs supporting sinewy hips and thighs, the stunning beauty stepped out of her bathing pool. Her skin bore an olive complexion. Her dark eyes were wide, alert and evil, her lips full and luscious and her sleek black hair measured down to her waist. Civilisation quivered when her name was spoken. Her dominions cowered in dark corners, terrified of gazing upon her lest she randomly snuff out their life without remorse. Birds refrained from singing. Fables related her transmutation should she be touched intimately, yet no man could doubt her integrity when such beauty radiated before them. Despite their fear, they wanted to take her and make her their own, prevented only by the tragic and terrifying sounds of torture emanating from those who had been bold enough to try. The cries of those who succumbed to desire beyond their control could be heard from the furthest edges of the domain.

Ancient legend prophesied that King Meng Tuu-Kyi would meet his death twelve moons into his daughter's eighteenth year. Today Shariyan's birthright would be complete. She would inherit the Kingdom and rule harshly during her dark dynasty. The Meng Tuu-Kyi rubies would be looted during the Palace's demise and would lie buried for centuries, until a random act of kindness would send them on a journey which would ultimately bring them back to Mya Palace for eternity.

Young ladies darted about the palace, each one augmenting their desire to complete their task, lest not to displease the princess. Some brought bowls of dates and fruit, whilst others laid out her attire. Mylula, the princess's most favoured lady in waiting, gently massaged fruit oil into the princess's silky body. The aroma was that of a delicious citrus cocktail and the substance cooled her skin from the already burning heat of the sun. She draped Shariyan in a finely woven diaphanous silk sari, lightly embroidered with a fine gold thread. She beckoned to the princess to be seated whilst she slipped on her golden sandals. To every eye that would gaze upon her today she would seem flawless, a perfect apparition befitting her title. Her external appearance was indeed unmistakably that of a princess. Shariyan knew her beauty beguiled all men and her political status allured intrigue. This day all men would revere her. The prophecy was imminent and with this thought foremost in her mind, she walked slowly up the opulent stairway to her father's chambers. The shutters on the heavily carved doorway swung back and forth as she entered. The King heard and knew Shariyan was present.

"Good morning my King", she whispered, and curtsied. He knew not whether she mocked him, or if she were merely saying goodbye. He knew doomsday was upon him and did not reply. She turned and left the chamber as slowly as she'd entered. King Meng Tuu-Kyi detected a muffled laugh, followed by raucous laughter as his daughter disappeared through the doorway and he wept.

The North of England 2005

"Carrie – why are you talking so loud? Anyone would think you were excited!

"Excited? Me? Well, I mean - is my itinerary for the next two months anything to get excited about? I'm only flying to New York for the first time in my life. That means serious retail therapy. I keep having oxygen attacks when I think about the plane. How do those things just hang there in the air? Mel said I have to get up and walk about or else I'll develop LVT or something."

"DVT", Fiona corrected, hoping to give Carrie time to draw breath. Carrie continued. "Anyway, I remember the first time I flew. My bottle of wine fell off the tray and rolled to the back of the plane. I was too scared to stand up, so I crawled down the aisle to retrieve it. Mel was sat across the aisle, happened to glance across and I wasn't there. He spun round to look for me and saw me on the floor with a bottle. He says I should conduct myself in a more civilised fashion this time! Then there's the big yellow taxi going over the Hudson. Lisa says it's fantastic when you see the Manhattan skyline for the first time. She says that huge metropolis reaching out before you is breathtaking. And I simply have to ice-skate in Central Park. Our Lisa's Graham says it's a date and he won't take no for an answer."

Carrie momentarily lost herself in a time-warp, remembering vividly the ice-rink on a Saturday afternoon when she was a little girl, a bus ride away for her and her best friend Fiona. The building had been constructed with authentic rustic materials and

Carrie had fantasised she was in a log cabin in the Canadian Rockies with a frozen lake outside the back door. The smell of the ice and the contrasting odour of racks of worn sweaty boots filled her senses. She could still feel the pinch of the gnarled brown boots used by hundreds of other skaters. She remembered her determination to try and get a pair that fitted better next time. How excited she and Fiona had been when they acquired life membership and swore they would ice-skate forever, no matter what.

Carrie jolted back to reality and resumed her chatter with gusto. "The Empire State will be lit up for Valentine's Day, ... and no, I'm not going up!"

"You'll have to go up Carrie. You can't go all the way to New York for Valentine's Day and then not go up the Empire State."

"I don't do heights, remember?"

"Yes, I know but ..."

"No buts. I won't be going up and that's that."

"So what are you going to do? Let Mel go up to the most romantic place in the world on his own? How can you even think it?"

"He can buy me a coffee at the bottom. He can go up and down and we'll meet at the bottom, instead of the top!"

"You're crazy." Fiona was exasperated.

"And, there'll be the hotel", continued Carrie not paying any attention to Fiona's frustration. "I wonder how posh it is. I'm soooooo excited, I can't wait. The Statue of Liberty and Wall Street, and the hotdog stands and everything!"

"The hotdog stands?" quizzed Fiona. "What about the hotdog stands?"

"Well, Lisa says you walk up to a little man at the stand. You'll be freezing cold with drips coming off your nose. You smell the aroma and ask for a hotdog, which you can watch being cooked. He wraps it up and hands it to you and says in a loud American drawl, 'That'll be waaaan daaarllar.'"

"You're mad Carrie!"

"And then you can go to another corner stand and order hot roast chestnuts, and walk to the next interesting bit while you warm your hands on the chestnuts. Macy's and Doodlebugs'll be fun."

Fiona smiled and corrected her again. "Bloomingdale's."

"Well, whatever. It'll be shopping heaven and I'm packing a suitcase inside a suitcase to bring things back."

"What things?"

"Just things. Christmassy things, American things. Is there anything you'd like?"

"Just for you to come back safe and not get into any mischief. Things always seem to happen wherever you go."

"I'll be fine. There'll be far too much for me to do to get into any mischief. Just a few days and nights to pack an American lifetime into. Oh, and Fee, there's the steam coming out of the grids like you see on TV. I have to have my picture taken beside one. Oh, Fee, I'm so excited. Then when we get home, it'll be all the planning for the wedding."

"I'll put the kettle on and we'll have a cuppa. Would you like any biscuits or a piece of cake?" asked Fiona.

"No ta, I'll be cooking a dinner for Mel when

I get home so I'll wait thanks."

The two girls sat drinking tea, exchanging stories about their families. Fiona's eldest daughter had just returned from a trip to Australia and had related a few hair-raising tales of banana plantations and jungle life. En route back home she and a boy she'd met had traveled to Thailand, Fiji and Bali. There were so many exciting opportunities for youngsters these days they both thought. Carrie and Fiona saw one another at least once a week, and there was always much to talk about. Their time together always flew and they never had time to completely fill one another in on all the family happenings. Fiona had only just begun to enjoy life again. Her newfound love, Alan, had completely swept her off her feet. She was always jet-setting off somewhere exotic and Carrie was overjoyed for her. Her best loved friend in the whole world had eventually found the happiness she deserved. Carrie found it difficult to keep up with the tales of Fiona's comings and goings these days, but enjoyed every second of hearing everything when they met. Fiona was besotted with Alan. He had very special qualities, and made her feel secure. They had just moved into their first house together and Fiona was happier than she'd ever dreamed possible. Her life was now complete. Carrie was delighted that her friend had found happiness and contentment.

"Well, I'd better get off and get the dinner on", said Carrie.
"What time's Mel home tonight?"
"Oh, the usual, unless he's stuck on the

motorway in a traffic jam again."

"Ok then, see you next week."

Carrie laughed. "Yeah, how excited will I be then?"

"See ya, take care."

"See ya." Carrie ran down the path, slid into the tattered leather seat of her car and Fiona waved her out of sight. Just as Fiona got back inside the house, the telephone rang. It wouldn't be the girls and Alan was on his way home. She answered inquisitively. Alan's voice was a whisper. Their lives were about to take the most dramatic turn imaginable.

Burma WWII

Through the steaming jungle at midday along the extreme Himalayan mountainous terrain, a colonel led his battalion of soldiers. Their mission, behind enemy lines, was to sever Japanese communications and their lines of supply and capture places of tactical importance. Along the way, soldiers fell from malnutrition and dysentery. For some malaria struck and typhoid was rife. Those who could fought valiantly and heroically.

Jack Masters stumbled over a protruding tree root which sent him and his array of military equipment plummeting to the rotting ground beneath him. It was this incident that saved his life. An enemy fighter plane overhead had released its payload seconds earlier and blown the ground to smithereens just in front of him. He feared the inevitable loss of life and when he finally managed to raise his bruised and battered body from the filth beneath him, his worst fears were founded. Two of his buddies lay dead, wounds gaping horrendously, already filling with a multitude of jungle life, and drenching the ground further with grisly red liquid. He vomited violently but feared he had no time for self-pity and shouted out for anyone who might be listening for survivors of the blast. For the second time that day, his luck held out, and he heard someone shout back. An English sounding voice came from ahead and he staggered in agony towards it, praying it would be one of his own battalion. He knew if it were not, he had signed his own death warrant.

They moved as quickly as the terrain would allow, dodging flying shrapnel from the Japanese artillery that had opened fire on their small platoon. Every fibre of their being pulsated, imagining the horrific consequences of capture. They trod the dense quagmire beneath them. Fatigue dragged them back and slowed down progress. In addition to battle injuries they were plagued with infected skin lesions, bites and scratches. Personal hygiene was non-existent causing further persistent physical conditions. They were weary from the heat and miserable from the nightmarish threat of tropical disease. Casualties from the enemy assault were rising and the stench of death and decay surrounded them, filtering through the foliage and entering their nostrils like an alien form of life. Their physical and mental condition was pitiable yet they pushed themselves forward, wounded animals seeking refuge. The few remaining soldiers prayed they would reach that refuge, wholly reliant on their scout leading them to safety yet not knowing if he were still alive.

The firing ceased, but the deathly silence increased their haste to exact some distance from their oppressors and forge on to the village they hoped to find. God willing, they might indulge in some respite from their gruelling march. They were only three now. Visions foremost in their minds of the harrowing end their comrades had met spurred them on. They came upon a clearing. Optimism provided enough curiosity to engage them in a carefully planned investigation of their surroundings. An

11

undisputed air of relief surged among them when they realised they had found the remnants of a makeshift village outpost. They used every ounce of willpower to remain upright and reach what they believed to be a place they could rest their broken bodies, if only for a short while. They were given that opportunity. Extensively trained in the art of detecting booby-traps, they found an empty hut free from any ghastly shocks, and entered. They agreed a rota, two resting, one guarding, and so they spent their first night of respite. The night was extremely cold and they hardly dared breathe or sneeze. Every noise made the nerves down their spines tingle. Exhausted, and having used the last of their rations, they hoped sleep would gain them strength for the arduous journey still ahead of them. They knew they were within the boundaries of their journey's end and although the environment would test them to the limit, their goal was in sight. They were to liaise with their battalion at a small town just north of their current position. They were frightened, hungry, thirsty, and the jungle penetrated and possessed their bodies.

They embarked on the remaining part of their journey with a jagged hope engaging them in a positive step. They attempted to keep their spirits raised as they forged through swampy land up to their thighs in mud and water, hacking through overhanging mangrove trees on the edges of the swamp. Their bodies itched relentlessly from fleas and lice. Other creatures stuck to their skin sucking their life blood. Five hours later, they were at the perimeter of the town. The operation had involved the evacuation of all civilians and it was evident this was still in process. The town lay in a dip in the landscape and from their vantage point, the three soldiers were able to watch, unnoticed, the other soldiers who were ushering adults and children along the streets. From everywhere, entire families emerged from the doors of primitive tin houses. Appearances suggested three or four generations might be living under one roof. Grandmothers carried babies and older children carried whatever small items they could, while the adults bore the heavier loads. They trod the pathways wearily, leaving their homes, not knowing when or if they could return. The town was a strategic point for engagement in a larger manoeuvre, and the risk to civilian life would have been too great.

Jack watched intently, with an overwhelming sense of sadness enveloping him. Momentarily he forgot his own suffering and felt bereft of anything but pity for the sight in front of him. He picked out one particular family and watched them. They appeared to be chattering away to one another, and although he had no hope of hearing, or understanding their conversation, he wondered what they were saying to each other. It struck him, that although these people were leaving their very roots, there was no sobbing and wailing. Apart from their incessant chatter they were simply following instructions, totally dependent upon the authority of the ranking officer endorsing the mass departure. Jack and his buddies kept low to the ground and moved in a little closer. Military personnel were few, so they began advancing to take up position and follow their orders. In the distance, Jack thought he heard gunfire and prayed that another attack was not imminent, at least until all the people had left the small town and reached their refuge.

The family he had been watching was led by an old grandmother with a child in her arms. One of the men seemed to have a leg injury as he held onto a wooden crutch and clung onto another man for support. They moved slowly along the street towards the other evacuees who were a good distance in front of them. Jack and the others were moving at a steady pace now towards the hub of activity. From where the edge of the town rose up again at the other side, they could see army vehicles beginning to set off north out of the town carrying as many refugees as possible. The town was an eclectic mix of ancient and slightly less primitive dwellings and moving through the streets, they felt uneasy with dark shadows looming at every turn. As no army personnel were bringing up the rear, Jack and his colleagues assumed that position. Weapons primed they stealthily followed the stream of wretched humanity. There was an incredible aura about the place, a mystique, which may have lured Jack back under different circumstances. It was as this thought passed through his mind, that another one followed it and he quickly and quietly indicated to the others that they should increase their step and shorten the gap between them and the last straggling family. His intuition was about to be rewarded as it was this decision that would ultimately change the course of history for his descendants.

Pegu 1323AD

King Meng Tuu-Kyi's chambers exalted the architecture of the era. Beautiful perforated windows, stone carvings of lotus flowers, floral designs, hamsa birds and peacocks adorned the room. Heavily fashioned artwork embellished the frieze and archways, and a golden Buddha shrine which he had believed protected him, dominated one corner of his bedchamber. Candles flickered in an array of coloured glass lamps beneath the plinth and the drapes and soft furnishings were of a heavily embroidered and bejewelled silk. He stood beside the window purveying his land. He recollected the wars and earthquakes which had fashioned it, and before the thought had passed, he crossed the room and opened a shutter door which led to his bed chamber. He asked the two guards to leave and take up position on either side of the outer chamber. They watched mutely, as down a narrow corridor leading to the outer parapets, they saw Princess Shariyan gracefully stepping into the royal barge which would take her to the Danan Pagoda where palace officials whispered she practised ancient love arts. The Princess of beauty secreted an intense dark force and no man, prince or warrior was permitted to retain any body part which could unfold her secrets. Muted guards were testimony to the whisperings. Ancient sexual rituals performed to heighten pleasure only served to enhance her sadistic desire and none were left alive or able to discuss their conclusions. The connection between her visits to the Pagoda and her lovers' visits to her bed must remain inviolate.

King Meng Tuu-Kyi had prepared his mind well for the prophecy. He had secretly removed the rubies from the orb and placed them with his private collection. He knew well enough that he could not escape his fate and although he knew not which form it would take, he would now make his final desperate attempt to avoid the inevitable, whilst preparing to meet his maker. Ancient Burmese warriors had believed that a ruby inserted beneath the skin generated mystical forces, and protected all those who performed the ritual from accident or attack. Once in his private chamber, he opened a wooden chest, and retrieved a baroque dagger which lay beneath reams of silk. He took the dagger and swiftly crossed the room to the partition behind which sat the golden Buddha and inserted the tip of the dagger into a notch in the wall. He turned the dagger ninety degrees, it locked into position and he used it as a handle and pulled. A small door cracked open. He gripped the edge of the door with his fingertips, opening it wide enough for him to see the bundle of cloth which lay inside. He quickly lifted it from the space, sealed the door again, took the dagger and returned to the chest. He lay down the dagger and began to unfold the cloth. There were a number of items inside, but he chose only one and then refolded the cloth and placed it beneath the reams of silk in the chest. He sat down on the mezzanine floor beside the chest. Out of his pocket he took a small bottle containing a colourless fluid and some cloth. He pulled off the stopper and poured a few drops onto the cloth, wiped the dagger, then rubbed the fluid on the fattest part of his arm and made a small incision creating a flap of skin. He inserted a large gemstone into the wound and pulled back the skin closing the incision as best he could. Mopping up the blood he wrapped a long length of cloth round and round his arm several times pulling it tight. For a few minutes the blood seeped through. He sat there repeating the bandaging until the flow of blood subsided. Thirsty and faint, he managed to reach a seating area where there were goblets containing water and wine. Letting go of the bandage to pour a drink, the King sat down.

King Meng Tuu-Kyi called his guards. They did not appear. In his desperate attempt to protect his life, he had not heard the commotion within the palace walls. He could now smell burning and crossed the room to the window. Fires were raging around the perimeter wall, bushes were alight, armed warriors fought with palace guards, his army nowhere in sight. Bodies lay dying, horrifically mutilated by the barbaric weaponry. He called out for his daughter but she had long since left the palace and had commanded his army to another battle. He moved away from the window toward the doors of his chamber, and could now hear screaming within the palace. The corridor facing his rooms seemed empty and he ran to the opening, passing no guards. He was alone. He could see the river ahead and fled down the corridor and over the courtyard, hardly daring to look behind him. He heard hooves clattering on the stone behind him and hastened his speed, hoping to get to the river where he might hide. As he was approaching the opening he believed would provide his freedom, he tripped as the bandaging on his arm unravelled. He heaved himself up and without looking back,

17

surged on toward his goal. The sound of hooves was gaining on him. He was well practised at throwing a dagger and in a split second decided to spin round and take aim. He did this with absolute precision. The dagger hit the rider through the throat, blood spilled out and the warrior fell, but the horse continued galloping. Running for his life, he thought his heart would burst. He reached the opening but too late. The massive beast had caught up and in the narrow space flanking them, the King was trampled. His leg was broken, the pain in his back was excruciating and the wound on his arm was now open and bleeding. He had smashed his face on the stone floor and blood was oozing from the wound. He crawled forward, aching to get into the water, but he was an easy target. On the ground beneath his crushed body, he could feel the reverberating thud of hooves. His palace burned behind him and the screams were becoming faint as he was beginning to lose consciousness. Pushing himself along, becoming weaker and in agonising pain, he could smell the water approaching and knew he was near. The thunderous noise was getting louder and as he gained the strength to lay one hand on the water, his most trusted warrior plunged the sword. The thrust of the weapon was so severe it rocked his body, forcing the ruby to slip out of the wound onto the ground beside him. A pool of blood quickly formed around it.

The warriors continued to raid the inner sanctum of the palace, hoping to glean what treasures they could before the fire engulfed them. Two of them went into the King's chambers and filled sacks with intricate gold and silver goblets, priceless trinkets and artefacts and their eyes rested on the wooden chest. They each grabbed a handle, believing that there would be more loot within its confines. They escaped from the flames which were now threatening to burn them alive and ran to the stairway. The chest was awkward to carry whilst running and they came upon a stone enclosure and decided to rest the box there and have a look inside. There appeared to be nothing more than reams of cloth, and disappointed their efforts had gone unrewarded, they left the heavy chest where it lay. The palace continued to burn, the blood-spattered warriors galloped away with their spoils and by nightfall the once magnificent royal palace was reduced to little but rubble.

When Princess Shariyan heard the news that it was over, she rejoiced by engaging her battle-weary army in a bloody massacre. She then rode with her army back to her father's still burning palace. She found the ruby beside her father's body, believing it to be a priceless gem from his ancient private collection. She scooped it up from the pool of blood and placed it in an amulet which hung around her neck. Showing no emotion, she gave orders for the King's corpse to be taken to a burial chamber within her new palace. Her coronation was a lavish affair and her dark reign began.

Princess Shariyan repeatedly sent her armies back to the pile of rubble which was once her home and on occasion rode there herself, searching in vain for a cloth bag. Her lack of triumph in this quest infused her with such venom and hatred, that her external appearance began to change. Her once beautiful countenance now matched her macabre soul. Neither man nor woman wished to look upon her and the people became reclusive, retreating into their own conclaves and living out their lives without rebellion. Her warriors lived in loathsome fear as she would execute mercilessly. The kingdom was in darkness. Her disposition trapped in its own web, lay in wait for some unsuspecting prey to enter its boundaries. Her reign continued for twenty-five years. Rage and bitterness consumed her and her empire crumbled, resemblent of the palace she had once lived in. Villages were burnt to the ground and her armies searched through every inch of the land. Hundreds were executed, but the cloth bag eluded her.

The chest had been of wooden construction heavily fortified with metal. Secluded in its stone hiding place, it had not been damaged by the fire, but the weight of the disintegrating palace had crushed the roof above the enclosure, falling heavily on the chest pushing it into the soft sandy soil upon which it rested. It remained there half in the ground and half covered by the heavy stonework and rubble, completely hidden for centuries. Landscape would soon claim the area and when would-be treasure hunters learning of the Queen's reign and the reason for her demise came searching, they would leave empty-handed. At forty-three years of age, Queen Shariyan took her own life by concocting a lethal poison. She entered the burial chamber, draped herself over her father's cask, took the ruby from the amulet and swallowed it along with the poison. The toxic substance disintegrated her flesh rapidly. Her bones were incarcerated in the cask with those of her father. The ruby was placed in a glass cabinet. Hope returned to the land and birds sang once again.

The North of England 2005

Carrie drove slowly, contemplating the few days ahead, and all that had to be achieved. This holiday had come up so fast, that there had been no time to plan anything. She was just being carried along and didn't dare dwell too much on the subject as she was positively petrified about the flight to New York. Her daughter Lisa was marrying Graham this year and New York was their favourite place in the world. Lisa wanted to buy her tiara in New York and look for other exciting goodies for her wedding. The opportunity had never arisen for Carrie to go with them but right out of the blue, a fabulous deal appeared on her email and she begged Carrie and Mel to come with them. Carrie was extremely excited. She would just have preferred not to fly! She and Mel had taken Lisa to the viewing platform at the airport for picnics when she was little. Carrie used to get so excited, jumping up and down and trying to touch the underbelly of the planes as they roared overhead. The little set of binoculars came out every trip and were glued to her eyes while the others tucked into a feast of chicken, pork pies, salad, scotch eggs and mini trifles. It was a regular enjoyment for everyone, and watching the antics of Carrie watching the planes, was much better entertainment than actually watching the planes. Never did Carrie imagine she would travel on one.

While she was driving along, the thought occurred to her that Alan hadn't been at home tonight and Fiona hadn't given her any clues where he might be. They usually discussed the men and what they were up to. 'Maybe he'd gone out with the lads', she thought. 'No, that was usually Friday.' She dismissed the thought and decided she shouldn't be so nosey. Nevertheless, she was curious. It had been a busy year and Carrie was looking forward to spending some time with her daughter in New York, and mused about the great time they would have doing all the fun things that Lisa had planned for her parents.

Carrie switched on all her lamps and chuckled as she remembered Mel's comment the night before when he locked up at bedtime. It took about five minutes to turn all the lamps, fires and electrical equipment off. She went into the kitchen and her bounding rotweiller Megan went completely bonkers running round and jumping up. As soon as Megan saw the rubber bone which Carrie offered, she began twizzing round and round, chasing her tail. Carrie lifted some spaghetti out of its packet. 'That's what we'll have tonight', she thought. 'Mel loves bolognaise.' The phone rang. Carrie nearly tripped over Megan trying to get to the phone. Megan always bounded in front of her wherever she went, making it difficult for her to put one foot in front of the other. She fell onto the sofa and grabbed the phone just as it stopped ringing.

"Damn you Meggy", she bellowed.

Meg's ears went back and she sloped off and lay on her bed. Carrie dialled 1471. Number withheld. That was always happening these days and she kept meaning to have the number changed. She assumed it was someone trying to contact the previous owner, who seemed to have more relatives that anyone she knew. She nearly tripped over Meg's bed.

"And you're going in a dog's home." Megan had raced out in front of her again, nuzzling up against her.

"Dinnertime, is it? You're on tripe and tuna tonight. You'll just have to wait a minute while I get your Dad's dinner on."

Carrie heard the doorbell ring. Mel had a key and lately there'd been a spate of canvassers so she decided to ignore it and carried on making the bolognaise sauce. She went into the breakfast room to turn the on the radio and heard the doorbell again. En route to the door the telephone rang. She stopped to pick it up.

"Carrie, is Mel home yet?" Carrie detected something in Fiona's voice and it made her panic.

"No, not yet. Why? Fiona, is everything alright, you sound weird, like something's wrong?"

"I've just had some news and I'd like to see you.'

"What's the news? Is it good or bad?" asked Carrie, beginning to feel very uncomfortable.

"I'll wait until I see you. Can you come after Mel comes home?"

"Yeah, no prob", said Carrie. "Are you going to give me a clue?"

"No" replied Fiona. "I'll see you when you're ready. Bye for now."

"Bye." Carrie lowered the receiver and looked out of the window to see who could be at the door. She realised that whoever it was had gone while she was on the phone. 'Oh, well, they'll come back if it's important', she thought and made her way back to her task of making the sauce, wondering what on earth Fiona's phone call was about.

Carrie struggled to get proportions right for two people. She was at her happiest when catering for more. Nevertheless, she always laid the table with as much precision as when she catered for the masses. She walked across her newly laid Indian tile floor to the dresser and rummaged through until she found a suitable candle for the hurricane lamp. The telephone rang again interrupting the usual pantomime of retrieving the old one from its glass tomb. "Oh, for goodness sake", she mumbled, yelling at Megan to 'Stay' so she didn't go headlong over the boisterous animal again. She yanked at the receiver in time to hear the line go dead. "Damn", she growled. "I'm going to get a phone extension put in the kitchen, this is ridiculous." She looked out of the darkening window. Street lamps were on. The trees looked a bit blustery and people walking past were huddled in hats and scarves, no sign of Mel yet. "Where on earth is he?" She went back to her chores. Dinner was beginning to impart a wonderful aroma through the house and she picked up a spoon and gave it a good stir. She finally managed to extract the old candle and replaced it with the new hazelnut scented one, laid the table carefully, and made a coffee while she waited. She wrapped her hands around the steaming cup of coffee and sat at the breakfast table. She reminisced about a German beer festival they had been to in a small village along the Rhine. They had loved one of the beer kellars so much, that when they moved into this house, the little snug had been the perfect space to recreate it. They enjoyed the challenge enormously and it had become the place where they did all their chatting. The ceiling was decorated with wooden beams adorned with strings of fresh hops and bench seating flanked three sides of the wooden table, accessible from all angles. A large oak dresser stood in one corner and wood effect tiles were laid on the floor. With a wood burning fire in the inglenook fireplace, it was their favourite part of the house. She straightened the gingham tablecloth, lifted the condiments down, and settled to have her drink. Her thoughts wandered to the events of the evening so far. 'What could Fiona possibly want me to go back for? Is there something terribly wrong? Why wouldn't she tell me or at least give me a clue? Is it something wonderful that's happened for both of them? What on earth can it be? Come on Mel, hurry home, have your dinner and then I can go and find out.' She reproached herself for this selfish thought.

There was much to do in preparation for the New York trip, not to mention Lisa's wedding later this year. It was without doubt going to be another busy year. They were planning their annual caravan holiday to Italy later in the year and couldn't wait to once again explore the mediaeval streets in the resorts around Lake Garda and sit at pavement cafes watching the world go by as they drank wine and cappuccinos in the hot sunshine. Carrie finished her coffee and wandered into the lounge and fluffed the cushions. She looked round and thought back to three months ago when they began their epic task to remodel the lounge before Christmas. Carrie and her daughter-in-law had been out shopping one Sunday, when Carrie had disappeared into a furniture shop.

She had purchased the suite of her dreams, plus a dining room suite, plus some occasional furniture which were on a special offer if you bought everything else, and a couple of complimentary pieces. Carrie didn't realise the nightmare that would follow her purchase. Organising delivery times, incorrect furniture being delivered, parts of it broken when it did come etc, and wondered if she really wanted the suite after all. She was still waiting for the men to come and put a new base on one of the sofas.

Her thoughts were stopped abruptly as she saw Mel walking up the path. She ran through into the kitchen and flicked the switch on the kettle. His cup was ready. Meg was twirling round and round in circles beside the hall doorway, chasing her tail. The clock in the hall was clanging and in came Mel, bobble hat, flask, newspaper and a big grin on his face.

"Hi, I'm home!"

Carrie went through to greet him, battling with Meg to get anywhere near him as he was showering attention on his beloved animal. Carrie eventually kissed him hello and took his flask.

"Sorry I'm late love. Had to be a Good Samaritan and help one of the lads with his wife's car."

"Is it alright now?" asked Carrie.

"Yeah, it wouldn't start when she came back with the shopping. She said she'd just got the baby strapped in the car, piled her shopping in, got in and it wouldn't start. Luckily she had her phone and rang Joe. He's not very good with mechanics, so he rang me and asked if I could take some tools. It was something and nothing. Jump started it and followed her back to make sure she was OK."

"Good, I'm glad you got it sorted for her. Dinner's ready, do you want your drink first?"

"Ai love, that'll be fine thanks. Have you heard about Ken?"

Ken and Sarah were their next door neighbours at the previous address.

"No, why what's up?"

"He and Sarah have split up."

"Oh, my goodness, when? Why?"

"Don't know. Saw Ken today at the yard collecting some crates. He looks terrible. Poor lad's devastated. Says he'll call and see us over the weekend."

"I can't believe it, they've been married for years, and the kids are grown up. They should just be starting to enjoy a new life together."

"I know love, I can't work it out at all, we'll just have to wait and see what he says."

"Poor loves, wonder what on earth happened. Drink your tea love and I'll dish up."

"How's Fiona, did you see her today?" asked Mel, genuinely interested.

"I'm coming now, and I'll tell you while we have dinner." Their idle chit chat continued.

Mel sat contentedly by the flickering candle thinking how lucky he was to have all that he did. They did seem to have more than their fair share of traumas and money was usually tight despite the exceptional year they were looking forward to, but they always came through and were still together to tell the tale. Mel would not have swapped his life with anyone else and was very proud of his family. Carrie caught his look as she walked through with the dinner. He looked cheeky and mischievous in the candlelight, and she loved him to pieces.

"Right", said Carrie, "I have to swallow this, and then nip back to Fee's."

"Why?" asked Mel. "You not finished putting the world to rights?"

"No, it's really odd" said Carrie. "I saw her today. Alan wasn't there, and it's not that I think she should have told me where he was, but she didn't mention his absence at all. After I arrived home she rang me. She sounded really weird and asked me if I would go back after you got home. I don't like the sound of it. I'm scared something's happened."

"There you go again Caz, making assumptions. It could be absolutely anything. Alan's probably taking her off on another holiday."

"She would have told me that while I was there."

"Well you said Alan wasn't there, maybe he only told her when he got in."

"Well, I have to go anyway, she sounded desperate."

Mel raised his eyebrows.

"This spag bol's fab. Here have another piece of garlic bread." They sat for five minutes after they finished eating, talking about the events of the day.

Carrie wondered all the way back to Fiona's house what on earth it could be that would cause her friend to ring her and ask her to go back. The front door was already open when she approached. She knocked and shouted.

"Come through, I'm in the kitchen," Fiona shouted. "Tea or coffee?"

"Coffee please", replied Carrie, as she entered the kitchen. It was triple the size of her own and beautifully fitted out with an array of mod cons. When Fiona turned with the coffees, Carrie thought she saw signs of a very faint smile quickly cross Fiona's face.

"Come on through, Alan's in the lounge." Carrie went through the middle doors into the sumptuous lounge and Alan went over to greet her. They hugged and Alan gestured to Carrie to be seated. Fiona handed her the mug of coffee and took a seat next to Alan. Carrie detected a bombshell was about to be dropped and held her breath slightly. She took a sip of coffee, put the mug down and looked across at the pair of them. "Right then, what's happened?" she inquired.

Fiona asked her to recall a conversation she and Carrie had two years ago about Fiona's father. Carrie could remember every syllable. It had seemed so poignant at the time as Fiona had been concerned for her father's sanity. He had been doing strange things which Fiona could not understand. He lived in a Victorian flat conversion on the other side of town with Nellie. They had met a couple of years after his divorce and had been together ever since. Fiona saw her father a couple of times a week. Then she wouldn't see him for a few months. She never enquired why and he never offered an explanation. That was just how it was. About six months ago he had asked Fiona to meet him at the flat. He began opening drawers and cupboards pointing to this and that and asking if she liked the contents. Fiona asked him why he was doing this.

"Well, I'm not going to be here forever and it will all belong to you."

Fiona had protested saying it was his stuff and she didn't want to take it. The first time it happened, he accepted her protest. Fiona told him she didn't want to hear any more about him not being here. He was very healthy and there was no reason to suggest he was going anywhere. He had said nothing. A couple of weeks later he rang and asked her to visit again. This time her father told her he'd had been diagnosed with a terminal illness. The doctors didn't know how long he might survive. He had been advised to live as normal a life as possible but there was nothing they could do for him. Fiona had been devastated, but her father had been strong and she eventually began to accept the facts. She also began to accept the gifts her father showered upon her. She didn't want to upset him by refusing and had accumulated quite a collection of cardboard boxes.

She had arrived home from work one day, opened the porch door and found another cardboard box, full of the usual bric-a-brac. Two days later, she received a telephone call from the hospital. Her father was asking for her. He died twelve hours later.

"Yes I do recall", said Carrie.

"Do you remember the last cardboard box he left in the porch?"

"Yes?"Carrie wondered where this was heading.

"Well it just got put under the stairs and

forgotten. I was having a sort-out and found it. Underneath all the usual rubbish, there was a cloth bag. I couldn't believe my eyes when I opened it. It was full of jewels and jewellery. There was a card inside it saying, 'To my dearest Joan, with all my love, Jack.'

"Were they your grandparents?"

"Yes, from my Grandad to my Gran when he came home from Burma. He must have passed them on to Dad."

"So how do you think they came to be in the cardboard box he left in your porch?"

"I think when Mum and Dad split up the boxes got mixed up and Dad finished up with the jewellery. I don't think Mum ever actually wore the jewels. She wasn't one for large costume jewellery. I think they'd been forgotten about until I found them."

"So let's have a look then" said Carrie, not understanding what it had to do with her or why Fiona had brought her back to tell her all this.

"I haven't got them. Alan said he thought they might be worth a few bob so he's had them valued. The jeweller nearly fainted when he saw them, valued them at £10,000 and wanted Alan to sell there and then. But Alan thought if this chap's willing to pay that much for them on the spot, what are they really worth? He asked a friend at work who has contacts in the business. He advised him to take them to London and made him an appointment for this morning."

"I got back about an hour ago" ventured Alan.

Fiona continued. "Apparently the jewels are priceless. They belong to a collection which was originally owned by a Burmese Princess who bequeathed them to her son on her deathbed, King Muchi or something like that. I know it sounds far fetched and I can hardly believe it myself. The fellow in London has a book which describes the jewellery in minute detail. During a palace raid in the fourteenth century the jewels went missing. There are legends and prophecies surrounding these jewels. The King who owned them at the time had a crazy daughter who committed suicide because she couldn't find them after her father died. Searches were conducted but they were never recovered."

Carrie couldn't contain herself and began to laugh uncontrollably.

"And these priceless jewels from King Muchi whatsisname and his loopy princess daughter were lost and found their way into a cardboard box in your front porch? That's very funny! Well, you really got me with that one. It was worth it though for the laugh."

Carrie was rolling about now, and at the same time trying to take another sip of her coffee and nearly choking on it. Fiona was giggling too, but trying to tell her friend it was all true. Alan tried to bring order by continuing the tale.

"During the Second World War Fiona's grandfather was serving in Burma and the story goes that he helped a family to escape from some Japanese soldiers. The old grandmother had been grateful and gave him a gift. Nellie found the card which accompanied the gift to my grandmother when she was sorting through Dad's papers. Though she never found the said gift, the card referred to some jewellery that had been given to the old lady while she was a governess at the palace." Carrie had stopped laughing now, and was intent on Alan's tale, hardly believing her ears.

* * * * * *

Burma WWII

Jack and the other two soldiers heard men's voices shouting and a burst of machine-gun fire. People began screaming and running. The old grandmother carrying the child began to increase her pace, intermittently turning her head encouraging the others to do the same. The old man lurched forward. His stick came down on a loose cobble and he fell bringing the younger man down on top of him. They were struggling to get up, when the deafening sound of aeroplanes seemed suddenly overhead. The deadly cargo was released. Jack rushed forward to help the two men up from the ground.

"You look after these two", he yelled to one of his friends.

"You help the others", he yelled to the other. He lunged forward grabbing hold of the old lady.

"Come on, hurry, I'm here to help, we'll get you to the vehicle. My friends are helping the others." He indicated to her that he would carry the child. The woman nodded and handed the child over, grabbing hold of Jack's arm to steady herself.

It was extremely difficult for him to carry the child, and still help the old lady from stumbling while maintaining his firearm position, but the old lady clung on and they began to run a little. They had only gone a few yards, when they heard a horrendous noise behind them. The old lady's heart nearly gave out, not knowing if her family had escaped the missile. Jack shared her distress and quickly turned his head to assess the situation. He squeezed her hand and nodded. She knew full well, that had they not been

35

helped and hurried along by these soldiers, they would have perished in the explosion.

They were nearing the edge of town and there was one vehicle standing unoccupied. There were no soldiers left at the pick up point. Jack prayed that he would be able to start the vehicle and prayed again when he saw a key in the ignition. It fired up. The family climbed in, Jack's friends helping the two injured men. They said their swift goodbyes and the other two soldiers retraced their steps to ensure that no civilians had been left behind. Jack sped off with the family, in pursuit of the convoy ahead.

The truck's wheels left the ground on a number of occasions as it bumped perilously along the rough terrain, and all the time the old woman chattered at him, her smile revealing a less than perfect row of front teeth, some black, some missing. But still her smile lit up her face and he prayed his efforts had not been in vain and he could get them all to safety. It wasn't too long before he caught up with the convoy trundling along in front of him and he hoped that their journey would be swift and safe. Once again his luck held out and some while later they were climbing a steep hill through a magnificent landscape of lush vegetation and vivid fauna. A sense of easiness began to overwhelm his passengers.

The convoy travelled uphill for about three miles, and then the narrow track they had been traversing opened out into a much wider track, and straight ahead of them was a sight Jack would never forget. Flanked by two gigantic statues beside which

36

stood military personnel was a magnificent structure. In Jack's wildest dreams, he could never have imagined such a place existed. He thought it resembled an exotic illustration from a fairytale. The large gates were open for the vehicles to enter and they drove into the courtyard. Soldiers seemed plentiful here and Jack began to think he might at last be able to satiate his hunger and thirst. The sound of gunfire became distant and intermittent and for now there was no sign of aerial activity. This was to be their sanctuary and he thanked God.

When he finally brought the truck to a standstill, the old woman took his hand. She beckoned him to look at her and began to speak very slowly whilst looking deep into his eyes. He could only guess that she was thanking him. The child on her knee, looked up at her and smiled, and as they all climbed out of the truck onto the cobbled courtyard, there was kissing and hugging and the loudest chatter Jack had ever encountered. Two young ladies approached them and began to bow to the old lady as if they knew her. Not understanding a single word of the language, again Jack could only hazard a guess at the gist of the conversation. It quickly became obvious that they all knew one another, although Jack wondered how a poor family, ushered from such a simple dwelling could have any connection with what he could only believe to be a royal palace. The two ladies now beckoned the group to follow and this they did with haste. Jack happily followed, only too pleased to be behind the walls of this magnificent place, and in what he assumed to be comparative safety. The family were very tactile and ecstatic to be alive. The old Grandmother constantly looked up at Jack and uttered words he could not understand and bowed to him. He bowed back.

They were shown into an opulently decorated room with dark furniture and comfortable looking seats. Jack wandered over to a window and peered out. Looking out over the panorama he could see plumes of smoke in the distance and the sun was an incredible orange ball in the sky. The scene was breathtaking. Moments later, he was taking his first sip of tea in what seemed weeks, and crooning over the array of food which had been laid before him on a gigantic patterned pewter tray. They all had their fill of food and drink, and were shown to a dormitory style room, with a triple carved wooden screen dividing the room into two halves. Jack presumed one for the women and one for the men. The old grandmother had left the group. They were shown the facilities and then left alone. In a quieter moment, he wondered where the other soldiers were. 'Had they made it? Where they being afforded the same privileges, or was there some reason for this special treatment?' They each picked the bed they were going to sleep on, and the children were put to bed.

A young girl entered the dormitory dressed in a vivid yellow and green wrap. She was stunningly beautiful with long dark hair, big brown eyes and a smile which seemed to light up the world. Jack was about to climb up on to his bed when she approached him. When she spoke, it was as though all his prayers had been answered. She said

"Hello, what is your name?"

Jack began to laugh, and she laughed with him.

"Jack", he struggled to say amid his laughter. "What's yours?"

"Ardonna", she said, smiling at him. 'I have come to speak with you on behalf of Letta, the old lady who you helped. She wants you to know that her family owe you a debt of gratitude. She says you saved their lives. Without you and your friends stopping to help them, their entire family could have been killed."

"Do you know Letta and her family?" asked Jack inquisitively. Ardonna replied,

"Many years ago, she used to live here as a nanny to the palace children and was Princess Kin-Kin's companion. This dormitory you sleep in tonight was the place all the children of the palace slept. The King wouldn't separate his children from the others so they all stayed together. Letta looked after them all, and was held in great esteem by all the palace officials. The King didn't know what he would ever have done without her. It had been her work at the palace that provided her family with enough food and drink to survive. The time came when she found it difficult to divide her attention between her family and still maintain her responsibilities at the palace. The King reluctantly released her from her duties. She went back to live among her own people but was always a welcome visitor at the palace. She is considered an exceptional lady in our lives, and she wishes you to know that you are a most highly honourable gentleman."

"Please will you tell her she's welcome, and

that it was my duty to help."

"But Letta says you did not try to save yourself from the gunfire and the bombs. Instead you tried to save her family and risked your own life for them."

"I did what I had to do, no more, no less", said Jack, overwhelmed and a little embarrassed. "Although I have to say" he continued, "we had been watching from a distance and noticed they seemed to be straggling. It became evident their progress was hampered and we moved in closer in case they needed help."

"Will you come with me in the morning to see her?" asked Ardonna.

"Yes, it will be my pleasure" said Jack smiling.

"You need to get a good night's sleep. I will see you in the morning."

Ardonna left the dormitory and Jack climbed onto his bed, happy to have found someone to talk to. Less than two minutes later he was sound asleep.

The following morning, the young lady came back and Jack followed her to where Letta had been sleeping. Letta bowed towards him slowly. He reciprocated. She took his hands and faced his palms upwards side by side, and she looked at him and smiled and put a package wrapped in cloth into his open palms. She began to speak and the young girl began to interpret. Jack could hardly comprehend what he was being told. Letta wanted him to have her only remaining possession. His kindness to her had saved the lives of her family. His reward was the package she now placed in his hands. The young girl went on interpreting and the story unfolded.

The North of England 2005

"So where did you say the jewels are now?" asked Carrie, unable to conceive she was sitting in Fiona's lounge listening to a tale that was more akin to an episode of Aladdin, than a current affair of her lifelong friend.

"In a safety deposit box at the bank", said Alan. Fiona fished in her pocket and swung a key in front of Carrie.

"And I'm the keeper of the key" she laughed. "We've been advised to keep it quiet for the moment until we meet with the expert on antique jewellery."

"And when's that going to be?" asked Carrie.

"As soon as they can locate him" said Fiona. "Apparently he lives in – you'll never guess in a million years...."

"Well, go on, the suspense is killing me" said Carrie.

"New York" replied Fiona.
Carrie remarked slowly, "Oh, my, God."

"Yes", said Fiona, 'and as soon as they've found him, we're flying out with the jewels.

"You don't think ...."

"Yes, if they find him quickly we could be going at around the same time as you."

"I just don't believe it. Have they indicated how much the jewels might be worth?"

"The chap in London said if they turn out to be the centuries-old missing jewels, they'll be priceless."

"And what will happen to them? Will you have to give them back or something?" Carrie was getting a bit edgy and she didn't know why. She had a feeling that there was more to come.

"Well, that's where you come in, Carrie", said Fiona in her usual non-committal way.

"How do you mean? I don't understand."

"Well, as I mentioned before, there is a legend attached to the jewels. The legend insists that whoever recovers the jewels and returns them to their rightful geographical location with other ancient artifacts, must be accompanied by a most trusted companion. That person must have neither the inclination to avert the journey of the jewels, nor be a member of the finder's family, nor have any external interest in the gems. They must have a compassionate ear for the bearer and duplicate a desire to return the Mystical Meng Tuu-Kyi Ruby.

"This is like something out of a fairytale", said Carrie. "Do you believe in all this stuff?"

"Carrie, if you could see the jewels, you would know. They are the most beautiful pieces of craftsmanship you are ever likely to see in your life. They seem to have, as the legend says, a mystical quality. There is something in it, I'm sure. So I'm asking you, if it comes to it, will you accompany me on this journey?"

Carrie wondered how on earth she would get the time off work. 'Work', she thought, 'Lord above, fancy having to think about going to work when I've just been talking about a collection of priceless jewels that belonged to a Burmese princess centuries ago, which have a legend attached to them, requiring me to go with Fiona to God knows where.'

"Well, I'm going to suggest to the chap in New York, that we come at the same time you're going with Lisa. That way I wouldn't be asking you to take any time off work. We could go our separate ways once the accompanying bit is done. It wouldn't be interfering too much with any plans you and Mel have, and Alan and I would get a short break too. We could maybe meet up and have a meal somewhere. Perhaps on Valentine's Day if it works out."

"Sounds good to me", said Carrie. "OK, just let me know what's happening. Goodness. What will Mel say when he hears all this?"

"Yes, tell Mel", answered Fiona. "But please don't tell anyone else. We don't know what sort of publicity this could unleash. We don't want subjecting to media interference. We just want to do what's right and be done with it."

Carrie already had her coat and gloves on. She could hardly wait to tell Mel. He would of course be scornful, just as she herself had been. In fact, she didn't expect he would believe it at all. Well who would she thought and smiled!

"Ooh, Carrie", Fiona exclaimed suddenly. "Could you drop me at the corner shop? I could do with another pint of milk and it'll save me taking the car out again tonight."

"I'll take you and bring you back again" said Carrie.

"Thanks. I'll take the ride with you to the shop, but I'll be fine going home again. It's not far and I could do with the walk. I need the exercise."

Carrie and Alan exchanged goodbyes. They gave each other a huge bear hug, and the girls ran off down the path.

On the way to the shop, there was a black sedan behind them with three occupants in black suits. Were they following them? Carrie's imagination ran riot. She dismissed the thought and told herself she was being stupid. All the same, she visited Fiona every week and never before when she pulled away from the house, had a black sedan suddenly appeared behind her. It followed her route round the narrow streets back to the main road. She was glad when the junction appeared in sight and the lights were brighter. Having just listened to an unbelievable story like that and told to keep it quiet, it was a bit spooky. Carrie's car came to an alarmingly abrupt stop at the give way sign. The way was not clear for her to take her turn. There was an articulated vehicle on the main road to her right. She glanced in her rear view mirror and imagined she saw the black sedan hurtling towards the back of her car and drew a sharp intake of breath. Fiona looked behind. Momentarily everything went black.

Letta's Story

Letta made her debut into the world on 18 May 1868, the daughter of a farmer. Her mother lost her own life bringing her baby girl into the world. Her grief-stricken father swaddled her and held her close to his own body warmth. An intense bond was created between father and daughter in those precious moments after her birth, which Letta was to retain all her life. Their culture had been largely unchanged through the centuries and her father knew that while he would grieve intensely for his wife, life must go on. He must care for this tiny baby and bring her to the ways of his people. He must find her some food. Kwei lay Letta down gently on top of her mother's still-warm body. He lay down beside them both and held his daughter's upturned face to her mother's nipple. He moulded the breast towards his baby with one hand, while pushing Letta's mouth towards her mother's nipple with the other. The two met and Letta's crying stopped as she attempted to suck hard to obtain whatever sustenance she could. After a few moments he saw Letta swallow. He wept. He did not know if his daughter had suckled well, but in his mind she was feeding. He created a makeshift sling garment out of his wife's clothing and lay the baby down, tightened her swaddling and laid her in the sling. After laying his wife to rest, he hoisted Letta up and on to his shoulders and set off to walk the gruelling journey to his sister's house. She would know what to do.

Suu-Kyi made them both welcome and told her brother that she knew of a young mother with a three-month old baby. Suu-Kyi approached the young girl and begged her to consider suckling Letta for her. The young mother agreed. And so began Letta's story. She was amazing as a baby, curious, bright as a button, happy and contented and rarely cried unless she was hungry. It soon became apparent to her father that she would be a clever girl and the special bond between them continued to grow. They were always together and he would often take her to work with him. Letta watched, learnt and gradually began to do small tasks to help her father. She busied herself helping Suu-Kyi when she was at home and learnt in a very short time how to do the chores. She was always skipping and singing, a very happy little girl. She went with Suu-Kyi to get vegetables and became aware of her much larger surroundings and kindled with curiosity, she asked hundreds of questions. She would not let them be pushed aside and pleaded for answers to them all. Her young brain had a vocabulary completely alien to a child her age. People in the village loved her charming ways and were always willing to talk to her. Word about the clever little girl spread through the province. Officials from the nearby palace began to query her whereabouts.

While Kwei was out working in the fields one day, two soldiers from the palace approached him and asked him to accompany them. Once inside the palace the King led him to a private room. Kwei gladly took the refreshment offered and listened while the King asked him to consider allowing Letta to join the young Princess Kin-Kin as a playmate at the palace. In return they would feed her, clothe her and privately educate her with the palace children. Kwei would be permitted to visit Letta in the palace twice a week, and she could pay an overnight visit home once each month. The King asked Kwei to consider his request an honour. He should not deliberate too long and he should take into account what might become of Letta, should he decline the King's request. At the palace her future would be safe and secure. Kwei was very proud that the King should want his daughter to become a part of palace life, but did not want to appear too enthusiastic. In the sternest voice he could muster, he replied that his daughter was highly sensitive and devoted to her family. He would consult with her this evening. Kwei thanked the King for his hospitality and for his offer and the two soldiers who brought him to the palace appeared and escorted him back to the field.

The North of England 2005

Carrie turned right onto the main road, and when the steering wheel straightened up, she looked in her rear view mirror. The black sedan was no longer in sight. She heaved a sigh of relief and accelerated. The girls hardly spoke on the way to the shop and Carrie wondered if Fiona had sensed anything wrong. The shop came into view and she dropped Fiona off. It was always against her wishes to let Fiona walk, and she insisted that she take her back home, but Fiona wasn't a bit perturbed by the short walk and Carrie bade her friend goodbye. Fiona hadn't mentioned anything but both girls felt decidedly edgy and wished they were already at home. 'Had there really been a black sedan behind them?' thought Carrie. 'It's probably all in my imagination.' Fiona waved goodbye and disappeared into the shop. Carrie turned the radio on and tried to listen to some music. It was disturbing her train of thought and she turned it off again. She accelerated harder, desperate to get home and tell Mel the strange tale. Just as she arrived home, the snow began to fall. 'Brilliant', she thought 'ice skating on Central Park!'

The snow was falling heavily by the time she parked and walked up the drive to the house. Carrie felt as though every move she made was in slow motion. Mel had seen her coming and opened the door for her.

"Come on, hurry up out of the cold" he said.

Megan behaved as though she'd not seen Carrie for a month and bounded up to her almost knocking her down. Carrie knelt down and gave her a hug. They all went through to watch the snow from the patio doors.

Carrie had been right. Mel threw his head back and howled. Then he bent over double and howled again. The tears poured down his face. He said he had never laughed so much in years. Carrie tried to keep a straight face whilst telling the story, but Mel just laughed and laughed and laughed.

"And you fell for it? Carrie, this is the 21st century, did you not try to convince Fiona it's all a big joke?"

"It isn't Mel. It's deadly serious. Fiona and Alan are trying to get a flight next week with us. They're going to New York to see this antique chappy……."

Mel started laughing again.

"Is he centuries old too?" he drawled, trying to invoke his spookiest voice.

"Oh, there's no use talking to you" said Carrie. "Wait until they're sitting in New York with us. Then you'll believe it. They'll be able to tell you straight."

Carrie ran off upstairs, remembering the suitcase she had bought earlier in the week. On the way down, she glanced through the landing window. She gasped as she saw a black sedan parked a few houses up on the opposite side of the lane. She rubbed her eyes and looked again.

"Mel!"

Carrie's scream brought Mel running to her side. She beckoned to the window for him to look out.

"What on earth's the matter? What am I looking

at?"

Carrie could hardly speak. Her heart was racing.

"The black sedan parked in the lane", screeched Carrie. "The one that followed me from Fiona's house all round the narrow streets back to the junction."

"What sedan, where?", asked Mel, drawing the curtains back further and craning his neck the better to see. Carrie nuzzled in beside him, peering out of the window.

"The one that's parked over there ….."

There was no car. Just crisp clean snow.

* * * * * *

Letta's Gift

Kwei was beside himself with excitement. This King ruled the provinces fairly and was noted as one of the most intensely humble royals the country had ever known. He had heard tales of a royal family who lived in the old palace centuries ago which made his blood curdle. But this royal family held a national reputation for kindness and compassion for the people. He believed it to be a wonderful opportunity for Letta to grow up in the palace and knew her mother would have been proud of them both. When he saw his daughter that evening, her face beamed up at him and she hugged him quietly, almost knowingly, and sat and listened while he told her what had transpired.

So began Letta's life at the Palace. She loved every single second. She adored her father and missed him on the days she didn't see him, but the advantages and benefits of living in the palace were wonderful for them both. Suu-Kyi also benefited, as Letta brought large baskets of vegetables and meat when she visited and the family feasted together, enjoying Letta's tales of Palace life. She told them of the beautiful Princess Kin-Kin whom she loved as if she were her own sister. They had become the best of friends and had lots of exciting secrets. Letta didn't reveal the secrets, but wholeheartedly launched into tales of her adventures within the palace grounds. The Princess was about two years older than Letta, so at six and eight years of age, their friendship was sealed. They had made a secret den accessible only by climbing through the thick walls of the palace courtyard. They had to move one huge stone, which between them they could just move out of position enough to slip through to the other side into the forest. Not too far away from the wall, they created their secret place secluded amongst the trees and hidden by tree branches and bracken. They took sweet titbits to munch on, and one of the youngest maids in the kitchen, who dearly wished she could join them on one of their adventures, made them up a container of fruit juice. They wrote notes there, and swapped ideas about their futures, and what they thought would become of them. They had taken small bags in which they stored all their most treasured childhood possessions. They had dug a large hole in the ground and stored everything in a piece of tarpaulin-like material in the hole. They pulled a stone slab across the hole and covered the stone with bracken. Their secrets would be safe from the world for ever.

The years sped by and the palace had long considered the Princess eligible for marriage. For many years suitors had been brought before her, but she had not been inclined to pay them any attention. Letta had a feeling that this was about to change, as she had begun to notice slight differences in her friend's behaviour. Kin-Kin spent hours with her maids helping her to bathe and preen herself, and so it was that Letta became Kin-Kin's highest-ranking lady-in-waiting. Letta considered this privilege the focal point of her existence and felt ultimately fulfilled that she, born into a small farming community, should exist in complete luxury and happiness beside her best friend within the palace confines. Inevitably Kin-Kin married and the wedding was a supreme occasion with no expense spared. The festivities lasted for many months before and after the wedding. Letta's father and Suu-Kyi were amongst the guests and in his wildest dreams, Kwei had never imagined his life could contain anything as extravagant as being a guest at one of the biggest royal weddings his country had ever seen. He had been blessed to have such a wonderful daughter and their relationship remained as poignant as ever.

Letta's life began to change, slowly at first, but gathering momentum, as predictably, Kin-Kin spent most of her time with her husband, her new best friend. They became inseparable, and Letta was delighted for her friend, but often consoled herself by remembering their secret place. It was difficult, if nigh on impossible for her to visit the place now, because two people were required to remove and replace the stone on both journeys. In order to do that she would have to relinquish their secret, and Letta considered that to be a betrayal.

For two years, Letta threw herself into her work at the palace. She was always happy at her work, always singing and pleasant with others. She continued to wait on Kin-Kin whom she found always to be a joy. She visited home regularly and spent precious time with her family. Her innocence carried with it a loveable renown and as she blossomed into an incredibly beautiful young woman, lion-hearted young men, valiant and resolute, began to attempt to court her. She celebrated her youth in harmony with expectations of romantic interludes and the more she groomed her appearance to entice possible liaisons, the more exalted she became and her fame spread throughout the province.

"But she's not of royal blood", one would-be suitor said to another.

"But she lives at the palace, doesn't she?" asked the other.

Legends of a beautiful princess who once lived in the palace and performed horrific rituals with her lovers were circulating the eligible gentlemen keen to pursue Letta's affection, but their partiality to their own bodies was preventing them. The heroic stalwarts amongst them, however, were prepared to risk their lives if necessary for just a smile from her, and one of the most exciting times of her life began. There were small men, fat men, tall men and thin men, some with lots of hair, some with none, some in soldier's uniform and some she considered as outright dimwits. But of them all, there was one, who possessed an inner strength she detected through his smile. His eyes were cobalt blue and she was smitten. They had a wonderful courtship, and on her twenty-first birthday she married Kwan-Kywa in the palace. They were to be given their own quarters in the servants' wing, and Letta would continue her work in the palace. Her new husband was to recruit for the King's army.

On the morning of Letta's wedding, Kin-Kin was enjoying role-reversal, and was helping her friend and mentor prepare herself for her marriage to Kwan-Kywa. It was very early morning, before the palace was awake. She asked her friend if they could go to their secret place one last time. The two girls hurried to the wall and removed the stone, climbed through to the other side and ran to their hiding place. Kin-Kin asked Letta to close her eyes and hold out both her hands. Letta did as she was asked. She felt a heavy weight placed upon them. When she was told to open her eyes, Letta gazed upon the most amazing sight. A largish piece of material opened out, revealing an array of sparkling gems, jewellery and in the midst of them all, a stone so large she barely dared to touch it.

"These are for you my Letta", said Kin-Kin. "For all that you have done for me and for all that you mean to me, my very special friend. They belonged to my ancestors who discovered them centuries ago in a wooden chest beneath these palace grounds. They are believed to have mystical powers and bring good fortune to those with a true heart. You gave up your life for me, to be with me, to grow with me, to learn with me and to have secrets with me. I would like you to have them. This is our ultimate secret. You are my very special Letta and I wish you and your husband to have an incredible future together."

Letta could hardly believe what was happening, and tightened her hands around the jewels, encasing them back in their cloth. She bowed very slowly and reverently to Kin-Kin, tears pouring down her cheeks.
"I have spent my life so far with an incredibly special person, and I am privileged and honoured to have done so. You have been my best friend and will continue to be forever. Wherever our lives now lead

us, and whatever we will do in the future, I will always remember our time together. I love you as my own sister and am overwhelmed that you do this for me. Thank you. I think though, my special Kin-Kin, that the emotion of the day may induce your generosity, and therefore, I will place the jewels in our secret place. Should you ever wish to rescind your noble kindness, please take them back with my blessing. We will share this secret to the end Princess Kin-Kin. Your ancestors will be very proud of you. I will only return for the jewels if it would be an appropriate and similar gesture. Otherwise they will remain the property of your ancestors."

Both girls sobbed and hugged one another before opening up the hole in the ground, placing the cloth bag containing the stones into one of the bags and placing it in its earthy tomb. They pulled the slab over, covered it with bracken and made their way back to the palace. The palace had come to life and was a buzz of activity. The two excited girls continued with their preparations for Letta's imminent wedding ceremony.

Kwan Kywa and Letta were happy together and were blessed with little ones. Letta became increasingly uncomfortable about her diminished responsibilities in the palace, needing to spend more time with her ever growing, demanding family. She approached the King and Kin-Kin with regard to her moving back out into the community to rear her family. And so it was that Letta, Kwan Kywa and their two children went back to live with Aunt Suu-Kyi and Letta's father. They were both delighted to have Letta back amongst them as were the villagers. Their children grew in the special love of family life and Suu-Kyi and Kwei considered themselves extremely fortunate that the King and Kin-Kin had been so benevolent, allowing Letta to leave the palace.

Shocking war-torn years followed and the provinces were ransacked by destructive war-lords, keen to gain the riches of the kingdom for themselves. Fighting became an integral part of every day life, and families considered themselves fortunate if they were all together for the next meal. Some families suffered terrible losses, and Letta became the one to whom they all turned for solace in their grief. As her children became independent their demands on her lessened and she spent most of her time looking after her father and aunt, and listening to the woes and sufferings of her local community. Kwan Kywa continued in service to the King, becoming a high-ranking officer and leading counter-attacks from which Letta often wondered would he return. He always did. She often thought back to her wedding day, and wondered if indeed the jewels bestowed some fortune on their family, even though they had not seen the light of day for many years.

Her daughter gave birth to two children, a boy and a girl, three years apart, and though her young family continued to expand, her father and aunt were becoming more dependent on Letta for their needs. She visited the palace often and spent precious time with Kin-Kin, and always came away laden with gifts for the family. The family were highly favoured and incredulous that they had been exonerated from the hardship surrounding them and tried as much as they could to alleviate the suffering of others. Inevitably Kwei was reaching his time and Letta devoted most of her spare time sitting with him, talking to him and stroking his hands until one day his heart expired. She wept uncontrollably.

Letta was never lonely, always busying herself helping others. She was happy to look after Suu-Kyi who was also becoming frail. She tended her grandchildren and mentored other less capable citizens. She had always been able to visit the palace with her children, and now she enjoyed taking her grandchildren, who played with Kin-Kin's grandchildren, and all their lives were enriched from the association. Her palace connections always foremost in her life, Letta began to visit more often and inevitably began to assist again wherever she could. Her own family were coping admirably, her children with their own offspring, her husband away with the army, and Suu-Kyi comfortable enough to be left for a few hours. Kin-Kin and Letta began to spend a lot more time together, and both girls treasured each moment. They knew their lives had been set apart from the rest, and although both were ageing, they were able to cope with whatever life brought their way. They had drawn enough strength from the good times to cope with whatever the future may hold. There had been rumours about unease around the world and both were au fait enough to realise their country could be caught up in another war. Sadly, their premonitions had been accurate and before another year had passed, the country became occupied. Atrocities beyond belief were reported. People tried to flee and became refugees in their own land. Four years later, the country had been ravaged and still the people fought on with their daily lives, desperately trying to avoid the persistent corruption and melancholy that enveloped their small community.

Ultimately the area was to be evacuated. The old and the young had to leave their homes, taking with them whatever possessions they could carry, and seek refuge at the nearby palace. It was during this mass evacuation that the massacre began. Soldiers of the warring faction had violated the palace and murdered the King and Princess Kin-Kin. When the word came amongst the people, Letta thought her world had ended and she had died too. Why were they going to the palace if it was occupied? Had the Army re-taken the palace and was it in the hands of allies again? Letta didn't know if she wanted to go there now that her friend was no longer there. She would probably never recover from the shock of losing her. Letta decided that she would stay in their family home for as long as she possibly could and stayed right up to the bitter end, until she thought they were the last family to leave, unaware that they were being watched by Jack Masters and his two friends.

Letta knew when she arrived at the palace that her life was coming to an end. She had long suffered with stomach pains, but refused to recognise the suffering as anything of importance. That would have impeded her work for others. The shock of the news of Kin-Kin and her father had devastated her, the evacuation of their village, the loss of their home and the almost tragic circumstances of their journey to the palace, forced her to visit her secret place for the very last time. This time, she had sought the help of one of the palace guards to help her remove the stone. He was a trusted soul, and never once did she consider that his newfound knowledge would be a threat. She would return with all the contents of their hidey hole, and distribute them as she wished. The bags were heavy and she couldn't wait to get them back to her quarters. She relived each moment, as she traced her way back through the years, searching through the contents of both bags. There were treasures untold, small gifts that Kin-Kin had bestowed upon her over the years, now revealed themselves as a ticket to freedom for her family. Priceless artefacts, small and weightless would generate enough money to allow them the lap of luxury for generations to come. Letters which Letta and the Princess had written to one another would form part of historical archives in a museum. But the item she was intent on finding was a large piece of cloth containing precious jewels and gem stones. This was not just a collection of precious stones or jewellery. There was something more to these jewels. They had an aura about them, something beyond words, and it was these with which, tomorrow morning, she would reward the soldier who had saved her family's lives. He had risked his own life to save theirs. She remembered some of the words Kin-Kin had spoken the day she gave them to her. "For all that you have done for me and all that you mean to me. They will bring you and your family good fortune. You gave up your life for me ……..." Her Father had been willing to sacrifice his own life and his daughter's life for the sake of helping the King and the Princess. She had promised Kin-Kin she would only retrieve the jewels in similar circumstances. Without the help of Jack Masters, her family could have been maimed or lost their lives. Their very existence was because Jack had risked his life to save theirs. She would reward him. She hoped they would bring him fortune the way they had for her. Her life almost over, she knew she had to act swiftly. She gathered her family together that evening and gave to them two bags and all their contents. To Jack, she gave the bundle of cloth containing the jewels. There was a great sadness, as they all knew she would soon be setting off on her longest journey. The whole community would be saddened. Her death would be a huge loss to her family and those remaining at the palace.

Letta died from the intense stomach pains two days later. Her final wish was to be fulfilled. Her mortal remains were to be put to rest beside those of her best friend the Princess Kin-Kin. That evening their husbands and families floated their funeral pyres out onto the river, candles burning, tears rolling and hearts aching.

* * * * * *

Jack's Return

Jack Masters had never felt like this before. He didn't know the person who had given him this gift, yet his heart was saddened by what had happened. He wept for Letta. He had been permitted to view the proceedings the night before and now he wondered if it had all been some bad dream. But he felt the weight in his bag and knew it hadn't. He extracted the package for the second time that morning trying to decide if his wife would like the jewellery. He was sure the big gem would be worth a few shillings at least, and considered himself very fortunate to have come across this old lady and helped her. He wondered if she had told her family that she had given him this package. He wasn't going to risk having to hand it back and decided to say nothing. He wrapped it all back up, and this time undid his back-pack and pushed the package deep into the bottom of his bag. He wouldn't look at the jewels again until he arrived back home to England. It would be a surprise seeing them again. He had to admit to himself that he felt a strange presence and couldn't help wondering why he felt like this. He shook off the feeling and went in search of food. This he found in the palace kitchen, where a lovely young lady was cooking rice and eggs. He took a liberty and patted her bottom gently; asking her to cook slowly and then he could watch her for longer. She didn't understand what he said, but smiled back at him, screwing up her button nose and fluttering her eyelashes at him in a flirtatious but sarcastic manner.

It was easy to forget at this precise moment in time, that there was in fact a war going on outside these walls and all too soon, he would have to set foot outside the safety of the palace and take his chances with the rest of the world.

Finishing the last traces of food on his plate, he picked up his rifle and back pack, which had been carefully placed at the side of him, walked over to the lady who had prepared his food, turned her face towards his, kissed her full on the mouth and left the kitchen in search of Letta's family. He found them in quite a state of shock. They were distraught, their lives shattered by her demise. Further distress had befallen them that morning as well, with the untimely death of Aunt Suu-Kyi. Jack left the palace that morning not really knowing or understanding what had happened in the last few days. It was incomprehensible and a thick mist of obscurity clouded the issues so he couldn't see them at all. He decided at this point that he should put it out of his mind and keep his wits about him. He gave one last passing thought to the items secreted in the bottom-most corner of his rucksack and the image danced before his eyes. He knew it was absurd, but he suddenly felt like a safety net had completely engulfed him and he knew that he would make it home. His belongings all gathered and positioned correctly about his person, he wandered out into the courtyard.

Everywhere seemed quiet and he wondered what had happened to the two soldiers who had helped him save Letta and her family. He wondered if they had survived. He hadn't seen them since his arrival at the palace. He knew that thanks to them, the family had arrived safely at the palace. He made a mental note to enquire about their whereabouts. They too deserved thanks for playing their part in rescuing the family. He felt completely alone. His intense early training would have to kick-start to allow him freedom of passage back through the worst terrain he had ever encountered. Just a few days earlier, he had been in stinking rags, his nervous system almost at meltdown, and his dishevelled appearance doing nothing for his self-esteem. His matted beard and dirty long hair had congealed into a tangled mass. His short visit to the Palace had enabled him to get himself clean somewhat, and the girl in the palace kitchen had cut his hair and beard to a respectable length. Invigorated and with a single thought in his mind, he set off to find his regiment. He was confident that he had full capacity ammunition, his machete fastened to his belt and a canteen of fresh water was strapped to his side.

He was seriously aware of the possibility of an ambush. He smelt the aroma of food as he passed deserted villages obviously abandoned in haste. At one point he actually wondered if he should scout round for something to eat. Maybe some cooked rice had been left behind. He kept as low into the undergrowth as he could and his sheer sense of survival curbed the pangs of hunger and he passed the huts by. On a number of occasions, he dived for further cover, as bullets flew past from the crossfire of other groups of soldiers and their oriental enemy, battling for supremacy in the squalid jungle conditions. He hid behind a huge tree and heard an almighty thud as a bullet hit the tree, his luck still holding out. At least now he knew there were other soldiers in the vicinity and hoped he could find a travelling companion. It emerged that he was caught up in the middle of a two-man combat. When the guns stopped firing, he waited, keeping right down, hating the feel of his belly against the squelching ground and eventually, the British soldier, to his intense relief, emerged the hero. Inevitably, after moments of anticipation and suspicion, Jack showed himself, and the two men conversed briefly, shook hands, and resumed their journey back to civilisation.

It began to rain. Large intermittent spots at first, changing within seconds to a torrential downpour. The huge elephant grass bent under the weight of pounds of water per second. They were drenched to the skin, the noise deafening out the sound of any would-be ambush and slowing down their already waning advancement. With Jack's water the only rations available, the rain was welcome. It washed away the dust from their clothes, cleaned their faces and quenched their thirst. Darkness fell quickly, another ally. They agreed to continue their passage through the jungle, hoping they would stumble on some means of transport. Jack's newfound fellow traveller, Vinny, still had his compass which made their decisions about direction somewhat easier. They chose to travel east for a while, believing themselves to be within a half day's journey of a railway line. Jack had felt uneasy about his worsening condition. His brain seemed to be processing the wrong waves, and even to himself he appeared confused. His legs seemed too heavy to lift to put down again in the quagmire beneath him, and lifting them back out of the mud was a major operation and he felt like he was doing everything in slow motion.

Jack could see coloured lights, a bright spectrum of colour, like rainbows, and thought he'd said to Vinny "Can you see those lights pal?" If he had, the words died on his lips and he crashed to the ground, displacing massive quantities of mud and earth, which spattered up high into the face and clothes of his friend, who trembled, fearing that Jack had been shot, and almost as quickly, voluntarily flung himself on top of Jack. When it became apparent there was no enemy in close proximity, Vinny began to investigate Jack's injuries. He discovered nothing, and realised quickly the man was suffering from sheer exhaustion. He further suspected a case of malaria. His suspicions would turn out to be correct.

He quickly looked at the situation and what he could do. He placed the open canteen against his lips and took two sips. He then positioned the opening against Jack's lips and moistened them. He checked his compass for the correct heading and guessed he was about two or three hours away from their destination. He thanked his lucky stars and deftly began to hack down the thick boughs and branches of trees. He pulled up reeds and any foliage resembling thick twine, and began to make a primitive stretcher upon which to lay his friend. He kept a close eye on Jack whilst being acutely aware he was in a very precarious position should the enemy locate them.

The rain eased off making his job less difficult and he worked hard, bringing all his army training into play and before long, he had produced quite a sturdy bed for Jack to lie on. He wouldn't notice it wasn't duck down, nor care if there were no clinical white sheets to lie over the top of him. If he survived, he would just be eternally grateful that he had come across this heroic man. And so it was that Vinny, having heaved Jack's body from the mud onto his life-saving creation, began the arduous task of pulling his friend across the hazardous landscape. Behind them and a little to the West, began one of the bloodiest battles Burma saw during that time. He heard, and hurried, grateful for the courage bestowed upon him and whispered prayers into the wind that he could bring them both to safety.

More than four hours later, and almost dying from exhaustion himself, he found himself approaching the railway. He wondered how long he would have to wait for a train, and again wondered if it would take him to safety or to his doom. Would the enemy occupy the station, would they be operating the train? He told himself he'd come this far, that his God would not desert him now. His faith bore fruit and in the distance he thought he could see a group of men, whose uniform he could swear was British. Half smiling, he wondered how on earth could you tell in these conditions what nationality sat beneath the filth of the clothes they wore. He prayed some more and edged a little closer. He listened for their voices carrying to him on the wind, and believed to his delight that they were speaking English. He shouted and waved, and when three men came rushing over to him, he asked for a medic.

"Tommy, get yourself over here now", shouted one of the men.

Tommy sprinted across, opening his medical bag whilst running, and dropped to his knees at the side of Jack. He confirmed Vinny's suspicions. Jack was suffering from malaria. He told Vinny his platoon was waiting for the train back to Rangoon. There was a massive camp near their destination, where Jack could be tended and convalesced, if he was lucky enough to make it through the train journey.

The sun was burning hot. The men waiting for the train were literally dropping from exhaustion. Still cautiously on guard, they never believed for a second they would be lucky enough to actually board this train which was going to take them for a short break, to recover their lagging senses, and put them on the road back to the jungle in just a few short weeks. Some fainted, dropping like dead weights on to the parched ground a few yards away from the tracks. Some of the wounded were crying out, their pain becoming too much for them to bear. Flies were furiously buzzing around their open wounds, but most were too tired to bother swatting. The soldiers lying on the ground were the first to realise that their salvation was but a few short miles away. The ground rumbled beneath them, and one or two thought the earth was quaking. The carriages trundled along the track, heavily laden with military, some alive, some dead and some just clutching at a mere thread of life. Soon the entire group were able to hear the train and began to rally. When the engine came into sight there was a big cheer, their excitement evident by the plumes of smoke emitting from the mouths of those who lit their last vestiges of cigarettes, willing to gamble they could replenish their supplies from others on the train.

Jack Masters was not classified as able, and was still lying on his makeshift stretcher amongst the wounded. Vinny didn't stray far from him as they waited for the train to chug to a halt. He squinted in the sun, trying to see beyond the carriages that now sat in front of him and wondered where their small group would fit into the already overcrowded carriages. A little man wearing a British uniform leapt down from the engine and began running up and down the line of soldiers. He assessed the situation in a matter of seconds and ran along the track until he reached the penultimate carriage. He jumped inside and quickly scanned the dying soldiers to see if any had already crossed the threshold to another place. Two had.

He shouted out, "Bill, over here, two more lad please."

Bill was a medic tending the wounded wherever he could and when he appeared the two men carried the dead men down the steps, along the track and up the steps into the next carriage. When they opened the door, the stench exuding from the enclosure was repulsive. They knew what had to be done. They tried to lay the bodies of the two dead men as humanely as possible, hurrying so as to avoid inhaling.

"Come on, we have two stretchers."

They hurried back to the group and carried Jack Masters and another unconscious soldier to the carriage containing the wounded.

"You better stay with them Bill", said the little man. "Looks like this one's got malaria. You got anything left you can give him?"

"No sir, we used the last lot. I'll stay with him as long as I can. How long do you think it'll take us to get back?"

"Couple of hours I reckon, all being well".

"Here's hoping sir. Do you want a lift with the others?"

"No, you stay here now, it won't take me long to organise the ones that can walk."

With that, he leapt back out of the carriage, and ran back to the group, who were becoming impatient for a place. Five minutes later, the engine stoked and everyone on board, the engine began the final part of its journey. It wasn't up to speed when they heard a familiar droning sound above them. Those standing up hit the floor in a heap, some sustaining further injury from banging the heads of other soldiers doing likewise. Those who could distinguish enemy from ally waved from the carriages at the supply plane flying overhead and heaved a sigh of relief. They all hoped for a swift journey's end. Some slept, others sang quietly in small groups. Younger ones chatted excitedly about the nurses they might encounter while they recuperated, and those who smoked enjoyed their cigarettes. The two hours passed without incident and the train finally drew to a halt on a deserted part of the track. They weren't taking any chances. They were going in the back way.

A number of men appeared, evidently having done this before, and quickly evacuated all the walking wounded from their carriages. They filed up the embankment where other soldiers waited to escort them into the medical centre to assess their injuries. Others were commandeered to help carry those on stretchers and the dead bodies were carried to a separate enclosure where digging was already under way. Other soldiers were instructed to take the dog tags and rucksacks from the dead.

Jack's condition had deteriorated. Vinny was now back beside him, but there was something missing. Something was different he thought. Jack was hallucinating and the words were very hard to detect, but Vinny heard enough to know that Jack was mumbling about a bag. 'That's what's missing' he thought. 'His bag's gone. He guarded that bag with his life. It must contain all his worldly possessions. Where the hell's it gone? I must find it for him'. He turned just in time to see another soldier disappearing round a corner with Jack's bag slung over his shoulder. Vinny ran over to him.

"Hey. That's my mate's bag sir, please."
"Sorry soldier, I have instructions to take all the bags from dying soldiers."
"But my mate's not dying, he's gonna be Ok."
"Why d'ya say that? What makes him any different than the rest?"
"Because I've been with him, and he's improving. He ain't gonna be too pleased to find all his stuff missing when he comes round, not to mention what he'll do to me for not looking after

them."

"You sure that's his, or are you after fags."

"Don't smoke, just want my mate's bag." Vinny was unsure what to do next. If he pursued it vehemently, there was no doubt in his mind the sergeant would be pedantic and refuse to give him the bag. The thought crossed Vinny's mind that the sergeant could be looking for cigarettes himself. If he made too much of a fuss, the sergeant would assume there was something inside the bag worth having.

"Ok. You have it. Probably only a few mouldy samples in it anyway."

"What d'ya mean, mouldy samples?"

"Well, the guy works in a lab, and he has to collect soiled dressings and take them for analysis. He'll get more." Vinny turned his back and began to walk away, priding himself on thinking up such a rouse and hoping it would work. He heard a thud behind him. When he turned, the bag lay on the ground, and the sergeant had hurried away. Quickly retrieving the bag, he hurried back to Jack and laid it on top of him. He was never to know the affect on the future his actions had that day.

Jack Masters went in and out of delirium over the next forty eight hours, and Vinny didn't believe he'd make it. When he did, he was beside him asking him if he wanted a beer. Of course Jack did, and their friendship was cemented. The fact that he'd brought him out of the jungle on a makeshift stretcher, looked after him, helped him find the way to the train, and stayed with him through his darkest hours, was enough for Jack to bestow upon Vinny the title of 'best bud forever'. Vinny didn't mention the incident of the bag, and Jack never knew how close he'd come to losing his precious gift.

His recovery was slow and the authorities considered that he wasn't well enough to go back into action. Arrangements were made to send him home. He was about to embark on yet another journey, but this time, he was excited. This time, he hoped he'd be able to smell a piece of brisket boiling on the stove in his kitchen at home. If he was exceptionally lucky, he'd be tucking into a freshly made treacle tart. The thought made his mouth water, and he considered himself one of the more fortunate ones. Vinny was being sent back to the front line in one week's time. They exchanged addresses and promised to look one another up when the war was over. They said their goodbyes and the jeep taking Jack on the next leg of his journey left the centre amidst clouds of dust. Jack looked over his right shoulder. Vinny waved. He would never see Jack again. He was shot with a single bullet wound to the head on his first manoeuvre back in the jungle.

The ship carrying its human cargo left Port Said in February 1945. Although an uncomfortable journey Jack made it back to England without further incident. He hitchhiked home from the docks, encountering some interesting folk along the way. Hardly believing he was back on home ground, he was eager to return to his home town as quickly as possible and did not sleep for the two days it took him to arrive at his front gate.

Jack often wondered how he had ever

managed to arrive in Rangoon still clutching his back pack. What a different story could have been told. It could have been lost to the jungle floor a dozen times, or claimed by other soldiers, stolen or otherwise. It never ceased to amaze him how the bag had remained firmly in his clutches, and what fate might have befallen him if people had realised what the bag contained. People would steal for only a few bob, and he thought the jewels might be worth at least that. Anyway, he thought, 'Joan might like them and want to keep them'. He firmly believed that somehow it was the contents of the bag which had kept him alive. He had felt it when he left the palace. 'Lucky jewels', he had thought. He could never have imagined in a million years what he actually carried half way across the world, dragged through the putrid floor of the Burmese jungles and almost lost a dozen times. Nor could he have imagined neither their beginnings nor the journey they now embarked upon. He was just sure of one thing. A special lady had given them to him and he had guarded them with his life.

Joan Masters had been watching through the window and seen him coming. The excitement in the house was at an all-time high. The old brown radio was blurring away in the corner, and as Jack had predicted there was a pot roast on the stove and a wonderful and much missed smell filled Jack's nose as he opened the front gate to walk up the path. He thought he saw his youngest son Tom, peeping round the corner of the rose trellis at the side of the house just as the door flung open and his wife and eldest son, John ran down the path to greet him. There were lots of hugs and tears and questions. Jack laughed.

"Is there a cuppa love?"

Joan Masters straightened her pinny, kissed him on the forehead and squeezed her husband's hand. She muttered something under her breath about Tom being missing when his Dad came home, and scurried off into the kitchen to make her husband his first cup of English tea for many a long month. The kettle was boiling away merrily on the stove and seconds later, she placed a china cup and saucer in his hands. She sat down beside him and began bombarding him with a thousand questions. The warmth in the house, the knowledge that his belly would soon be full, and the sheer joy of escaping the past few months virtually unscathed, made Jack sleepy, and as he settled further and further into the old comfy sofa, his eyes began to close. Joan gently took the china from his hands and placed it on the hearth, dragged a small footstool over and lifted his legs up onto it. She took off his boots as gently as she could, and left him to sleep. Joan Masters together with their eldest son John left the room and began the process of creating a hearty supper for the miraculous homecoming. They set the table in the small cosy kitchen. A clean, white tablecloth, freshly pressed, and the best cutlery set out. Joan placed a creamy coloured bud vase in the centre with a couple of fresh flowers from the garden and a bit of greenery.

"There", she said "a table fit for a King."

"Ay" answered young John, "King of the Jungle!!" and they both laughed. Two hours later, they were all sat round the kitchen table while Jack recounted some of his escapades. His sullen youngest son, also present for supper, was utterly disinterested, except to ask if Jack had brought him anything home.

"There might be a little something for my two boys", replied Jack.

"Whar is it?" asked Tom in his most slouchy voice.

"I'll show you later" said Jack and winked at Tom. Tom finished his food and left the room. Joan Masters was beside herself with worry about Tom and confided in John that she didn't know what would become of his brother. John was also concerned about Tom but refused to let his brother's sullen mood spoil the wonderful homecoming evening. Jack chose this moment to give his wife her gift. He laid the cloth on the table, opening it slowly and said, "These are for you. I hope you like them." He told her the story of how he came to be in possession of such lovely looking jewels. The three of them sat there long into the evening while Joan and John listened to Jack's stories. Joan clutched the cloth until their talking was finished and then decided to put her precious keepsake in a 'safe' place, kissing and hugging Jack on her way. Though none of them knew it, the jewels would soon be in John's possession. Joan Masters passed away within the year.

Uncle Tom

Three years his brother's junior, Tom had always felt inferior to John. Tom felt his parents doted on his brother, and left him to more or less fend for himself. His brother always had lots of friends calling after school, but he, Tom, was always left to walk home from school on his own. Arriving home one afternoon, when the nights were beginning to darken early, he opened the back door and John and his friends jumped out on him from behind the wash house. The shock made him trip and he fell through the opening and onto his school bag. Inside the bag had been a model aeroplane which had taken him weeks during woodwork lessons to make. When he recovered and opened the bag, he discovered that the aeroplane was squashed and irreparably damaged. He went absolutely berserk, screaming and lashing out at the other boys, shouting obscenities and the million things he would do to them all for frightening him and making him fall and ruin his work. The other boys including John were laughing uncontrollably. They thought it was hilarious. This made Tom fifty times worse. John wondered afterwards if Tom would ever actually get over it.

Tom was sullen for a whole month. He became incredibly moody and sulked for the slightest thing. He never missed a chance to yell abuse and sarcasm at his brother and his dark moods worried his parents. Tom's grades at school worsened and during his final year at school, he was expelled for hitting the Headmaster. Mr Adamson never knew what hit him, it happened so fast.

"Masters, where do you think you're going?"

Mr Adamson knew exactly where Tom was heading, and it was his duty to prevent it. Tom had been severely reprimanded in the Maths lesson for letting the ink drip out of the pen onto his jotter, which soaked it up like blotting paper. He was supposed to have been doing algebra. He never listened in any of his lessons, and didn't know how to do the exercise. The Maths teacher had been walking up and down the line of single desks, cane in hand, and Tom had made no attempt to hide his activities. The teacher had whacked the cane across his hand, which made the pen in Tom's hand spurt ink out again. The ink splattered Mr Jones' trousers, which made him extremely mad and he lashed out again, catching Tom's fingers with a mighty crack. Writhing in pain, Tom slammed the pen down on the desk and ran from the room, holding his throbbing fingers under his armpit, then shaking his hand fiercely and putting them back under his arm again. He needed a cigarette and was heading straight for the kitchen. He knew the kitchen staff would have gone home for the day and he could sneak out of the back door without being seen. But he didn't reckon on the Headmaster being in the corridor. Mr Adamson, a large daunting figure, now running, boomed again.

"Masters, come back here, now."

Tom was hurting, angry, and extremely annoyed at being discovered, preventing him from his much needed nicotine boost. Quick as a flash, he turned and as Mr Adamson approached him and tried to grab the sleeve of his blazer, Tom clenched his already throbbing hand, and launched it straight into

Adamson's chest. The ferocity made Greg Adamson stumble backwards and he never actually knew if he'd been more shocked at what had happened or in terrific pain. The thumping chest pains continued for two days after the attack.

There was an investigation, and two days later, there were rumours in every corner of the old Victorian boys' school. Little groups huddled in corners discussing the events. Some were exaggerated beyond all proportion. Somebody thought he'd stuck the pen in Adamson's chest. Others added that he'd twisted the pen and made the wound twice its size. But none were sorry to see Tom in trouble. He had no friends of his own and the younger boys were scared of him. His moods could swing as quickly as the pendulum in the Grandfather clock in the foyer. Larger groups of the older boys gathered, bets were laid and money exchanged hands. Would he be expelled? When would it be? How would it be?

It was a dark January morning. Every light in the huge auditorium was lit. Every pupil was wearing the smart navy and grey uniform. The snow was beginning to fall outside. The windows were high and the dark grey clouds sauntered slowly past. There were hushed whispers amongst the eight hundred boys standing there, as they wondered what would happen. Teachers in customary cap and gown were lined up at the front of the auditorium facing the boys. Behind them loomed the large dark stage, which had seen so many happy events. Nativity plays, drama productions, practising Shakespeare texts, Speech and Awards days, not to mention the staff play on the last day of each summer term. All those old enough to remember the staff play two years ago, when Mr Adamson played the part of a tree in the forest of Snow White, would ever forget it. The auditorium nearly burst its roof when all the staff taking the part of 'trees', turned very slowly round to face the audience, revealing themselves. Today the big black and gold curtains remained closed. In front of them an empty foreboding stage except for the single walnut lectern.

The room became hushed and silent. All that could be heard was the rustling of Adamson's black gown swishing against his trousers, as he began his journey down the centre of the auditorium towards the stage. He ruled the school with a rod of iron. All the young boys were frightened of him. He had no reservations about the punishment befitting the crime. Those who had stood outside his room awaiting the inevitable, seldom went back a second time. The older boys eventually relinquished their mischievous ways and became quite reverent in his presence, ultimately showing respect for him, though none liked him. The Deputy Headmaster moved from his place in the line, climbed the four stairs up on to the stage and demanded silence. There were two members of staff missing from the line up. The row of older boys at the back could hear sounds and one or two turned discreetly to distinguish the origin of the noise. They saw Tom Masters in his school uniform flanked by the two missing members of staff, rather big burly men also in their caps and gowns. Each had hold of one of Master's arms. Some snivelling could be quite clearly heard from the younger boys.

Mr Adamson reached the line up of his staff, and bent down to whisper something to one of them. He continued his journey up the stairs and onto the stage. He took his place behind the lectern against which he leant his cane and faced everybody. He began in his loud booming voice.

"Any boy who mutters one syllable, or moves half an inch will be standing up here as well. There will be absolute silence, do you understand?"

There was complete stillness. Some said later the loudest noise was the snow fluttering outside the grubby windows. Mr Adamson didn't speak again for at least three minutes. Boys tried to stifle coughs and nobody dared to breathe lest their exhalation be considered a noise. There was no shuffling. Everyone stood completely still. The school bell rang, shattering the silence and making everyone jump. The shrill sound echoed around the vast space for the fifth time, and although still ringing in the ears of all, Mr Adamson began his speech, shouting every syllable as loudly as his lungs would allow.

"Our school has been dishonoured, by this contemptible boy", he yelled, emphasis falling on this, as though describing something inhuman.

Tom was nudged by the two men holding him, and the three began the walk up the aisle towards the stage. Mr Adamson continued while Tom was walking towards him.

"Lift your heads up" he shouted "and look upon Tom Masters. His despicable behaviour has brought disgrace to St Edward's Boys' School. I have no alternative but to deliver this punishment."

Some shuffling could be heard amongst the

boys stood watching in stark horror, as Mr Adamson prepared to cane Tom right there in front of everybody. Tom was ushered roughly up the stairs until he stood at the side of the Headmaster, who was now red-faced. He took out a handkerchief and mopped his brow, lifted his gown slightly, stuffed the piece of cloth into his trouser pocket, and roughly straightened the gown.

"Boy, you will stand perfectly still and hold out your right hand. You will keep your hand still. You will not withdraw it."

Tom was inwardly shaking. He knew he deserved this punishment. He didn't know what had come over him the day he'd hit old Adamson. It was like the devil himself had possessed him for those few seconds, and now the inevitable was about to happen. There had been a lot of discussion. His parents had been brought into school. They knew exactly what would happen today. Arrangements had been made. Tom didn't offer out his hand. One of the members of staff holding him forced his arm out, and reluctantly Tom opened his right hand, palm facing upwards. Mr Adamson directed his next statement to the two staff.

"Step aside please."

They did so, and left Tom still holding out his hand and gritting his teeth. He knew he had to retain some dignity. The hundreds of boys stood watching this would never forget what they saw and heard today. He had to harden himself and become brave. He had been to the toilet half a dozen times, and hoped he wouldn't disgrace himself in his moments of pain. Mr Adamson slung his gown over his right shoulder, bent down and retrieved his most flexible cane, and before anyone had even seen his arm rise, the cane came down on Tom's hand with such force, and made such a loud crack, everyone thought Tom's hand had broken. Tom's face reddened and tears sprang to his eyes. Whilst he controlled their flow, Mr Adamson delivered two more blows down on Tom.

"Other hand." bellowed Mr Adamson.

Tom didn't dare but comply, and shaking uncontrollably now, he stuck out his left hand. Mr Adamson spoke again. "There will be one blow for every bell. You will remember, Masters, the five bells of St Edward's Boys' School." He swiftly raised his arm and Tom felt the remaining two whacks on his left hand. Mr Adamson replaced the cane against the lectern. The two members of staff regained their stance either side of Tom.

"Turn and face your fellow pupils", screamed Adamson.

There was perfect silence in the room, everyone wondering what would happen next.

"Undo your jacket boy."

Tom tried. His hands hurt too much. One of the men standing beside him quizzically glanced at the Headmaster, who nodded. He stepped in front of Tom and undid the buttons. Mr Adamson walked to the back of Tom, and dragged his arms back, removing the jacket. He held it up in the air.

"Tom Masters is not fit to wear this jacket. Let every boy see this and remember."

He tore off the badge bearing the crest and coat of arms for the school, located on the jacket breast pocket and placed it on the lectern. He threw the jacket behind him. It slid a little on the shiny wooden floor, and lay there, crumpled.

"Face me boy."

Tom turned to face him, eyes lowered.

"Hold your head up. Up, I said."

Tom tilted his head backwards. Every boy in the room, holding their breath, imagined that Mr Adamson was going to thump him in the chest. 'An eye for an eye', was the thought running through the minds of all who witnessed the day that Tom Masters was expelled from St Edward's Boys' School. But Mr Adamson had no intentions of hitting Tom. He was going to remove the last vestige of St Edward's uniform from him. He turned to face the silent throng again, saying, in a slightly quieter tone.

"Bear witness today, all pupils of St Edward's, that Tom Masters has disgraced this school, himself, his family and God, and is irrevocably expelled from this school."

He reached out towards Tom, and there was a sharp intake of breath from every boy. He slid the knot of Tom's tie down, and pulled the tie over his head, and placed it on the lectern with the badge.

"Get out of my school", he bellowed.

The tears welled in Tom's eyes again, as the two members of staff, placed their hands on his elbows and frog marched him down the steps, and down the aisle, past eight hundred boys not daring to turn their heads. A couple of boys at the back sniggered as Tom went past. His parents were waiting outside.

The auditorium took on a new mood now. What would Adamson do or say next? Mr Adamson stood there, stiffened his back and bent down to pick up his cane. He tapped his left hand two or three times with it, looking all around the room. He marched down the steps taking long strides back down the aisle, eyes down, gown swishing.

John was glad he hadn't still been at the school to witness the spectacle of Tom's last moments at St Edward's. In a way he felt guilty. 'If I had tried to be more pleasant to my brother', he thought, 'this wouldn't have happened.' He determined that he would, from that day forward, endeavour to befriend his brother. Tom, happy at last with some attention, led everyone to believe that at last he had reformed. Of course, he hadn't.

Preparation for the Journey

The next few days were the usual mixture of work, eat and sleep, intermingled with an extortionate array of washing and ironing. Carrie was particular about clothes for special occasions. Visiting New York was one of her most special occasions yet. She had originally considered a glamorous image, for the cameras of course. She had seen a long grey faux fur coat, which was just what she wanted, but thought about the hem dragging through six inches of snow. How would she ice-skate on Central Park in a long coat? She would probably do herself a mischief. She considered all her options. She wanted to save what money was available for New York. She emptied wardrobes and drawers. Lisa had emptied the contents of her wardrobe the weekend before. As always some items came Carrie's way. Most of the time they were her own! Carrie had an eye for a bargain but seldom got to wear any of her new clothes, for daughters seemed to know instinctively when mums have bought something new. Quite how baffled Carrie, but she felt that even disguised bags, once inside the house, developed a phenomena invisible to all except daughters, displaying a note: 'new clothes in this bag, please help yourself'. Carrie was alarmed she couldn't even call her underwear her own. This had been a real sore point when Lisa was younger. If she bought any new underwear, she would have to hide it in a coat pocket or somewhere equally inconspicuous. It didn't matter that she regularly spent a fortune buying new lingerie for Lisa, the veritable second she got any new for herself, the daughter thing happened again. Coat pockets became the hidey place. The older the coat, the more chance she had of being able to wear her new underwear, at least once anyway.

Carrie had collected half a bin bag of goodies from Lisa's, and had gone through it with a fine toothcomb. There was her favourite black top, a little less favourite now it had been stitched with white cotton, and a t-shirt which had seen better days. But for the most part it was a good collection. Carrie had been delighted and started her selection process. Her suitcase would be packed and unpacked a dozen times, and they were only going for a few nights. 'Well you just have to get it right' she thought, 'and of course, you have to have items for every conceivable occasion. What if you only had one pair of jeans and you got soaked to the skin, well you just had to have another pair with you. And what if you spilt gravy on your favourite top while you were out to dinner? Well, that can happen to anyone. You'd have to have at least one or two others to be able to change into.' Catering for climate was abysmal. You had to cater for every eventuality: ice and snow, warm sunshine, rain, wind, and so on. It really was a serious business packing a suitcase. And Carrie did that, the same as she did everything else, with gusto, sincerity and a huge amount of enjoyment.

She periodically turned her attentions to Mel's suitcase. To be truthful, she could have packed a carrier bag for him. She would meticulously pack his best clothes, buy at least one or two new outfits for him and invariably he wouldn't take them out of the packaging. They would still be in the cellophane collecting dust twelve months later. His excuse was always the same. 'I'm saving them for me hols'. Still every time they went away, Carrie would wash, iron and pack all Mel's favourite clothes. New smellies, favourite aftershave and a selection of shoes, although she knew he would wear only one pair. She also knew however, if she didn't pack at least three pairs of shoes, he would ask why. 'Men!' she thought. And so the packing saga began. Carrie was disinterested in glam now and was thinking more casual, perhaps a bit sporty. She had two lovely sports t-shirts that had been gifts at Christmas. 'I'll team them up with a pair of track-suit trousers' she thought, 'pair of trainers, my Ralph Lauren cardy, and a body warmer. Yes, that's what I'll do, lots of layers. Then if I get too hot, I can remove a layer. Wooly hat, scarf, gloves and a suitable jacket'. She decided that the coming weekend was a 'sort my clothes out for America' weekend. She had an early hairdressing appointment on the Saturday morning and afterwards she would carry on into town and get some last bits for their trip. It looked set to be another busy weekend. Since they had moved into their new house, there had rarely been a weekend with nothing to do. There was always something going on. Lots of catching up to do with family and friends, apart from the jobs they had to do around their own place and this weekend they had been invited to a friend's birthday party.

Carrie had planned to have the Wednesday afternoon off work before they flew to America early on Thursday. She would clean the house, finish packing and then have a lovely soak in the bath, wash her hair, and have all Mel's stuff ready for him when he came home from work. Megan would have to be taken to the kennels. What a fiasco that would be. Megan didn't object going, in fact quite the opposite. Once the kennel owner, Cynthia, was mentioned, Megan would nearly have a seizure. She was an extremely intelligent animal, and knew that the word Cynthia meant she was going on her holidays. The trouble was that Megan was very difficult to control in an excitable state. Carrie remembered with horror the first time she had attempted to take her to the kennels on her own. The drive to the kennels was a long single track road with deep ditches on either side. If traffic was travelling in the opposite direction it was literally a case of fend for yourself. Carrie hadn't liked the drive and Megan hadn't liked the car, so they were both wound up like coiled springs by the time they arrived. There hadn't been anywhere ample to park. Carrie had had to position the back end of the car sticking out into the road, and hope that another vehicle wouldn't need to get past. She had opened the door gingerly and caught Megan's lead, but the dog hadn't wanted to wait. She had leapt out of the car yanking Carrie's wrist and as Carrie twisted her body to keep hold of the lead Megan had pulled her flat on her face into the middle of the road. The yank on the lead nearly suffocated Megan and they both finished up limping like wounded soldiers up the path to reception. Carrie had not wanted a repetition of that incident. She would wait until Mel got home and they would undertake the chore together. 'That would be best', she thought.

More about Tom

Tom had been rooting through his mother's bedroom drawers. He had come across a small cloth bag. 'Mmmmmm, wonder what this is', he'd thought. He lifted the cloth bag out onto the bed. His mother was chatting to her friend downstairs and would be at least another hour. They gossiped about all sorts. He sifted through the contents. 'Bits of jewellery', he thought. 'Never seen mum wear these. Wonder why she never wears them.' He would ask his mother when her friend had gone. But no, he couldn't, cos mum would know what he'd been up to. It didn't take him long to come up with a solution. He put all the jewels back into the cloth bag, and placed the bag on top of the underwear lying in the top drawer. His mother kept her precious talcum powder in that drawer, which is what he'd been looking for in the first place. When Elsie had gone, leaving that awful red lipstick around the rim of her cup which Tom despised, he ran back to his room and called to his mother.

"Mum, mum, come quick." Mum raced up the stairs at the sound of one of her offspring calling her.

"What's the matter son?" she enquired.

"I've got a rash mum. Can I have some of that talcum powder that you use?"

"Why would you want that for a rash?" asked mum, not really taking too much notice.

"Frank says it makes rashes better", said Tom. He followed his mother into her bedroom, and stood beside her as she opened the big top drawer. Immediately, Tom said "What's in that bag mum?"

91

His mother looked puzzled.

"I don't know what it's doing there."

Tom said again, "What's in it?"

"Oh, a keepsake your Dad gave to me when he came home from Burma."

"Can I have a look, mum please? Please mum, let me have a look."

His mother relented and took out the cloth bag, and walked over to the bed. For the second time that evening, the jewels were tipped onto the pink bedspread and he sat fingering them. His sneaky plan had worked.

"Are they worth anything mum?"

"No, I don't think so. Just sentimental value. I rather think they're too big for me, but they're nice to keep."

Tom was silent for a moment.

"Can I have them?"

"No son. Now what would you want with them?"

"Don't know. Just like them", said Tom sullenly, annoyed at not getting his own way again, especially after having devised the devious plan to have a proper look at them. "Didn't want them anyway", he muttered and slumped out of the room.

"I can't find the talcum powder Tom."

Tom didn't hear his mother. He had closed his bedroom door and was sulking. Little did he know that he had actually had a stroke of luck tonight, discovering the jewels. The next time he saw them again, was when he saw his father Jack Masters giving them to John after their mother had passed away. His temper had raged inside him for months and he became almost reclusive.

The night Joan Masters died was a warm summer's evening. She was out in the back garden. The sun was low in the sky and their west-facing rear garden caught all the beautiful sunsets. She had been collecting lavender and marvelling at the aroma imparted from her favourite plant. The bees were in profusion that particular year and as every other year, were extremely partial to the large fragrant bush. When weeding, she would always linger by the bush, so sweet was its perfume. Whilst she wasn't frightened of the bees, she preferred not to be too near them and waited until they had finished collecting their pollen before she snipped her flowers. She had just stood up and was straightening her back, when a large bumble bee flew past startling her and caused her to fall backwards against the sturdy thick wooden garden bench. She felt the corner of the bench jab against the middle of her back and the pain was excruciating. She continued falling into blackness. The doctors said the shock had caused her heart to fail. The coroner pronounced a verdict of accidental death and the funeral was held five days later.

She had been very much loved by everyone who knew her and utter disbelief engulfed her family and friends. When Jack Masters had to sort through her personal belongings, his grief overwhelmed him. He sat in their bedroom pouring over photographs of their happy times and he wept. He forced himself to continue his task, and came across the cloth bag. He cried out loud. He wasn't aware she had kept the jewels. He knew she hadn't cared to wear them and always assumed she had given them away, or sold them for a few pounds to meet periods of hard times. He was looking at them really for the first time. He remembered so well the lady who gave them to him and memories came flooding back. There was a knock on the door and his eldest son John appeared.

"Are you ok Dad?" he whispered gently.

He was an astute young chap and unlike his brother, had gone out of his way to be more helpful. He looked at the cloth bag and the jewellery lay scattered on the bed. Tears began to trickle down his cheeks. His father embraced him and he patted his father's arm.

"I'll be just downstairs if you need me Dad."
As John opened the door to leave the room, his father quickly scooped all the jewels up from the bed, dropping them back into the cloth bag.

He shouted, "John, would you like to keep them? There may be a lady in your life one day?"

John turned and walked back towards his father, tears still welling in his eyes.

"Yes, I'll look after them Dad, but there'll never be another lady as deserving of them."

He took the bag from his father and left the room. As he walked across the hall, he saw his brother disappear back into his room. Tom ransacked his sibling's room every time he was in the house alone, as he did in his mother's room, but he never found the cloth bag. He made it his life's ambition to own the contents. Jack Masters survived in abject misery without his wife and died of a broken heart.

The North of England 2005

Carrie had had a particularly bad day at work. She had spent most of her day hopelessly lost, with a map and a magnifying glass, trying to find her next port of call. She had recently started a new job which involved a lot of driving and her sense of direction was notoriously zilch. She loved the work, but had hardly ever driven outside her own town. To be travelling on motorways most of the time was a shock to the system, and Mel, who was a skilful driver and a wizard of direction, was mystified by her perplexity. He could have driven to China and back without so much as a map reference. Unfortunately Carrie didn't share that talent and left her family in dread at the trail of devastation she could leave behind her, whilst summoning up the courage to decide which lane to be in. The inhabitants of the vehicles behind her wouldn't have a clue what her intentions were, because neither did she until the last second. This was the burden you had to carry when you didn't know your East from your West, she would inform everyone.

She came straight home from the city centre, without calling back to base. She was already late, and there was much to be done. She collected the mail from the porch and switched the light on. The bulb popped. "Oh, not again" said Carrie out loud. They popped with such frequency, she wondered whether there was an electrical fault. She dropped the mail on the coffee table. Megan was nearly knocking the door down, trying to get in. She had a five-star kennel packed with five-star straw, and was a most comfortable guard dog during the daytime, but in the evening she expected the same home comforts as her owners, and being indoors when Carrie was in, was one of them. Carrie unlocked the door and let her in. The animal nearly flattened her. After the usual five minutes bedlam, Megan finally ran off into the lounge to 'bury' a bone which she retrieved from her bed. It was the funniest thing to watch. She would 'bury' in corners, pushing the article she was 'burying' into a corner until it was at a right angle, and then scrape her nose along the carpet towards the thing, as if pushing some imaginary soil over it. She would spend a considerable amount of time doing this, then patting it down with her nose every now and then. Satisfied that the job was done and the bone 'hidden', she would trot away and lie down some two or three feet away from it, pretending not to look at it. Then, two minutes later, she would go back and eat it. Even funnier, were the times that she would choose to bury a bone in the middle of the room and after all the nose scraping and patting was accomplished, it was obvious that she thought no-one could see it.

Carrie decided on a mixed grill for dinner and set about skinning the mushrooms. Megan came along and poked Carrie in the leg with her wet nose.

"Alright Megan, you can have yours in a little minute, just let me get Dad's dinner on first." Megan went and sulked in the breakfast room. The telephone rang. Carrie leapt over the top of Megan, and ran to the phone. Lisa's voice boomed out shrill, and sounded very excited.

"Guess where I'm going Mum?", she asked in a breathless state.

"Go on, tell me", replied Carrie in the same excited way.

"Amsterdam on Saturday morning. Graham booked it right out of the blue. I knew nothing about it. Isn't he a sweety?"

"Wow, that's fab", squeaked Carrie. "How long for love? Don't forget we fly to New York on Thursday morning."

"I know" gasped Lisa. "We fly Saturday morning and back Monday. The flight should land as we're just about to start work." Lisa and Graham both worked within the airport complex. "We only have to do three more shifts and then we fly to New York on Thursday. How good's that!"

"It's absolutely fab" said Carrie. Her daughter's flighty wings had not yet been clipped. She had itchy feet and loved to be on the move. She had inherited that from her parents and couldn't sit still for more than five minutes. They chatted for a few more minutes and then, as always, Lisa finished the conversation abruptly. Carrie was mulling over the possibility of inviting Fiona and Alan for dinner on Saturday evening. Since starting her new job and working longer hours it was virtually impossible to do anything after work. She rang and asked. A delighted Fiona accepted.

Carrie put the mushrooms into a colander and walked towards the console table housing the phone. She wondered if her imagination was running riot with her. Her heart nearly stopped again as she glanced out of the window. Parked opposite was a black sedan with three inhabitants. She dismissed it as utter nonsense and decided it was probably someone visiting the house across the lane. Nevertheless, she felt a chill down her spine.

They ate their grill with gusto, and then just vegetated in front of the television, a rare treat these days. They enjoyed some chocolates left over from Christmas. Carrie had a glass of claret and Mel drank a bottle of Christmas ale. They were completely chilled, enjoying each other's company.

Carrie decided the next morning, that she'd go to the shopping park straight from work and buy a few things they needed for the forthcoming trip. She rang Mel and said she may be a little late home. She wandered into one of the stores, collected a basket and wandered around looking for inspiration. She didn't find any. Her mind seemed to be preoccupied. She was wondering what the jewels were all about. 'Was this a hoax? Could it be real?' Her thoughts were racing ahead when there was a tap on her shoulder. She jumped a little when she turned round and saw Fiona's stepsister Sophie. Fiona considered them all a bad lot. Lenny and Bart were Sophie's brothers and believed to have been fugitives fleeing the country some years ago. Sophie always seemed to be in trouble with the police and had a distasteful boyfriend called Elliott. Carrie was surprised that Sophie would even recognise her, let alone want to make contact. She politely said hello and made an excuse that she was in a hurry. She didn't want to be accused of aiding and abetting any funny business, which Carrie was sure Sophie would be up to. She scurried along and ensconced herself amongst the pyjamas and dressing gowns, keeping her head down.

She soon forgot about the encounter.

Carrie chose some new underwear, two jumpers and a pair of jeans for herself, and a sweatshirt and some underwear for Mel. On the way to the checkout, she was reminded of her encounter with Sophie as she saw the girl skulking around the jewellery counter. 'Up to no good' she thought, and hurried on her way. She paid for her purchases and left the shop.

Excited again about all that was happening she drove home listening to her favourite radio station. The traffic news wasn't good. There had been an incident on the motorway and long delays were forecast. "Oh, no, that means he'll be late again" she thought. "Oh well, only a few more days and we can spend some real time together. I wonder if Fiona has managed to sort a flight out. I must remember to ask her."

The following morning was Saturday, and when Carrie returned from the hairdressing salon, she began to prepare an old favourite meal. Japanese steak was simple and absolutely delicious. Profiteroles and pouring cream would be the desert and tuna pancakes and side salad for starters. She chose a couple of bottles of Fiona's favourite red wine and some beers for the men. Quite suited with her preparations, she went to Fiona's for a coffee. When she pulled up outside, she was more than surprised to find Fiona cleaning the windows. Fiona didn't do windows. Inside there appeared to be a spring-clean occurring and there were delicious smells emitting from the kitchen.

"What you up to?" asked Carrie nonchalantly.

Fiona grinned, and said "We're having a visitor."

"Is it the Queen of Siam?" retorted Carrie in a sarcastic tone.

"Not quite" said Fiona. "But I'm glad you're here. Maybe you can help me fathom why Alan suddenly decided yesterday that we're selling up. We have viewers coming in about an hour.

"And you're baking for them!?" Carrie was in a wicked mood, but Fiona wasn't amused.

"No, that's for Uncle Tom."

"Since when has Uncle Tom ever come for a meal?" quizzed Carrie.

"Well, not very often, but it seems he's going back abroad and wants to see us both before he goes. The least I could do is cook him a meal", said Fiona.

"What's really going on?" asked Carrie.

Fiona looked like she was going to burst into tears and Carrie wondered if she should really be giving her friend the third degree. After all it was nothing to do with her. It was just so odd, but then again everything seemed odd these days.

The girls enjoyed a cappuccino while Carrie tried to decipher Fiona's garbled sentences. Why would Alan suddenly announce they were moving, and where did these viewers miraculously emerge from so soon? Why was Uncle Tom visiting for a meal when she knew Fiona and Alan hardly ever saw him? And why did she get the impression that her friend didn't really want to talk about it? Carrie decided to make her exit under the pretext of having to get the meal underway. She gave Fiona a hug and wished her luck with her viewers. She wished her well with her visitor too and left.

"See you later for dinner" yelled Carrie when she was almost at the gate. They blew one another a kiss. Carrie felt her mind in turmoil. 'What on earth was going on?'

Fiona had informed her that their flight to America would be the day after Carrie and Mel's. The meeting with the antique jewellery expert had been arranged. Fiona had stated this in a matter of fact manner and not in any way indicated her excitement about the venture. Mulling all this over in her mind, Carrie went back home.

Mel had had a busy day too. Amongst all the mayhem organising his daughter's wedding, and a million DIY jobs, he was also trying to trace his family tree. He had been stuck on a particular ancestor for a few months and didn't seem to be getting anywhere. There was some mystery surrounding the gentleman in question, and the tale was quite bizarre. He had been trying to sift the truth from the fantasy, but no matter which way he turned, he kept coming up with blanks. He had been to the reference library that morning to look at some articles about the Wars of the past couple of hundred years. His grandfather had also served in Burma and he was looking up some newspaper articles when he remembered the story about Fiona and the jewellery. He searched on the Internet to see if he could find an atom of truth in the story Fiona had told them. He was surprised to find that indeed centuries ago, there had been feuding in Burma and ancient palaces had been burnt and pillaged. Carrie would be thrilled he'd taken the time to do some research. They sat and chatted about each other's news and agreed that the turn of events was amazing. Carrie told him they would be meeting Fiona and Alan in New York and that she would accompany Fiona to the antique expert. Maybe he and Alan could go for a beer while the girls did that. Mel thought that was a sound idea and they both went about their business for the afternoon.

Fiona and Alan arrived about eight o'clock, laden with bottles of wine and goodies for 'afters'. Carrie had presented the dining table beautifully, and they sat by the candlelight and enjoyed their meal, drank a couple of bottles of wine and listened to Frank Sinatra singing in the background. Enjoying each other's company they chatted excitedly about their trip to New York.

The next few days were a whirlwind and last but not least was the trip to Cynthia's with Megan. She had been very good, and hadn't pulled much on the lead except when Cynthia appeared on the other side of the gates with Megan's two canine friends, and she'd nearly pulled Mel's arm out of its socket. They parted company, which was always sad for Carrie and Mel, although Megan didn't appear to be one bit perturbed by the separation. They set off to Lisa and Graham's where they would stay overnight and travel to the airport together the following morning. They had to rise at the crack of dawn to be at the airport three hours before the flight. Carrie could feel her stomach welling up. She hated flying and remembered many years ago working for a financial advisor, who flew his own small plane. He had invited her to go up with him one morning, and she was feeling brash and said yes. They were taxiing along the runway when she begged him to stop so she could get out. Her thoughts had been, 'Oh, my God, what if something happens, and the plane crashes, and Mel doesn't even know I was here'. And so, she had clambered out, disbelieving that he had flown off by himself anyway, leaving her completely alone at the small aerodrome to await his return. Another incident she could recall involving planes was when she'd been flying back from Dublin and was sitting beside Lisa waiting for the plane to start taxiing. There had been a disturbance about a suitcase which didn't belong to anybody. The authorities had to remove every suitcase from the plane and identify them all, until they found the one that must have belonged to the absent passenger. This had unnerved Carrie to the point of being frantic, and she had begged Lisa to let her off the plane saying she would get a boat home instead. Lisa had not complied. All these thoughts were rushing in and out of her head and she finished up with a migraine, the one she always seemed to get just before she flew. They arrived at Lisa's, drank a couple of glasses of red wine, and flopped excitedly into bed. Carrie lay tossing and turning, her thoughts rolling over and over but eventually from exhaustion, she fell asleep.

She felt a gentle kiss on her face. Mel was up and dressed. Carrie went into panic. "Are we late, are we late?" Mel passed her a cup of tea and said she had twenty minutes to get ready. She piled her hair on top of her head, gathered it up into a clip and ran downstairs to find everyone waiting. "Right, let's do it", she said positively and hurried out of the front door and down the grassy bank to the car leaving the others flabbergasted. Carrie normally dragged her feet where planes were concerned. They decided not to question her enthusiasm and followed with the suitcases.

The drive to the airport was a pleasant one. Hardly any traffic on the road, and they were there in a little over half an hour. They were collecting an airport car and leaving their own in the compound. Carrie and Lisa stood in the early morning mist with the cases, while Mel and Graham took their car to exchange it for the lovely Mercedes that would take them to the terminal. The boys appeared in the car, and Lisa and Carrie jumped in and the excitement began. Lisa was so looking forward to this trip. Carrie had decided she was not going to let the plane journey spoil it. This was for Lisa and she would let nothing dampen the anticipation.

They disembarked in Amsterdam with a waiting time of three hours until they could board their flight to New York. They meandered round the airport for a few minutes getting their bearings, and then sauntered into an Irish bar. They positioned themselves in a corner of the bar from where they could watch the fascinating things people did when they thought no-one was watching, unbelievably funny things, bizarre and sometimes dangerous. Carrie was watching the waiter carry drinks to another table where a young couple were scrutinising a Dutch map. Two back packs were perched precariously on the bench at the side of them and she found herself wondering what nationality they were, and what they were doing in Amsterdam. Her mind wandered once again into the past. The back-packs had reminded her of a special friend whose partner lost his life in a mountaineering incident some years ago. That thought evoked the word dangerous, and that in turn reminded her of when they had been caravanning in Loch Ness. They had taken Lisa to hunt for Nessie. They were sited on the banks of the Loch and every morning at first light, a man appeared in a wet suit, a balaclava and goggles. They watched him jump off the 'edge' and naturally assumed he was jumping into the Loch. One morning, Mel decided to get a little closer, so he donned hat and coat, left the caravan, and wandered over to a position from where he could observe the man a little more closely. When he came back to the caravan he was doubled up with laughter. When Carrie questioned his jollity, he could hardly get his words out, and the more he tried to tell her, the more he laughed. Eventually, he managed to blurt out that the man wasn't jumping into the Loch at all. There was a small ledge just beneath the banks of the Loch, and he was jumping onto that, wandering back along the ledge and emerging back on the banks of the Loch, and going back to his caravan. She remembered watching that ritual every day and laughing heartily at the man's antics and wondering why he would be performing such a peculiar ritual. The man had been sarcastically nicknamed 'Dangerous Brian'.

Carrie was summoned from her meandering thoughts by a noise in the far corner of the bar. The waiter appeared with their drinks and sensing Carrie's alarm at the rumpus in his bar, asked her not to be alarmed, informing them that a particular local vagabond had been banned from the place for upsetting customers because of his unwashed smell. Every day he tried to climb through one of the open windows in the gents toilets. Some days he got the windows mixed up and tried to climb through the ladies toilet window. Carrie didn't think this was at all amusing and wondered if the man in question knew exactly what he was doing. The thought occurred to her that if one day there was nobody to apprehend him climbing through the window, his mission could well be accomplished and she couldn't understand why the waiter thought it even slightly amusing. She decided not to pursue the topic and instead turned to watch a lady emerging from the ladies room. She was quite elderly, very straight-backed, her hair swept into a French pleat with a large comb at either side, bright red lipstick, tweed skirt and what Carrie assumed to be a mink jacket, but it was what she was carrying that made her appear odd. Instead of a handbag over her arm, she clutched a small briefcase. Carrie wondered what the lady could possibly be carrying in a briefcase and why she didn't have a handbag with her. She began to fantasise about the lady and the briefcase. 'What had happened in her life to bring her to this point today, in a bar at Amsterdam airport, emerging from the ladies loo with a briefcase?' Even Carrie admitted her thoughts were often absurd but she couldn't help wondering. She watched the lady walk over to a secluded corner, edge herself onto a bench behind a table, lay the briefcase down on the table in front of her, take a sip of the drink waiting for her and begin a conversation with the gentleman sat opposite. Carrie was so enthralled with her own ideas, that Mel startled her when he spoke.

"Have we got a secret agent in the place?" he said with a hint of sarcasm.

Carrie knew by his tone that he too must have thought the situation odd. Time rolled by and it was soon time to wander over to the departure lounge for their impending journey. As they got up to leave, Carrie knew instinctively that someone was watching her and she felt conspicuous. She decided that the someone else was just a people-watcher like herself and dismissed the thought. She instinctively turned to the secluded corner but the lady and the briefcase had gone.

Carrie shut her eyes tight, sucked like mad on a barley sugar and waited for the inevitable feeling in the pit of her stomach as the plane left the ground. It never got any easier. When the monstrous lump of metal began to accelerate, she once again felt the tears pouring down her face. She couldn't stop them, they were always there, an emotion which drowned her each time she flew. Once they were at the correct altitude, she slowly began to uncoil and so long as she couldn't see any land, relaxed a little as she watched the fluffy clouds beyond the man sat on the left next to her. He was wearing a very expensive after-shave. 'Nice smell' she thought. She observed that he was wringing his hands, and wondered if he too, hated flying. She scanned as much of the plane as she could for the lady in the tweed skirt, but she was not there.

She linked her husband's arm and snuggled against his shoulder while they looked at pictures in the in-flight magazine. Her eyes slowly began to close, the excitement finally betraying her intent to remain awake. A sudden immense feeling of descent, like being on a downward roller coaster jolted her eyes open and she tightened her grip on Mel's arm. It was only momentary and the turbulence soon abated.

"How long have I been asleep?"

Mel smiled down at her. "About twenty minutes hun." He squeezed her hand. The flight was thankfully an uneventful one, and after the cabin crew had fed and watered them a couple of times, they both fell asleep and only awoke when the stewardess tapped Mel on the shoulder politely asking him to put his leg back in front of him. She wheeled her trolley past him and the last drink of the flight was distributed. They both chose tea. As the aeroplane began its descent into Newark Airport, Carrie began to think intensely about Fiona and the Burmese jewellery. Was it going to be priceless? Had they simply just planned to be in New York at the same time as Carrie and Mel? Her thoughts would be put to the test over the next few days. Right now, she was just thankful that the plane had made its customary bump down onto the runway, and New York was hurtling past and it felt like the pilot had lost the ability to apply the brakes.

New York 2005 AD

The airport was teeming with people of every nationality and they were glad to emerge into the open. They instantly saw the placard with their surname, and behind the man holding it was the big yellow taxi which would take them across the Brooklyn Bridge towards the reason for Carrie's excited jibberish. As they sat on the back seat in the taxi, Carrie didn't know which way to look. She didn't want to miss a single thing and her head felt like it was on a pivot, until they started the approach to the bridge, and the only place she then wanted to look was straight in front. There it was. The Manhattan skyline as she'd perceived it in stories and seen on television. Never in her wildest dreams had she imagined it could be as beautiful in real life. Stretching out in front of them, tall, elegant, majestic, yet evocative of a city from a science fiction movie. She cried tears of joy and felt she would burst from excitement. She was electrified at the sight, igniting a flame of insatiable energy and stimulating an intense desire to explore the soul of this extraordinary city. Lisa had known her mum would feel exactly as she had herself on seeing Manhattan for the first time and for a moment there was an all-knowing silence between them, as Lisa squeezed her mum's hand. As the city loomed ever nearer and the delirium gained momentum, Lisa began pointing out landmarks and locations to her parents. She and Graham had been a number of times and their delight was evident. The city was magnificent from a distance and there had been no overstatement in Lisa's marvellous description.

Once across the Hudson River, the enormity of the architecture took their breath away. Carrie was doing somersaults inside the cab, trying desperately to see the top of buildings and categorically failing. Loud shouts of 'Oh my God, look at that, Lisa, Graham, Mel, just look at that, oh my God, it's fabulous', carried through the partly open dividing glass which made the taxi driver smile. Of Afro-Caribbean descent, he had lived in the city for ten years and loved his job, especially bringing people into the city for their first time. As the traffic lights turned swiftly to red, and the cab lurched to a halt, the middle aged driver turned and welcomed them, asking them where they were from, and how long they would stay. He slid the glass doors open a little further and enthusiastically enthralled them with tales of his exploits as a NYC cab driver. He pointed out directions to the Empire State Building, to the Rockafella Centre, Macy's, Bloomingdales and Central Park. To Carrie, this man would forever be an integral part of their trip and she hoped they might ride in his taxi again.

The vehicle came to a halt outside their hotel on Lexington Avenue. Carrie was so glad she'd decided to change into her flat knee-length boots. She eased herself out of the vehicle and let her feet sink into the foot deep snow. Mel paid the driver and they all made their way into the hotel foyer. By now Carrie's excitement was overriding all else and as she turned to give Mel a big kiss, her heart skipped a beat. Through the panoramic window behind Mel, she saw

110

a black sedan pull up outside the hotel. 'There must be hundreds of black sedans in New York', she quickly thought, and tried to ignore it, but the reality was beginning to dawn they were being followed.

"Passport please", barked the receptionist.

They had reached the front of the queue and although Carrie knew the hotel receptionist had a job to do, she felt he could have been a little more pleasant doing it, but nonetheless handed over her passport. When she returned her gaze to the window the black sedan had gone. Her thoughts turned to Fiona, who by now must be so excited. She would be getting ready to leave for the airport. Somehow she had the strangest feeling that the black sedan and Fiona's trip to America were not unconnected, although she tried to dismiss the idea as ridiculous. Mel was always teasing her about her vivid imagination, but somehow this time, she just knew her intuition was on the right track.

They took the oversized lift up to the fifth floor of the hotel and located their rooms. Carrie laughed and said "I think I'd have preferred the lift, it's twice the size of this." The silly thought of them in a bed in the lift going up and down made her giggle. There was an en suite and after retrieving some clothes from the confines of the case and hanging them on a peg, Carrie took a quick shower. Refreshed after their long journey, she rang Fiona to let her know they'd arrived.

Carrie and Mel were meeting Lisa and Graham in the foyer in about an hour, dressed for the snow and as it was only late afternoon, they would be able to do a bit of exploring before dinner. Carrie watched her handsome husband getting ready. He was very tall and slim, his once dark hair now receded and although a few age lines had appeared, he wore them well. They were hidden under his NYC bobble hat which Lisa had procured for him. He double wrapped the lovely warm scarf around his neck, zipped up his titanium snow jacket, slipped the gloves onto his pianist's hands and said "Right, are you ready love?"

"Will be in a sec."

Carrie began the process of donning socks, boots, coat, gloves, hat and scarf. It was now Mel's turn to watch. Carrie, as he kept telling her, was a handsome woman, and like her long deceased mother, age was eluding her. She constantly altered the style of her long dark hair to suit her mood. Sometimes she scrunched it until it formed a halo of curls, and sometimes she wore it in a pony tail with a variety of adornments and combs. Today's choice was a pony tail, which she pushed up under her thick cream woollen bobble hat, making her look as cheeky as Mel. She wrapped up warmly and tightly. Her cheeks displayed a warm rosy glow and her lipstick blended perfectly. Her cream accessories complemented the Tuscan coat and her eyes glinted mischievously at Mel. She was happy and it showed. Both raring to go, they closed the hotel room door behind them and set off on their adventure into the snowy streets of New York. Collecting Lisa and Graham from the foyer, they stepped into the biting wind and Carrie was so excited, she didn't know where to look first. There were yellow taxis trying to bully their way through the traffic but sliding along instead. There were people scurrying by, trying not to slip on the sidewalks. The immensity of the buildings continued to take her breath away. They went into a coffee bar for a minute from the cold, while Lisa read her street map. She wanted her mother and father to see as much as was humanly possible in the four days they would be there. Of course Lisa and Graham were not aware at this stage that Fiona and Alan would also be in the vicinity in a few short hours. Carrie and Mel felt awful about keeping it from them, but were more than a little concerned that the fewer people who knew, the better. Lisa opened up her map. Graham and Mel brought the coffees and a blueberry muffin each to the table. Lisa proceeded to lecture everyone about the avenues of Manhattan and they all agreed they'd like to walk to Times Square before dinner. Carrie couldn't contain herself, swallowed her coffee and picked up her muffin.

"Right then", she said. "Are we all ready, let's go, come on and …..'

Just then, she stood frozen to the spot as she saw a black sedan parked across the street. Three men got out and ran across the road to the hotel. The one the four of them had just come out of. She watched as they went through the swing doors and disappeared. Her heart was racing at ninety to the dozen and she decided now would be a good time to reintroduce Mel's memory to the night they peered out of the bedroom window at home. The others hadn't noticed her sudden reluctance to leave the coffee bar and were eager to start their adventure. She caught up with Mel as he was opening the door and grabbed hold of his hand, practically dragging him out of the establishment and on up the street. To

Carrie's relief, Lisa and Graham were lagging behind playing in the snow which had begun to fall quite heavily.

Mel listened intently as Carrie told him of the black sedan and its occupants.

"What could they possibly want with us?" asked Mel. "It's nothing to do with us, we're here on holiday. How could they even think we are connected to Fiona, and why aren't they following her instead of us, if in fact they're following us at all? I'm very sceptical hun. I think it's that oversized imagination of yours again."

"No" said Carrie. "You have to believe me. There's been more than one occasion when I've thought someone has been following us. Even the lady in the airport bar was odd, the one with the brief case for a handbag."

"Oh Carrie, now you're being totally paranoid."

"Well, if I am", quipped Carrie, "it's for good reason. I just know there's something funny going on. Maybe we'll feel better when Fee gets here and we can talk it over with them and see if they think there's any connection, or whether it's just simply coincidence, but there's too may coincidences for my liking."

Tightening her grip on Mel's arm, Carrie suddenly felt quite scared at the prospect of stalkers. She didn't see the men or their car again that day, and once distanced from them by a couple of blocks, she began to relax a little and enjoy her wonderful new surroundings. Lisa and Graham plodded along behind them, kissing, cuddling and totally oblivious to the trio observing them from a doorway across the street.

Fiona and Alan

The Boeing 737 careered along the runway, accelerating for take-off. Fiona and Alan were seated at the rear. Neither were concerned about flying and usually quite thrilled about take-off and landing. This time was different. Fiona felt a sense of foreboding she couldn't quite pinpoint. Alan dismissed her comments, suggesting that it was the reason for the flight that was making her jittery. Sitting in front of them was a lady with two small children and across the aisle was an elderly lady wearing a tweed skirt, red lipstick and clutching a briefcase.

The aeroplane lifted off the ground. Two or three seconds later there was a loud bang. The passengers drew a sharp intake of breath and one or two screamed. Further along the plane in front of them a passenger sitting by a window over the wing was getting uncomfortably warm. People were shouting questions. The fasten seatbelt sign was still showing as they hadn't yet reached altitude. The captain's voice came over the loud speaker.

"Good evening everybody, I'm Captain Seddon. Everything is under control. I'm sure you will all know by now, that we appear to have a minor problem, and as a precaution only, I'm taking the plane back to the airport. Please do not be alarmed and please keep your seatbelts fastened. Thank you."

The passenger by the wing was getting extremely agitated and called over the stewardess. There appeared to be a commotion and people stood

115

up screaming. The captain was turning the plane in preparation for their descent. People peered out of windows but the plane still appeared to be very high. The captain's voice was heard again.

"Ladies and gentlemen, please return to your seats and remain calm. We have clearance to land and everything is under control. Thank you." Fiona and Alan held hands tightly. Fiona looked out of the window and was extremely concerned that she could not yet see the runway, and the commotion seemed to be gaining momentum, particularly by the wing seats. Everyone at the back was desperate to know what was wrong. They were scared. Whispers came back down the rows of seats that one of the engines was on fire. Another loud bang seemed to make the aircraft veer sharply. Everyone's heart was racing and every passenger thought they were going to crash. Couples held onto one another and children clung to their parents crying. The stewardesses were trying to calm the situation by gently returning passengers to their seats. Fiona and Alan were holding one another in a tight embrace believing this was the end. Everyone on the plane thought they were going to die.

The plane's descent was swift now. People were vomiting from fear, and then the runway came into view. Everyone prayed. Silence enveloped the plane like a ghostly ship sailing through fog in the dead of night. Everyone prayed harder. Fiona and Alan didn't look out of the window any more. They just clung tightly declaring their eternal love for each other, tightly, tightly, kissing, crying, kissing again. Through their tears they felt the bump which denoted the plane had touched the runway. They each released their grip on the other and peered out of the window. It looked like pandemonium down there. Ambulances and fire engines raced along trying to keep pace with the plane. The co-pilot's voice could be heard over the loud speaker.

"Ladies and Gentlemen please do not be alarmed by the emergency services following the aircraft. Please remain calm and stay seated until your stewardess gives you further instructions." They felt the brakes being applied and after what seemed an inordinately long time, the plane began to taxi and eventually came to a halt. By now the fire was visible to everyone and people were in panic. The cabin crew positioned themselves in a line down the plane and gave instructions for leaving the aircraft. The emergency hatches were opened and the shutes blown. People were asked to leave the plane in an orderly fashion. The stewardesses stood by each row of passengers, and one by one, they all slid down the shute to people waiting at the bottom. Miraculously no-one was seriously injured. A few people were seen to be getting into an ambulance. Fiona thought it was the people who had been sitting in the row beside the wing. It was Fiona's turn to slide down the shute. They were ushered into a waiting bus which would take them back to the terminal. As the bus left the side of the aircraft, fire crews could be seen tackling the engine fire. Fiona activated her mobile phone to ring her family and tell them of their ordeal, and she rang Carrie and Mel to say they wouldn't be arriving on time as there had been a flight delay. Once in the terminal, passengers on flight 2279 were given a ticket to buy a drink courtesy of the airline and Fiona and Alan waited their turn in the long queue.

They exchanged their ticket for two cups of tea, and found a seat. Fiona took two pain relief pills. She had a headache and thought she was going to be sick.

"What do we do now", she asked Alan.

"We'll have to wait and see what flight they're going to put us on", replied her husband

"I don't know if I want to go on another one", cried Fee. "I can't believe that's just happened, it was like a nightmare. I thought we were going to die and I'd never see you or the kids again." Her voice was shaky and she began sobbing uncontrollably. Alan wrapped his arms around her. He smiled and said with a hint of sarcasm, "That legend thingy with the jewels might have saved us."

"What do you mean? What do you know that I don't?"

"Oh, nothing much, in fact I've only just remembered about it. Mel did a bit of research, and apparently, rubies are said to protect their owners from accidents and such. I know it's daft, but I wonder if there's anything in it."

Fiona had gone white. "Oh my God, that's unbelievable. We're up there, I don't know how many thousand feet in the air. An engine blows up, catches fire, and we land safely. How many planes have you ever heard of developing that big a problem in the air and landing safely?"

"Well I'm sure things like that do happen, it's just never happened to us before, and because the jewels are prevalent in our minds at the moment, I just wondered." He smiled at her. "Well I don't mind believing it just at the minute. 'If they've saved us, that's fantastic, thanks Ruby!"

Fiona managed a smile back at him but added "Don't mock them, we don't know what else they can do."

"No, well anyway, we're safe now, we're warm, we've had a hot drink and a rest, I think it's time to go and find out when our next flight is."

They got up to leave, and Fiona noticed the lady in the tweed skirt again. She didn't know why, but there was something about her that unnerved her.

"Don't you think that lady's a bit odd?", she asked Alan.

"Why? What's wrong with her? She's just a little old lady."

"Well she's hardly little but don't you think it's odd she's carrying a briefcase?"

"Perhaps she's carrying jewels for an expert valuation" laughed Alan.

Fiona saw the funny side and laughed too.

"Are ours safe", she asked, knowing full well that they were of course tucked safely into the bottom most corner of Alan's hand luggage. There had been a hairy moment, when the stewardess wouldn't let them carry their hand luggage off the plane, but they were reunited when their bus and the cage carrying their luggage met at the terminal.

"Yes", he said, "stop worrying Fee, you're beginning to sound like Carrie" and squeezed her hand. "It'll be ok. You'll see."

They quickened their step and hurried to the information desk.

There was a long queue at the desk and Fiona and Alan could see that many of the people standing there becoming agitated had been passengers on the same flight. The two children who had been sat near them were alarmingly noisy and were running round and round and darting in between people. One gentleman had a paper cup full of coffee balancing on his rather large hand luggage, and one of the children dived past him and knocked it off. The brown liquid spilt all over his luggage and quite naturally he was annoyed and began to shout that all parents should keep their misbehaved, rowdy children under control. Quite a commotion followed. Fiona and Alan crossed over to the window where they found two empty seats. They weren't sure how long they would have to remain at the airport but they would join the queue when things quietened down.

"I wonder if they'll put us up in a hotel if we can't get another flight tonight." said Fiona. "I was beginning to get quite excited, but now I'm wondering if we'll ever get there. We'll have to keep Carrie and Mel posted."

"That's a good plan", replied Alan. "As soon as that queue goes down a bit, we'll get over there and do some finding out."

They watched, through the window, the activity outside on the tarmac. Fiona broke the silence.

"It's a pity we can't sit looking at them. We don't know what's going to happen when this man values them. If they are the ones they're on about, they'll probably want to buy them off us to complete their collection, so we wouldn't have them any more, and their beauty would be lost to us."

"Yes", said Alan, "but look at all them luvverly pennies!"

"Let's not count our chickens, suppose we'll just have to wait and see. I'm beginning to get impatient. I just want to be there now."

"Come on love."

They held hands and joined the back of the queue, which had diminished considerably. The children, their parents and the shouting man had gone. The lady in the tweed skirt was up at the counter. Fiona watched her curiously. She was very tall for an old lady and held her back very straight. She wished she could get a bit nearer to her. Perhaps she'd have a better clue what appeared odd. She had the strangest feeling from a side profile she was vaguely familiar but that was bizarre. 'I've never seen this person before in my life. Have I?' Fiona was racking her brains trying to imagine where she could possibly know her from. They had been moving slowly up the queue. Alan gently pushed her forward and they were at the desk.

"May I have your name please, madam" asked the young girl at the desk.

"Fiona Oliver. Mr & Mrs Oliver", said Fiona. "We were on flight 2279 and we're wondering when our next flight will be."

"Yes, madam, the airline is proposing to accommodate you at the Cosmopolitan Hotel for tonight, and your new flight will be at 0900 hours tomorrow. We apologise for any inconvenience suffered, and of course your hotel room will be free of charge. However, you would be expected to pay for any meals and drinks charges that you may incur. Check in will be 0700 hours. May I just see your passports please?"

It was obvious there would be no further comment from the young lady about their trauma, and Fee refrained from asking if it would be the same plane after the repairs had been done that they would fly out on. She didn't really want to know the answer.

"Thank you madam", said the girl, handing back the passports. "All seems to be in order. If you would like to go to the blue bus stop by the main entrance there will be a coach along in a few moments to take you to your hotel. Thank you for travelling with us and for your patience. I hope you have a pleasant evening".

Alan wanted to bombard the lady in uniform with questions, but like Fiona, he felt he didn't want to know the answers, and even if he asked, she wouldn't be able to tell him.' Company protocol' they would say. They walked away silently, and found the coach stop. They didn't have to wait long before the coaches arrived.

It was a lavish hotel, Fiona thought, and although she would much have preferred to be on her way to New York to meet Carrie, she was extremely tired, needed to refresh herself, and was actually looking forward to taking a hot shower and sinking into bed. Luckily, she had put a few clean clothes in her hand luggage and was very grateful for that small luxury. She assumed the hotel would provide everything else. She was right. Room 260 was beautiful, decorated in a pale lilac, with a deep purple throw on the bed, and peeping from beneath the throw were fresh, clean, white Egyptian cotton sheets. She almost longed to climb into bed and sleep now, but she knew Alan would be hungry and want to eat. She put her bag down and took out a few necessities.

"I'll just have a quick shower. See you in a minute."

The hotel had provided them with a few toiletries and plenty of towels, and Fiona's shower was luxuriously hot. She draped the warm towel around her and went back into the room, where Alan had made her a cup of tea. She sipped the tea, and asked if they should have a look at their jewels again. Alan picked up his bag, and almost as if he was expecting them not to be there, he gently pushed his hand to the bottom of the bag.

"Oh no", he said, with a horrified look on his face, "They've gone."

Then he smiled and pulled out the bag. Fiona whacked him with her free hand almost spilling her tea.

"You rotten beggar, don't do that", she squealed.

They opened up the cloth bag and Alan carefully placed the jewellery on the bed. They stared at them, mesmerised by their beauty and as with every other occasion, the tantalising gems sparkled back at them and took their breath away. They were absolutely gorgeous. Some of the jewels were loose gems; big rubies, small ones, predominantly deep red. Even in the light of the hotel room their colour was vivid and extremely intense, yet they looked perfectly transparent. Neither Fiona nor Alan had expert knowledge of jewellery, but Fiona's Auntie had worked for a jeweller and sometimes told her of rich people who brought items in to be valued, so she felt she had a little knowledge. She knew the size of a stone was a contributing factor, as well as the colour, the translucency and the facets. And these rubies were big, some more so than others, but the largest one was the most amazing stone she had ever seen. Almost indescribable, wonderfully ornate, she was certain that it had special qualities. Some of the rubies were set into jewellery alongside what she believed to be diamonds.

"What do you think will happen?" Fiona said in a low voice.

She was almost too scared to ask, in case the inanimate objects became offended or turned into raging monsters and gobbled her up.

"I think they're genuine and I think this guy will try and rip us off. I don't think there's anything we can do about it and I think the jewels will finish up in a museum, raking in millions of pounds in an exhibition. That's what I think will happen", said Alan.

Fiona wasn't happy with any of the security options, but she didn't feel safe taking them out. She didn't much fancy bringing attention to the fact that they had valuables requiring a safe, so they unanimously decided to put them in the room safe while they went for a meal. They wouldn't discuss their possessions within a ten mile radius of another human being. 'The gems, if genuine, would generate a huge amount of interest from all sorts of unsavoury characters', thought Alan. He was already worrying about the worst case scenario, but hadn't voiced his fears in case it worried Fiona. They opened cupboards and drawers, looked under the bed, behind curtains, under the mattress, and finally opened a small built-in wardrobe.

"I've found it!"

Alan put the bag of jewellery inside the little box and turned the key to lock the safe. It didn't want to turn at first, but eventually the little key turned three hundred and sixty degrees, and the safe was locked. They turned out the main light, leaving a small bedside lamp on, creating a warm glow in the room, and left. They took the lift even though Fiona didn't like them. She remembered a hair-raising experience she'd had in a major chain store in the town when the children were little. The youngest had needed to go the toilet, and there were none. She'd asked one of the assistants if there were staff toilets she could use, as her child was desperate. The assistant was only a young girl, and indicated that if Fiona went through the door at the back of the store marked 'staff', she would find a service lift. Fiona had done as instructed.

Once inside the back of the store, it was like walking into another world. She could smell raw bacon and of course that was because the store bought huge sides of pork, and packaged it. She could smell the musty stone floor, and the smell of fresh fruit and vegetables. This deviation from the norm had reminded her of a fresh fruit and vegetable market she had been taken to as a little girl with her mother on a Saturday morning. Brightly coloured stalls piled high with all varieties of fruit and vegetables, giant leeks, cauliflowers as big as footballs, beetroots with the stalks and leaves still attached, the beets themselves as big as grapefruits. On the other side of the market was the fishmonger's stall. Fiona's mother had had to drag her away from them. She was completely fascinated by the creatures which still wriggled on the fish counter piled high on top of one another, the colours blending into one another like a hazy rainbow on a wet morning. She could still smell the familiar yellow Finnon Haddock, or 'finnie haddie', which her mother cooked in milk in the oven. Fish as big as an oval plate with red spots all over their skin, lobsters, and entities she had never known the name of, still squirming. She loved that market, and knew it would remain in her memory forever.

That memory was poignant now, as she remembered standing in the back of the high street store looking for a lift to take her, the children and the pushchair up to the toilets. Having found the lift, she had asked a man in a brown coat to open it for her. She stood inside the lift with the large pushchair, and the huge metal gate shut them all inside, as the heavy metal clanged into the other side of its holding. She was told to press the button showing the number one, which she did, and the lift slowly grinded, making odd jangly noises, and jerked into an upward movement. She assumed the bottom of the lift had just cleared the ground floor, when the thing jerked to a halt. She realised in stark terror the lift had malfunctioned with her and the girls still in it. There was no phone and of course there were no mobile phones. She would have to yell. This she had done loudly. She asked the girls to yell too, but they were too busy eating bags of sweets, so she continued yelling through the pattern in the heavy gates which were imprisoning them. It had seemed like an eternity before Fiona realised that someone had discovered the problem. They had pressed the button to bring the lift down and it hadn't obeyed. Five or so minutes later, two young gentlemen were apologetically escorting her out of the lift on the first floor, into even mustier surroundings, but she saw the toilet door and aimed the pushchair straight for it, weaving her way through cardboard boxes lining the route.

Their lift slid to a quiet, seemingly motionless halt and Fiona and Alan stepped out into the foyer of the airport hotel. The doors on the lift next to them had just closed and were going up. The lady in that lift pressed button five. She was wearing a tweed skirt and carried a small brief case. She had just received a telephone call from the man in Room 262 who was standing in the corridor. He had telephoned his sister Sophie minutes before and now disappeared quickly down the staircase, heading for the basement car park. He too, had been a passenger on flight 2279. The lift stopped at floor five and the lady stepped out, walked directly to Room 260, took a key out from a concealed pocket in her skirt, opened the door and disappeared quietly inside. The perfume which Fiona had just sprayed attacked her nostrils as she searched swiftly and silently for the prize she had come to collect. It didn't take her long to locate the safe. She had assumed nothing less than the room safe for the security of the valuables and was banking on the fact that their stay would only be for one night and perhaps they wouldn't trouble the manager for the hotel safe. She had guessed accurately. The only thing the lady in the tweed skirt hadn't banked on was the fire alarm going off.

Standing at five feet ten inches tall in his stocking feet and of slight build, Tom never thought in his wildest dreams he'd get away with this scam, dressed in drag, but here he was, fighting for all he was worth to recover what he truly believed was his rightful inheritance. The consequences of his actions had never entered his head. He thought his little game was over in the ladies toilets when some silly old pervert almost gave him away. He had thought it safer to go to the ladies, but hadn't reckoned on the tramp trying to gain access through the window of the cubicle he was in.

Loud bells always reminded him of the fateful day at St Edward's Boys' School, and this was no exception. The fire bell sounded loud in his ears and made him jump out of his skin. For a split second he believed it was the demons of old Adamson, who had come back to haunt him committing yet another crime. He immediately regained composure and realised the cause of the sound, making him hurry even more. The skirt was a nuisance. 'How do women wear these damned things?' he thought. Seconds later the safe was open. He seized his prize and placed the cloth bag into his briefcase. He slammed the door of the safe. The tweed skirt had attached itself to the clasp. Panicking he pulled the skirt free, tearing it slightly, relocked the safe and left the room.

It was absolute pandemonium in the corridor outside the room. Everybody was running this way and that, not really knowing where they were going. He sniffed the air, trying to establish if there really was a fire, or if it could be a drill. He decided to go with the latter. Of course it was a drill. Real fires were too scary and it couldn't be one of those. He began to run. He had the briefcase tucked tightly under his left arm. He wasn't familiar with the layout of this hotel, and wondered whether to take a lift, or use the stairwell. His nose caught a whiff of smoke but he dismissed it. 'It won't matter in a minute' he thought, 'I'll be out of here'. He decided to take the lift, and inserted his arm into the closing doors of one going down. It was a squash, but he didn't feel as vulnerable in amongst a crowd, as he would have done running about on his own. He clung tightly to the case and kept his head down as the lift began its descent. He could hear screaming in the distance. The others in the lift heard it too and immediately everyone could sense that something was really wrong.

"Oh my God, what is it?" cried one young girl standing at the back. Someone replied with another question.

"Is this a drill, or is there a fire?"

"Don't know", said someone else, "it's scary though. Hope this lift makes it to the ground."

The lift came to a smooth halt and everyone waited for the doors to open. They didn't. "Mummy, why don't we go out?" said a small girl standing in the far corner, hanging onto her mother's dress. The person standing nearest to the controls began pressing buttons in an attempt to open the doors, but they remained firmly shut. He pressed the alarm button. The alarm sounded. Tom imagined. He hated bells. They stood there waiting to be rescued from the lift. No help came. There didn't seem to be any air in the lift, and people became extremely uncomfortable. Tom felt perspiration forming into beads on his forehead and hoped his make-up wouldn't run.

Fiona had decided on a quick bar snack followed by a brisk walk. Alan chose a wrap filled with chicken, bacon, salad and mayonnaise and half a pint of bitter while Fiona munched on a bowl of cheesy chips and a glass of white wine. They were very hungry and it hadn't taken them long to consume the lot. It had been very warm inside the hotel, and although they knew it would be freezing outside, it would be very refreshing, and tire them so they would sleep. They had ventured outside and decided to walk around the hotel complex. They talked quietly about their adventure, and all that had happened so far.

"I'm glad we left the jewels inside", said Fiona. "I kept imagining someone jumping out on us."

"Don't be daft", snapped Alan. "And anyway no-one knows about them except Carrie and Mel, and they wouldn't be jumping out at us."

Fiona laughed and said "Well, they can't, they're already in New York, where we should be by now."

"Not long" said Alan. "This time tomorrow."

Fiona snuggled into his body.

"I hope nothing else goes wrong. Who'd have believed all this? It's absolutely bizarre. I can't really believe it's happening, and who knows what's going to happen when we get there. I could get quite paranoid."

"Well don't think about it, scaredy cat", laughed Alan. 'You're quite safe. You're with me and I won't let anything happen to you."

Fiona had been looking down at her feet while she was walking so she didn't slip on the icy patches. She lifted her head to the sound of the commotion going on just ahead of them at the entrance to the hotel.

"What's going on there?" she asked. "Alan, what is it, what's happening?"

"I don't know", he said, "But we're going to find out soon enough. That's the only way back in."

People were running out of the hotel. A few were screaming and there was pushing and shoving in the doorway.

"Think we'll just stand here a minute" said Alan. "I don't like the look of this."

Fiona's nerves were already on edge, and she didn't think she could handle anything else going wrong today.

"Are you sure there isn't another way in? We could try that."

"No", said Alan, "I think we should wait."

They walked on a little and stopped again. A couple who they assumed had come out of the hotel were just in front of them. Alan asked casually "What's happened?"

"Not really sure", said the woman, half smiling. "Some alarm went off, think it's the fire alarm."

"Do you know if there's a fire or is it a drill?"

"Not really sure", replied the woman.

"Well, if it's a real fire", said her partner, "They've not handled it well, it's pandemonium in there. We were quite near the door when the alarm sounded, but there's people screaming and pushing and shoving, and no-one really knows what's happening. The alarm didn't sound for very long, so it's probably a drill. Not going back in though till we know."

"How are we going to find out?" asked Fiona, bemused at the nonchalant way the pair kept flicking their cigarette ash behind them.

"Where's the fire brigade?"

As Alan spoke, they heard the familiar sirens.

"Oh, my God", said Fiona, "it must be real, they're here."

They watched as three vehicles screeched to a halt outside the hotel. Firemen jumped out and ran into the hotel, surging through the large conglomeration of people outside. Some people stood shivering in the cold, others huddled together, and some smoked cigarettes. Some had beer glasses in their hand. Some women were still in their nightwear, and most still wore slippers. Children were being carried, clutching their favourite bedtime toy. Amongst the tears of scepticism it was total chaos. Everyone kept looking up at the hotel, to see if they could glimpse any smoke giving a clue to the mystery surrounding the alarm. But there didn't appear to be any. A hotel official finally came out of the doors towards the crowd, which was now edging slowly back towards the hotel doors. He was armed with a clipboard and carried a loud speaker which he raised to his mouth.

"Everybody, please remain calm. We have everything under control."

Fiona remembered the same words from the Captain on the aeroplane and could hardly believe she was hearing them again.

"You will be able to go back to your rooms in just a few minutes."

Everyone began talking at once. People from every angle were firing questions at the official. The poor man looked more than a little bewildered by the whole procedure. Nothing like this had ever happened on his shift before, and he didn't know how to handle crowd control. He was only a small man, with a black moustache and a decidedly Italian air about him. He spoke perfect English but wondered at that moment whether he could get away with pretending to speak only a little English, and discharged a verbal barricade of Italian discourse. His second main duty that evening was to make an attempt at a roll call. He turned to go back into the hotel, with the crowd hot on his heels, and stood by the swing doors. As people made their way back inside, he took their names and crossed them off the list in front of him. The two firemen who had entered the lobby, were stood at the desk in a deep discussion with the blonde receptionist. The other occupants of the three fire engines remained in their vehicles.

Alan said to Fiona, "Come on love, let's get

back in out of the cold, and see if we can get up to our room."

They followed the rest of the horde back inside the hotel, where it could quite clearly be smelt that there had been a fire.

Confusion reigned supreme, and it was then that the other firemen appeared through the swing doors, armed with all kinds of equipment. The reception desk in the hotel came complete with a suite of rooms behind it for staff. They had taken a new member of staff on a few weeks earlier, and she had been in the kitchen making some toast for a customer with diabetes. She had heard her mobile phone ringing, and gone to the cloakroom to retrieve it. The toast had been forgotten, the fire had begun and was spreading rapidly. On entering the kitchen area again, she had seen the flames and immediately broken the glass on the fire alarm. The Duty Manager had decided that as the alarm had gone off and most people would have heard it, they would treat it as a drill and evacuate.

The hotel official, who had done the roll call, came running over to the desk, brandishing the clipboard and shouting in a mixture of English and Italian. The manager took the clipboard from him, and handed it to one of the firemen. During the fiasco one of the lifts had broken down. The computer had malfunctioned and the lift had stopped at the ground floor with the doors tightly sealed. One of the occupants of the lift had had the foresight to grab his mobile phone when the alarm sounded and had telephoned the desk to inform them that not only had the lift stopped functioning with twenty or so people inside, but that one of the passengers had collapsed and didn't appear to be breathing. The receptionist had asked was it a man or a woman. The reply had been very strange.

"Well we thought it was a woman but when she fell she knocked against someone and it dislodged a wig. She had obviously been very anxious and sweat has made her make-up run. She now looks like an elderly man although he's dressed like a woman."

The receptionist relayed all this information to the hotel manager. The firemen were working diligently outside the lift doors, and eventually managed to prise them open. Inside the lift stood some terrified people. In the tiny space there was panic. A person in a tweed skirt was slumped on the floor. Peeping out from beneath him was a briefcase. The bottom half of him was dressed as a woman. The top half now clearly showed a man's face with smudged make-up. The wig lay beside him. Tom was dead.

Some people stepped out of the lift as soon as it opened to make more space for the firemen to enter. The fireman who checked recorded no pulse. The paramedic team arrived and raced towards the lift with their stretcher, lifted Tom up onto it, and hurried off out of the hotel past Fiona and Alan who stood aside to let the trio out of the swing doors. Fiona looked at the stretcher as it went past and her legs wobbled. The entire colour drained out of her face and she took on a ghostly persona.

"Alan, look. No it can't be. I can't believe it. It's the woman in the tweed skirt, look at her face."

She thought she was going to be sick. Alan tried to stretch his neck to see more clearly. There was Uncle Tom in a tweed skirt with a briefcase lay on top of him. It only took a few seconds to dawn on them the harsh reality of the situation, and with no thought about the fire that could be raging anywhere in the hotel, they ran to the door leading to the stairwell. They bolted through it and up the staircase two at a time. Arriving at the fifth floor they raced hell for leather along the corridor to their room. Alan had the key ready and opened the door. They scrambled on the floor to the safe, opened it and confirmed their worst fears.

"Quick", said Alan, "we have to get the case."

They took wings, and flew down the staircase, Fiona puffing and panting. It was the most exercise she had done for years. They saw the ambulance take off and hailed one of the hotel taxis, yelling at the driver to "follow that ambulance." They clicked in their seat belts, not quite believing what was happening. They remained silent as the taxi driver pelted along after the ambulance, and minutes later, were pulling up outside the hospital's Accident and Emergency unit. Alan dove into his pockets to see what change he had, and handed it all to the driver. They leapt out of the car and headed into the hospital following the stretcher. They were told to be seated. Uncle Tom was taken into theatre, and the door closed tightly behind him. They didn't have to wait long. A doctor came out of the room and they jumped up and approached him.

"May I ask if you are relatives?" he questioned.

Fiona said, "Yes, he's my Uncle. Is he alright?"

"Come with me into my office." said the doctor in a kindly manner.

Fiona knew instinctively that everything was not alright, and refrained from asking again until they were sat in the Doctor's room facing him at his desk. Fiona uttered once again "Is he ok?"

"No", replied the Doctor, "I'm afraid there was nothing we could do for him. He's had a massive brain haemorrhage. There will have to be an inquest. I'm very sorry."

Tom had found it especially hot in the lift. He felt himself perspiring. He was most concerned that his hands appeared to be sweating, and he was frightened of losing his grip on the briefcase. There were a lot of people in the lift. He couldn't wait to reach the ground floor. He had his prize. Nobody was going to take this from him. This was his reward for all the unfairness he had suffered in his life. This would show them. This would more than make up for his suffering as a child, and the humiliations he had endured. He could feel his heart pounding in his head, and knew that he had become agitated when the fire alarm sounded. It had really struck a nerve and he was desperately trying to calm himself down, but it wasn't working. Like Fiona, he had an aversion to lifts, but thought on this occasion it would be quicker, if not safer, than trying to spring down the stairs in this darned female clothing, where he might run into more dangerous circumstances. His disguise had been a godsend up to now. Nobody knew or even suspected. A few people had passed strange glances his way, but he'd thought nothing of it. He checked himself very thoroughly and knew it was foolproof. He knew he was sweating. He could feel it pouring down his face. He lifted his free hand up and wiped the perspiration away, completely forgetting the make-up. He was so hot. 'Oh, goodness, I'm rich' he thought. 'I can do anything I want with the wealth contained in this briefcase. The first thing I'm going to do is buy ten crates of beer to quench this thirst'. His throat was bone dry and he couldn't swallow. What a stroke of luck all those years ago to see his father hand John the jewels. Nobody knew he'd been watching them.

Tom's memories of that evening induced an uncontrollable shaking. He tightened his grip on the briefcase. The handle was wet. His palms were hot and sticky. He felt nauseas and could feel the bile rising in his throat and thought he would vomit. He felt like someone was pounding his head like a drum. Others in the lift could hear gurgling noises coming from his throat and they tried to squash against the sides of the lift. One kind soul squeezed past trying to get to him, but it was too late. The case released from his grip, and Tom slumped to the floor like a demolished chimney. The wig had come off as he brushed against someone's trouser leg on the way down, and the profuse sweating and face wiping had left his make up smeared.

Fabulous New York

Fiona and Alan were dumbfounded. It was too much to take in. Fiona felt quite ill. The doctor asked them if they would like to go to the waiting room. He would have to take some details from them before he could release Tom's personal effects. He escorted them to a quiet corner and asked them if they would like some tea.

"Yes thank you. That would be lovely." said Fiona.

A pretty young nurse with big blue eyes brought two mugs of tea on a tray and smiled as she handed them one each.

"Are you the relatives of the man they just brought in from the hotel?" she asked.

Alan smiled back and told her "Yes. He's my wife's uncle. We had no idea he was in the vicinity. We're on our way to New York. We have to leave early tomorrow morning for an urgent meeting. How long do you think this will take?"

"I'll let you have your drinks, and then you can come to my office. We'll do the necessary paperwork and you'll be able to go", said the nurse. "How long will you be in New York, because arrangements will have to be made?" Alan told her that they were not sure how long their business would take, but that he would contact her when it had concluded.

"I'll see you in a few minutes when you've finished your drinks. Come through the double doors, turn left down the main corridor and my office is third on the right."

"Thank you", Fiona managed feebly.

They sipped their tea quietly. Neither spoke. They followed the nurse's instructions and found her small office easily.

"Can you tell me what happened Mr ..?"

"Oliver" answered Alan.

The nurse continued. "I'll have to file a report for the coroner'.

"We don't really know" said Alan. "We should have been in New York by now as I mentioned, but the flight developed problems and we had to land. The airline has put us up in the hotel for the night, and we fly out again in the morning."

He drew a deep breath before he continued. "We had no idea Uncle Tom was even here, what he was doing here, or why he was dressed in that ridiculous way. We just don't know." Alan related as much as he knew.

"Have you some form of identification with you Mrs Oliver? You'll have to sign for your uncle's belongings."

Fiona fumbled in the front pocket of her travel bag and pulled out her passport and her driving licence. She also had their marriage certificate with her, as she wasn't aware what ID the jewellery expert might ask for and had brought all her documentation. Two hours later all the paperwork was finished and to their immense relief, Tom's belongings were handed over, including the briefcase and the key which had fallen out of a pocket in the tweed skirt when he was undressed. Everything was in a plastic bag which the nurse handed to Fiona.

"We can expect you to telephone when your business in New York is finished?" she asked.

"Yes", said Alan. "We're rather hoping that the rest of this trip will be uneventful."

Fiona had given Nellie's name as a contact should there be a need to telephone for anything, and their mobile telephone numbers. Fiona would have to contact Nellie and inform her. She wasn't looking forward to that. Nellie was getting on in years, and had no time for her brother in law, but under the circumstances, there was nothing else to be done. They thanked the nurse for her help and promised to return as soon as possible. The nurse had informed them that the doctor was hopeful the post mortem would be carried out within a few days and the body could be released. They said their goodbyes. Alan gripped Fiona's hand tightly and they left the hospital. Once outside, he put his arm around her and kissed the top of her head.

"Come on love, we're going to get a stiff drink."

There was just too much to think of. The stark horror that was beginning to emerge didn't bear thinking about. "He must have somehow found out about the jewels", thought Fiona, "and it's him who's been following us. He somehow got into our hotel room, went in the safe, stole the jewels and then got caught up in the aftermath of the fire alarm and died in a lift that broke down. It's absolutely incredible. My brain won't comprehend it".

Alan hailed a taxi and they arrived at the hotel to find everything calm. Fiona made a mental note to make further enquiries.

Alan was unusually quiet and Fiona just thought he was, like her, disbelieving of all that had happened to them in such a short time. But Alan was wondering how he could possibly tell Fiona that he had suspected something fishy about Tom when he had come visiting a short while back. That was one of the reasons he had suddenly suggested a move. He wanted to live as far away from Tom as he possibly could and he wanted Tom to have categorically no knowledge of where that would be. He remembered the phone call. Fiona had been quite taken aback. Uncle Tom's infrequent visits always left them with a nasty taste in their mouth, but because it was her uncle, she felt unable to refuse. She had agreed to the visit and as usual had taken time to prepare him a meal. Tom, however, didn't have such charitable thoughts and the day he came for the meal, in an attempt to disguise why he was really there, told them he was going to live abroad. Alan had put two and two together, and thought he'd come up with five, but it seemed he'd done his sums correctly. Alan arranged for an estate agent to come and value the property the same day he got the first phone call from Tom. Fiona had been very uneasy about it. She loved the house they had bought together. But Alan insisted. Fiona remembered thinking she'd never known Alan so adamant about anything and asked him what had suddenly made him want to move. Of course he couldn't tell her the truth. It would terrify her, so the easiest thing to do was put his foot down. Fiona had gone along with it as Alan often made snap decisions.

There had been a few occasions when Uncle Tom had visited, and although Alan disliked his wife's uncle venomously, he always managed to force a smile. Tom harboured hatred. This hatred filtered down to his niece and bitterness chewed him up every time he remembered the day he saw Jack Masters give away 'his prize' to his brother. He had hated John's first wife, but Nellie …, she was different.

It was through him his brother had met Nellie. Tom and Nellie met in a nightclub and became lovers immediately. Nellie did not feel any loyalty to her own body at that time and within four hours of meeting they were enjoying each other in a wave of complete lust on Nellie's bathroom floor. Their relationship was based purely on sex and lasted for only six months, until she met John and fell for him, hook, line and sinker. Her relations with Tom had been suffering for a few weeks and she knew it would soon be over between them. She had no compunctions in changing brothers. John was gentle, where Tom had been harsh. John was attentive to her needs, while Tom had just wanted her for his own pleasure. Tom couldn't have cared less. He had been playing around for the last two months and was actually quite glad she was off his back. He didn't perceive however, that the relationship she would have with his brother would be long lasting.

As the years rolled by, he became more jealous of the relationship. He got drunk one night at a family gathering, and began talking to Sophie, Nellie's daughter by a previous marriage. In his drunken stupor, he had forgotten himself and began telling Sophie about the jewels. It wasn't long before Sophie had contacted her brothers in Los Angeles

143

telling them the story as Tom had related it. When Nellie informed her daughter that Tom was dead, Sophie's head began whirling. She feigned grief and ran to her bedroom, closed the door quietly behind her and did a little dance, throwing her clenched hands out in front of her, saying, "Yes, yes. What did old Tom want with them anyway? All the more for me."

The flight to New York was without incident and as the Boeing 737 landed, Fiona and Alan looked at one another, exchanged a quick kiss and putting recent events behind them, began to get excited. "New York, here we come", said Fiona, beginning to get butterflies in her tummy.

The plane taxied to a halt, and they peered out of the window while the surge of people from seats at the rear began to pass them.

"What time are we meeting Carrie and Mel?" asked Alan, reaching up into the overhead locker to retrieve their hand luggage.

"Well, because of our flight delays, it was left open" replied Fiona. "I said we'd ring while we're waiting at the carousel. We'll need to get to the hotel and freshen up and then, if they're not busy, we'll meet them soon after that. It'll still only be early afternoon, and we can get something to eat. It's funny isn't it. We should have been at the jeweller's now if we'd flown yesterday."

Carrie had telephoned and cancelled their appointment explaining what had happened.

"We're very lucky the man can fit us in on Monday", Fiona replied in a worried tone.

"He said he was flying over to Hawaii in the afternoon. It's very good of him to see us at all."

"Nine o'clock, isn't it?" asked Alan.

"Yes, we'll have to be up bright and early that morning. Come on, we can get out now."

All the people from the back of the plane had squashed further towards the front and Alan stood back a pace and let Fiona out in front of him. They slowly made their way towards the open door, hardly daring to believe they had actually arrived.

Although the tarmac was clear, it was evident there had been a big snowfall recently and as they approached the door, they felt the cold air whipping around their legs. Fiona was grateful she had put a pair of tights on under her jeans. They thanked the stewardess and walked through the windy tunnel and out into the arrivals lounge. They quickly made their way to the carousel and stood watching the array of luggage going round and round on the conveyer belt. Fiona telephoned Carrie and told them they had arrived. They had been lucky enough to get a room in the same hotel and arranged to meet in the foyer.

On a wintry afternoon in New York, Fiona and Alan marvelled at their surroundings as the taxi took them the same route as their friends had travelled two days earlier. They too, were dumbfounded by the beauty of the sky-scraping conurbation which lay before them at the other side of the river. They wondered what the next few days

145

would hold.

When Fiona and Carrie saw one another, they wrapped their arms around one another in a huge bear hug. So much had happened and there was so much to say, but no words would come. When they finally surfaced from their hug, they left the hotel and made their way to Planet Hollywood as Carrie had suggested. They chattered non-stop all the way there, the boys walking some distance behind them. They didn't have to wait long to be seated. A dark-haired waitress with a very short skirt and enormously high heels smiled and showed them up some steps to their table. The four of them were so engrossed in their environment, craning their necks to see all the movie artefacts, that nobody spoke until their first round of drinks arrived. Then the stories began to unfold. The two couples listened mutely while the others related their tales, and each of them became acutely aware of the stark reality of their situation. Carrie was feeling intoxicated by the state of affairs and getting more so with her third brandy, and Fiona felt decidedly tipsy after her fourth glass of wine. They exited the venue and hailed a taxi to take them back to the hotel. They departed to their own rooms, arranging to meet later. They were going to one of Lisa's favourite venues just a few blocks away for their evening meal. Carrie and Mel sat debating the best way to inform Lisa and Graham that they had spent the afternoon with Fiona and Alan, and why they hadn't told them that the couple were coming to New York. Carrie had a feeling Lisa wouldn't believe her. She needn't have worried. There was a knock on the door. Without any preliminaries Lisa confronted her mother and father with a barrage of questions. A big beam spread across her face.

"I can't believe you all kept it a secret for so long", she continued without drawing breath.

Her face was flushed from her skating activity and romantic interlude in Central Park. She always had a healthy glow but today her cheeks were bright and rosy and as she bent forward to kiss her mum, Carrie felt her cold cheeks brush against hers.

"What on earth are you talking about?" Carrie asked, trying to keep her face straight.

"Well, guess who we just bumped into downstairs?" quipped Lisa.

"Oh?", said Carrie, with a slight hint of a smile forming at her lips, not wanting to give the game away just yet.

"Fiona told me", said Lisa.

Without moving her lips to voice it, Carrie wondered just what Fiona had told her daughter.

"You could have told me Mum, I wouldn't have been bothered about them coming."

Carrie ventured to ask what exactly had Fiona told her. She inwardly heaved a huge sigh of relief when Lisa explained that Fiona had said their trip had co-ordinated quite accidentally, but they hadn't wanted to take the edge off Lisa's visit with her parents, and so had decided to keep it quiet and low profile.

"We're meeting them later and going out for a meal?"

"Yes", answered Carrie. "We thought it was about time you knew they were here."

"Well, it's fab. I can't wait. It's lovely to see

147

them both here in New York. How great is that! Of all the times they pick to come and it's the same time as us, and in the same hotel. Are you sure you're not keeping something from me mum?"

Lisa cocked her head on one side questioningly, but Carrie quickly changing the subject, asked Graham if he had enjoyed the afternoon. The topic diverted, Lisa and Graham both launched into details of their performance on the rink. Lisa had spent more time on her bottom with Graham in tucks of laughter. Graham had been many times with his parents and was an accomplished skater. Lisa was scared of everything and ice-skating was just one item on her repertoire of fears.

"Never mind, mum, it's your turn soon. Graham won't take no for an answer." Carrie smiled at her daughter, secretly remembering once again her exploits many years ago. She didn't let on to Lisa or Graham that both she and Fiona had also been accomplished skaters! Though she wondered. Oh goodness, it had been an awfully long time.'

"Oh well, we'll see. Come on, we'll have to get a move on, we're meeting them shortly. Mel, do me a huge favour and put the kettle on please. Thanks love. I'll just go and have my shower. Bye, see you in a mo."

With that, Carrie disappeared into the bathroom, leaving Lisa relating to her father the details of her skating expedition. From her vantage point on the ice, she had romanticised about the giant beanstalk proportion of the buildings surrounding the rink, and proceeded to inform her father of the advantages of being a film star and living in a New York skyscraper overlooking Central Park.

"Dad, it was fabulous", she began. The horse's name was Maddy, and I think his owner *was* mad! He never stopped talking, yada yada yada, all the way round. We had to stop talking back to him, and I think he finally got the message that we wanted a romantic twosome in the back of the carriage, and not listen to him yammering on. It was wonderful. He helped us climb up into the back of the carriage and pulled the big hood over us. He threw a thick red blanket on our laps and wrapped it round our legs. Then off we went, in through the park entrance. It was just starting to go dusk, and all the lights were coming on, and we trundled around the park up and down the little pathways, and all round you could see the enormous buildings towering and all the twinkling lights. It's absolutely amazing. Are you going to take Mum?"

"Yeah, I think we'll go tomorrow. Your mother's beside herself. There's just so much we want to do and the clock's ticking. It'll not be too long before it's time to leave. We'll have to come back and do all the things we haven't time for this trip."

"You like it then?" smiled Lisa.

"Yeah, it's ok!"

Mel never committed to anything, but Lisa knew her father well, and knew he absolutely loved it as much as she did. They finished their mugs of tea and the two youngsters left to go and get ready for the evening. Mel sat down by the window. The only thing he could see through the darkness outside were the lights of the building right next to them. It looked as though you could reach out and touch the building next door, they seemed so close. Without doing himself a mischief, he couldn't see the top of the building next door, but through the gaps between the two buildings, as far as his eye could see, were mirror images of the phenomenal twinkling towering blocks.

The six of them met in the foyer at precisely half past eight. They were all chattering excitedly and looking forward to their meal at a much recommended restaurant. They were too engrossed with their own chatter to notice three men sitting over in the corner on a leather sofa, watching them intently. As the six of them left through the swing doors, the three men rose and followed them outside. They meandered a safe distance behind them, taking care not to alert the unsuspecting visitors. Had Carrie turned around, her suspicions would have been immediately aroused, but she walked on oblivious to the danger lurking behind them. Fiona and Alan had decided to take the jewels with them this evening, but instead of the bulky flight bag, Alan had secured the jewels in a much smaller material bag with a long shoulder strap, which he wore underneath his sweater. By the time he had his jacket on over the top the presence of the bag was completely hidden. Although Tom was no longer in the picture, they weren't taking any chances and whilst they both knew there was a real possibility of being mugged, they felt they had taken the necessary precaution by hiding the bag. They too, walked on, unaware of their followers.

Lisa and Graham walked on ahead of the four friends, too in love to even notice three men walking at a fair distance behind them all.

Elliott was a bit wimpish, and hoped the two brothers weren't going to do anything stupid. They didn't even know for sure that there was any expensive jewellery. The two brothers had received a phone call from Sophie. Elliott couldn't understand what all the fuss was about. Why would he want to go trekking half way round the world, chasing what could possibly turn out to be a bunch of stupid costume jewellery. And what did it have to do with him anyway. He'd much rather have stayed at home eating burger and chips in front of the TV. In fact the attraction of the visit for him had been the American burgers. He needed to taste them. Why wasn't his stupid girlfriend there herself if she wanted to see these damn jewels so badly? Why did it have to be him? She always sent him to do her dirty work except when she was stealing lingerie. He refused to do that. If he got caught, they'd think he was a pervert and he wasn't having that. He didn't really get on too well with her brothers, but Sophie had insisted, saying it was about time they got on. They were family, after all. So, Elliott had tagged along to keep the peace. He hadn't the sense to realise that he was there as the scapegoat. Should they get into a sticky situation they could leave him to carry the can. The least they could get away with telling him the better. The only time they really spoke to him was to give him instructions or to question him about his knowledge of the jewels and his knowledge of them was sketchy. It took him all his time to remember how many burgers he'd eaten the day before, never mind intricate detail about some jewellery he'd never seen.

Sophie was indeed tiring of him and had intended to dump him until Uncle Tom had got drunk and told her things she thought her ears would never hear. Now, with Uncle Tom gone, she would soon give Elliott his marching orders, but not just yet. He was still useful. Her two brothers were in New York chasing what could be the beginning of a wonderful new life and Elliott was helping them. No, she couldn't get rid of him yet. She needed to be patient for a little while longer. She was beginning to think her dreams could finally be coming true. She just had to get her hands on those jewels. That wouldn't have been too difficult if stupid old Tom hadn't gone and died. That was too bad. That would have alerted Fiona and Alan to the fact that the jewels were causing interest and it was the last thing she wanted. His disguise had been a stroke of genius and Tom would have got away with it if he hadn't gone and died. Still, one less person in the equation meant more of a cut for her. Elliott definitely wouldn't be getting a cut. She just had to work out what she would do about her brothers. If she could help it, they weren't getting their hands on any either. A devious plot had already begun to develop in her mind. But she wasn't counting her chickens. It might all prove futile. She would be patient and wait and see what the next forty eight hours brought.

The meal was fabulous. The ambience of the restaurant was a perfect copy of a famous Australian development. They all chose the mixed grill.

Disbelieving what they were seeing, Carrie and Fiona wished they'd chosen something lighter. The dinners were served on huge pewter platters sitting on top of highly decorative wooden charger plates. The amount of food they contained was typically American but alien to Carrie and Fiona. On each plate was a thirty-two ounce steak, four thick barbecued sausages, four thick rashers of bacon, two large kidneys, two slices of black pudding, and a large pork chop. The waiter brought a tray of fried eggs and asked each in turn how many they would like and would they like them sunny side up or easy over. In the centre of the table was placed an enormous bowl of mixed salad leaves, rocket, dandelion, radicchio, cos, water cress and fennel tips. Next to that was a large rubber wood Lazy Susan, containing separate porcelain dishes of sun dried tomato, char-grilled peppers, cucumber, stuffed olives, a selection of onions including caramelised, Graham's favourite, and a hot salsa dip. There were baskets of small freshly baked buns at the side of each setting, interspersed with plenty of foil wrapped butter. On a raised shelf at each end of the table, were the condiments. Mel had ordered two bottles of red wine and a bottle of white. He had also ordered a bottle of sparkling wine which sat in a wine cooler at the side of the table. The waiter now shook out the large red and white gingham napkins, placed them on each of their laps, and poured their chosen wine.

Elliott and the two brothers had been watching the proceedings through the window and thought there had been a safe time lapse for the three of them to enter the restaurant. They were ushered to a table from where they thought they would be able to hear the conversation from the table across the walkway. That might have been conceivably possible, if there hadn't been an Australian artist singing and playing strange musical instruments which produced an incredibly loud sound, drowning out all hope of eavesdropping. The table of six, unknowingly, chatted through the evening, talking about anything and everything. Of course, the jewels were never mentioned in front of Lisa and Graham. The long Australian style bar extended behind their table and Lenny and Bart took turns to come and stand by the bar to order drinks. From there they could quite clearly hear the ordinary conversation which certainly had nothing to do with jewellery. Their efforts had been to no avail and in the end, the brothers sent Elliott to stand at the bar to do all the listening. He had no idea that Fiona would recognise him if she were to see his face, as it was many years since they had been introduced. He hadn't remembered their meeting, nor had he calculated in his mind that if she did recognise him, she would make the connection. There would be catastrophic consequences if she subsequently alerted the authorities. He just stood there drinking and trying to catch snatches of their conversation, none of which revealed anything unusual. He eventually reported back to his table. The three men had a lengthy discussion as to why they thought the conversation at the table of six was devoid of jewellery. They decided it was impossible to pursue matters further this evening, finished their drinks and left. They reported their failed mission to Sophie, who instructed them to be up at the crack of dawn the next day and to make sure they were seated discreetly in the hotel dining room before anyone came down for breakfast.

It took Fiona almost the whole of the evening and disrupting her flow of conversation it niggled sub-consciously, until eventually she had to introduce it to her conscious mind that she definitely knew one of those men sitting opposite them tonight. The one who had been stood at the bar most of the evening, right beside their table. He'd had his back to her most of the time, but when she had gone to the ladies room, she'd seen his profile and it was familiar. When the harsh realisation came, she wanted to dismiss it. She tried to tell herself she was being paranoid. But she knew now that Carrie was right. The danger wasn't over just because Tom was dead. He'd been in on it too, in that awful disguise, but now there were three more. She had sussed out who they were, and armed with that, would discuss it with Alan later. Tomorrow when the four of them were together they would decide what to do about their predicament. The meeting with the jeweller was set for Monday morning. They had a few short hours to come up with a counter plan.

Although Fiona knew the three men would almost certainly be there somewhere, she decided not to look for them. She would not give them a clue she was on to them and would conduct herself accordingly. They ate a continental breakfast at eight o'clock. Lisa and Graham were going to have some time to themselves and the other four would spend the day together. More snow had been forecast and they sensibly muffled up. Today was going to be great. They would try to cram as much as they possibly could into a few short hours and that's exactly what they did. They headed for the Empire State Building. Carrie's romantic mind wandered to a film she had seen about a meeting up on the viewing balcony, something like the 82nd floor. She also remembered a conversation she'd had with Fiona before she knew their trips would coincide, about how she would not be going up inside the building, and cringed as she knew she would now have to do it. Especially as tomorrow would be Valentine's Day.

She climbed into the lift very reluctantly and shut her eyes. It took longer than she thought to get to the viewing balcony. When she was actually stood on it, she knew that she couldn't do much viewing. It was extremely windy up there, and it was all she could do to open one eye and glance out into the distance. The others were wandering around taking photographs of the spectacular views out across Manhattan and the surrounding boroughs. They found a virtual ride on one floor of the building. Carrie gritted her teeth, and went along. It was fabulous. She enjoyed every second. The movement of the hydraulic seats gave the effect of actual movement and the magic of advanced flight simulation took them on a helicopter ride, a snow buggy race, an alien spacecraft flying between the New York skyscrapers, a roller coaster ride and other such fantastic experiences. She decided to keep her eyes wide open and just go with it, and found it utterly amazing.

There were other events taking place within the building, but there was so much they all wanted to do, they had to quickly move on. Because of the short margin of time, they used taxis to traverse the city. They sat and watched the skilled skaters performing professionally in front of the incredibly beautiful Rockafella Centre. They stood in awe of the sights and sounds around Times Square, deposited themselves in front of the web cam, and took lunch inside one of the Square's famous hotels. Another taxi dropped them off for a walk down Wall Street, which Carrie found incredibly weird. Although it was a darkish day, she felt as if there would never be much sunlight there at all. An incident had occurred just minutes before their arrival. There was a man lay bleeding on the pavement with a crowd of people around him. Police cars were everywhere and a team of paramedics arrived. Carrie and Fiona were too scared to look. They didn't really want to see, but the boys looked and said he'd been stabbed. Carrie wanted to get away as quickly as possible.

They moved on to Ground Zero and Carrie had never experienced anything quite like the way she felt. They had seen all the incredibly different zones of New York, each zone quite different from the last. When they were within half a mile of Ground Zero, the mood changed quite dramatically. There was a silence and no birds were singing. There was no traffic noise, there was no human noise, the whole atmosphere a complete contrast to the rest of the city. Bunches of flowers had been pushed through the gaps in the high metal railings which circled the expanse of space where the two buildings had once stood. There was a black tarpaulin seemingly draped around a nearby building. Other people stood beside them just looking. No-one spoke. There was an intense sadness hanging in the air which seemed to fill the hearts of those who stood there with an indescribable credulity. Carrie prayed for the souls of those who had perished at the site and her thoughts turned to their loved ones and an immense wretchedness and desolation seemed to engulf her and she knew the others felt the same. It was some moments before any of them spoke. They were glad to walk away from the site towards the harbour and the boat which would take them to Staten Island and the Statue of Liberty. They took the hour-long boat trip around the dockland and were astounded at some of the sights. When they had finished the boat tour, the light was fading. It was extremely cold and although they were huddled up in warm clothing, the cold was penetrating. The taxi driver dropped them off at Bloomingdale's. The girls were in their element inside the fabulous store. They didn't know where to look first. The boys were glad to be in out of the cold, but neither did shopping very well, and they found a cafe and left the girls to wander aimlessly until they'd had their fill of shopping. Armed with bags and packages, the girls finally sat down beside their men, and ordered a cup of well deserved hot espresso coffee. The girls handed their parcels to the men to carry for them and went back outside to discover a heavy snowfall. They walked the rest of the way back to the hotel, collecting the odd snowball here and there throwing them at Alan and Mel, who appeared unscathed by the attack. Later, they would meet Lisa and Graham and Carrie was looking forward to her challenge on the ice, then perhaps a pizza, a few drinks and maybe a show to wind the day down. Tomorrow was a trip into the unknown and they would all need their wits about them.

The Expert

Monday morning dawned and Carrie awoke with a start. She thought they'd overslept and panicked.

"Mel, we're late and we've got to go to the jeweller's with Fiona and Alan. Come on love, wake up."

Mel half opened one eye and winked at Carrie.

"Oh yes, we're off to see the ancient one!"

It turned out they weren't late at all. Carrie's alarm on her mobile phone hadn't gone off. They showered, dressed and went down for breakfast. Fiona and Alan were already there. Alan was tucking into a full English while Fiona was picking feebly at a grapefruit and not looking too happy at all. They sat down and Alan asked what Lisa and Graham were doing.

"Think they're having a bit of a lie in this morning" said Mel. "Not like us oldies. The younguns can't take it like we can!"

"We'll hopefully be back before they notice we've gone" said Carrie. "How long do you think the valuation will take?"

"Well, if this guy's as good as they reckon, not too long", replied Alan. "What'll happen then though?" questioned Carrie.

"Don't know, we'll just have to wait and see." replied Fiona. "Seems to me, we're in the lap of the Gods."

An exceptionally skinny waitress in a crisp white pinafore approached their table, pen and pad in hand, and deftly took Carrie and Mel's order for breakfast. She laid down their cutlery and napkins.

160

Seconds later, a large stainless steel teapot arrived together with a second, taller but much thinner one. Instead of hurrying along with their meal, they all seemed to linger, as though their individual fears were preventing them from movement. Alan strapped the bag around his shoulders, pulled up the zip and put his coat on over the top.

"There, safe and sound", he announced. "No thieving pickpocket ainta gonna get his mitts on this baby."

"Good", said Fiona. "Are we ready then?

They smiled unconvincingly at one another as their thoughts melded and stepped into the revolving doorway, out onto the street and left the hotel behind.

Lisa and Graham had decided to rise early, grab some breakfast and go for a lovely morning stroll in the crisp white snow which Lisa loved passionately. They were both wrapped up snugly and alighted from the lift just in time to see their parents disappear out of the hotel door.

"That's odd", Lisa said to Graham. "Where are those four going this early in the morning, and why did mum not tell me? Something's going on here Graham, come on, we're going to follow them. I wonder if one of them is in some kind of trouble? There's definitely something fishy going on."

They pulled their scarves up round their faces so as to disguise themselves a little and quickly slipped out of the hotel and paced themselves at a comfortable distance from the four adults in front.

The crisp wind caught Carrie's breath, and she pulled her scarf further up round her mouth. Her stomach seemed to be manufacturing the largest butterflies known to mankind but her mind was trying to link with Fiona's. She wondered what emotions her friend truly felt this morning. Would the day turn out to be life-changing? Would it be a wasted journey? She dismissed the latter, as their time together could never have been a waste, but she wondered would it turn out to be the biggest hoax of the century and something they would laugh at for the rest of their lives. She tried to ignore completely the niggling temptation to panic attacks at the thoughts that someone may try to snatch the jewels, or worse, try to snatch her friend. Her imagination was running riot.

Mel's voice cut through the biting wind as Carrie listened to his rendition of 'We're off to see the Wizard'. His hilarity was infectious and soon they were all tramping through the fresh snowfall, singing along and laughing uncontrollably between verses. They soon came to the street down which they had to make a sharp left turn. Fiona glanced at her watch and wondered if they would have time for a coffee before their meeting. She too, was now feeling decidedly edgy and voiced it. Alan squeezed her arm.

"Everything's going to be ok Fee", he said gently.

Five minutes later, in a small back street of Midtown East Manhattan, they found the place they were looking for. The shop was distinguishable from the other shop fronts by its fairytale appearance, perfectly befitting a Dickens novel, and further enhanced by its snow laden window panes. There were no lights on indoors, and the 'closed' sign was hung clearly in the glass section of the door. They were early, and satisfied they knew they were at the correct location, they walked quickly back to a coffee bar they had passed a few minutes earlier. There were a lot of people queuing for breakfast but those wishing to purchase only beverages were invited to jump the queue, which they did without hesitation. Alan ordered three lattes and an espresso. There appeared to be an unquestionable aura about the place, as though everyone in the world gathered here to share their secrets, and they each wondered whether it was because of their quest, or was this coffee bar strategically placed for the 'expert'. Each concluded silently they were mad. They finished their coffees and walked quickly back to the shop. Carrie had detected rustling of curtains and whisperings behind doors on the way back to the shop. She now couldn't believe her eyes. What had seemed a small back-street jeweller's with a closed sign on the door had become a bustling hive of industry. Light emanated from every pane of glass, and what they had believed to be a tiny shop front, had transformed into an endless corridor of light, of massive glass fronted display cabinets, of flawless décor, of impeccably presented assistants hurriedly lifting trays out from the glass topped cabinets in front of them, to show to innumerable customers. The door was still closed, but there was a definite 'Open' sign hanging where its negative partner had hung just a short while ago. They looked at one another without speaking and opened the door.

The noise almost deafened them when they stepped inside. They could hear chatter from every corner of the shop. Archways led into further corridors, again adorned with the floor to ceiling cabinets displaying every gem imaginable, the most ornate pieces seemingly more brightly lit. It was a breathtaking experience. The oddest thing about the shop was its 'pay' area. There was a small wooden hatch along one wall, looking like a ticket collectors office from a 1940s outback train station. Seated behind it was an old man who, to their amusement, looked very similar to the wizard they'd just been singing about. They continued their journey down the long corridor displaying arrows beneath which the name read Monsieur Boesflug, Master Jeweller. The mood was decidedly fictitious and Fiona and Carrie both felt they had been transported back in time as the further away from the front of the shop they moved, the more dimly lit it became. At the very end of the corridor, they approached a large wooden doorway, more in keeping with the front of the shop than the hugely commercially lit establishment they had just walked through. On the door was the name plaque they sought. Fiona knocked twice and a voice from within asked her to enter. She turned the brass knob and not knowing what to expect the four of them entered the space behind the door. It was an empty space except for an old window containing one pane of dirty glass high up on the wall to their right, another wooden door straight in front of them with some sort of intercom system at the side of it and a modern speaker on the wall to their left, from where it was obvious the voice had emerged. Apart from those things, it could have been a courtyard from some ancient palace. They almost expected to look down and see straw beneath their feet. They were holding their breath. What on earth had they come to, and what would they find beyond that door? Creepy was the word lingering on their lips and they were glad of each other's company. Should they hold hands like they would in a fairytale, or should they behave like adults coming for a valuation on some jewellery. They decided on the second option, and not hearing anything to deter them from moving on they began to walk across 'the courtyard' towards the door.

They had only gone two paces and heard the same voice speak again. Simultaneously they looked up to where the voice seemed to come from. As they did there was a flash. Their picture obviously taken, and a little disgruntled about that fact, they heard the voice welcome them through the door. Alan went first with Fiona close on his heels, followed by their two friends. What they found behind the door troubled them greatly. The man standing in front of them who they assumed to be Monsieur Boesflug looked like a gangster. Fiona panicked a little, thinking the whole thing had been a set-up by the jeweller back in England and that they were going to be victims of some terrible gangland mugging or even murder. Carrie sensed Fiona's fear and somehow knew instinctively she would have to mediate. She spoke for her friend and introduced the four of them to the person standing before them. He came forward and shook hands with each of them. He was a small man, immaculately dressed. He sported a Van Dyke beard, a pair of dark glasses and smelt of expensive after-shave. He smiled at them, a gold tooth gleaming amongst the row of otherwise perfectly white teeth. He introduced himself as Monsieur Boesflug's assistant, Bernard. He led them over to a table upon which there was a guest book which he asked them all to sign and date.

Bernard turned round and smiled. "Follow me please."

They walked to the other side of a very plush room furnished with soft leather upholstered sofas, beautiful suede rugs and fabulous tapestries. Bernard turned a dial set in the wall. The doorway led them into a vault. Thousands of handles lined the walls. 'Safety deposit boxes', thought Carrie, and wondered what treasures lay behind each of the spaces, briefly fantasising about her friend's valuables. There was a glass table with a small leather stool at one end of the room and a doorway at the other, which opened and a very tall, thin, bald man entered the vault, crossed the room, shook each of their hands and introduced himself as Monsieur Boesflug. In his left hand, he carried a small attaché case, which he now lay on the glass table and invited them to join him around the table.

"Mrs Oliver", he began. "I'm very pleased to make your acquaintance. I'm sorry you have had to experience our security, but we have to be sure you are who you say you are. I am sorry too, if you have experienced the feeling you were being watched during your stay in New York. With items of the calibre indicated, we feel we are well within our rights to ascertain the bearers of the items are the same people who contacted us in the beginning.

166

Please forgive this intrusion. It was for your own safety."

All four began to relax. Believing their paranoia to be unfounded, they began to talk excitedly all at once, feeling somehow safe and secure with this man they'd never met but who now seemed to be their friend.

Monsieur Boesflug laughed and said "Shall we get down to business?"

Alan took off his jacket and removed the bag from his shoulders, extracted the precious bundle and laid it down on the glass table. Monsieur Boesflug flipped open the attaché case, took out his glass, squeezed it into his eye socket and began to undo the parcel. The silence in the room became eerie and there was an uncomfortable few moments as he slowly unwound the cloth surrounding the stones.

The stillness was shattered by his long slow intake of breath when the gems were unleashed from their shroud. His eyes widened to saucer-like proportions and he gently picked up one of the smaller pieces. Carrie thought he looked at it like an optician doing an eye test, examining every facet from every conceivable angle possible, almost doing somersaults, his facial contortions indescribable. He placed the stone down, and picked up another, this time a jewel set in gold and repeated his earlier inspection. This he did with complete alacrity until all but the largest gem had been inspected. He had certainly been saving the best for last. Mel, who had remained dumb until now, inhaled and exhaled loudly and Carrie began to cry. They had never seen anything so beautiful. Monsieur Boesflug examined and inspected, almost inverting his entire body for at least fifteen minutes with this last piece. When he'd finished his inspection, he placed the precious jewel back into its cloth, folded everything back up to its original presentation, stood up, beckoned to Bernard to bring box number 826R. Bernard seemed to extract the stepladders from out of thin air, rolled the gigantic steel steps along the stone floor until he reached the appropriate place, pressed his foot on a huge lever attached to the ladders, which locked them in place. He climbed slowly up and up and up, and eventually reached Box no 826R. Pulling it slowly out of its cabinet, he carefully climbed back down the ladder, walked across the room and laid the box on top of the glass table. Monsieur Boesflug placed the cloth bundle into the box, which was lined with red velvet, resembling the colour of the stones he had just inspected. He picked up the box and asked the dumbfounded four to follow him once again. The box tucked under his left arm, he crossed the room and turned a dial in the wall by the door, which opened and they stepped into a comfortable looking lounge area.

Once again the soft leather sofas adorned the room and they all felt compelled to be seated in their welcoming warmth. A young girl in a black dress and a white pinafore entered the room, and placed a white cloth over the large coffee table in front of their sofas. She disappeared and reappeared with an enormous silver tray, resembling those used in a stately home, containing a silver tea and coffee service and china crockery. She poured their requirements, handed them

168

their cups and left. An open fire roared in the grate of a huge marble fireplace and they waited for Monsieur Boesflug to speak. It was almost a squeak. "Which of you is the companion?" was all he said. Their hearts were racing and they knew they had in their possession the product of fairytales and legend. What they did not know was the value of the treasure nor indeed the journey on which they would now have to embark. His next question addressed to Fiona would begin that journey.

The Expert's Room

"How did you acquire them?" The question that Monsieur Boesflug posed was racing round in Fiona's mind. She felt like she was in some sort of pantomime, where everything you did for a day was make-believe, with an audience out there who clapped and clapped when you did something funny. Only this was not funny, it was completely bizarre. Her head felt like it was spinning round and round in opposite directions. Her focus kept landing on Carrie and she tried to clasp her hands. Carrie clasped Fiona's hands in her own.

Looking into her eyes, she said, "I'm here for you. Whatever you need, I'm here." Fiona smiled at her best friend, looked at the two men, and turned to Monsieur Boesflug.

"Carrie here is my companion. She is not related to me in any way. We have known one another since we were five years old. I trust her implicitly and she has agreed to be my companion should the jewels turn out to be genuine. May I have another cup of tea please?"

No sooner had the question left her lips, than the skinny waitress appeared and poured the tea. Fiona took a large gulp, focused all her attention on Monsieur Boesflug and began questioning him. Carrie had been hoping Fiona would do this. They all felt the need to establish who this person was. How did they know he wasn't an imposter who had heard of the jewels and eliminated the real expert and taken his place? They knew it was impossible to ascertain with any degree of accuracy, but a few well put together questions might alleviate their fears and give them an incentive to accept this peculiar person as authentic and to have faith in his guidance. Both the girls kept thinking back to their childhood fairy stories and both were honest enough with themselves to realise they could legitimately fantasise about their immediate future and that they were actually embarking on a road untravelled for centuries. Twenty minutes later, Monsieur Boesflug had convinced them he was sincere, and informed them he would be frank with them as well, imparting all his knowledge of the jewels and the fantasy surrounding their retrieval and ultimate voyage home. Fiona inwardly conceded that Monsieur Boesflug was genuine and began her story to answer his question.

Right back as far as she could remember when she was a little girl, three years old. She told the expert how she sat on her mother's bed one day, all dressed up and ready to go to a Christmas play in which she was playing a fairy princess. Mrs Forrester, the props lady who came in twice a week during December, to help with such things as plays and nativities, had asked if the children had any jewellery that mummy would let them borrow for the play. Fiona had asked her mummy, and been carried upstairs wearing her costume ready for rehearsal. Her mummy had sat her down on the bed and gone to a drawer in the bedroom dresser, extracting a largish cloth parcel, unwrapped it and placed a necklace round Fiona's neck. Fiona had felt a tingling sensation coming up from her ankles.

"There", her mum had said. "Now you look

like a real princess." She had smiled and kissed her pretty daughter's nose saying, "Come on, we have to leave now or you'll be late."

As Fiona was telling this story, she wondered for the umpteenth time why nobody had ever had the jewels valued. They had just been simply treated as sentimental costume jewellery. Perhaps the jewels rendered themselves inane, whenever there might be a chance of their recognition, imparting the notion to all who handled them that they were worthless, perhaps originally purchased in some penny bizarre somewhere in the orient. Fiona had gone to her Christmas play and looked the perfect part of the fairy princess she was playing, and apart from the 'Oh, doesn't she look cute', and 'Oh, isn't she just gorgeous', the necklace had not invited comment. The play over and Fiona safely back at home, the necklace was replaced in its cloth sack.

Fiona told Monsieur Boesflug everything she knew. She knew that her Grandfather had been given the jewels in return for an act of kindness during World War II in Burma and that he gave them to her Grandmother when he came back home. When her Grandmother had died, the jewels were passed to her father for safe keeping. She never remembered her mother wearing them and over the years, after her parents divorced, possessions must have got mixed up and the jewels had been put into a box and forgotten. The box somehow made its way with her father who subsequently met and lived with Nellie. To the best of her knowledge, the jewels must have remained unused and left in the box that she found in her front porch when her father was having his clearouts. There had been the horrifying incident with her Dad's brother, Uncle Tom. She related the unbelievable story to Monsieur Boesflug, who did not take his eyes off her, nor speak, the whole time. She told of the feelings they had about being followed, and that it had turned out to be Uncle Tom undertaking a ridiculous scam to get his hands on the jewels. But that she also now knew Monsieur Boesflug had had them followed for security reasons. Now here they were, waiting for his advice. She told him as much as she could about her companion and Monsieur Boesflug turned his attentions to Carrie and Mel. He asked Carrie to relate to him everything she knew, from the beginning.

Carrie began her version from the night that Fiona had called her up and asked her to go back to the house. When they had all finished speaking, there was silence in the room for a few seconds before Monsieur Boesflug picked up the box, seemingly caressing it as he did so. Fiona imagined he was Aladdin rubbing the genie's lamp and smiled across at Carrie who immediately picked up her meaning and smiled back. They waited.

Monsieur Boesflug spoke.
"Do any of you have any idea about the contents of this box? Have you ever wondered at their beauty? Have you ever asked yourselves where they originate from? Have you ever wondered why nobody ever had them valued before now?"
"Yes", Fiona said quickly to his last question. "I have wondered but only just recently. It occurred

to me the other day that they have lain untouched, unopened, unworn, in their cloth parcel at the bottom of a drawer for decades, and nobody ever thought to have them valued. Now I'm here in front of you and there's a possibility they're special, I do wonder why it's never happened."

Monsieur Boesflug's reply to her statement made Carrie's spine shiver.

"Oh, it's not just a possibility Mrs Oliver. I am herewith obliged to inform you that you have in your possession the lost Meng Tuu-Kyi rubies, described animatedly in inscriptions from the region they were mined in tenth century Burma, and believed by the early monks to possess astonishing mystical powers and priceless wealth. We have a lot to discuss and many arrangements to make. I must first of all ask you if you can all extend your holiday. Do not worry about cost. All of your expenses will be catered for, as will everything else for the duration of your stay with us. Come, we will start the necessary paperwork. We must draw up an itinerary and precise description of everything contained in the parcel and register Mrs Oliver as the current keeper of the jewels. According to the legend, your companion must also be named in the documentation. You are each welcome to keep your partners with you as our paid guests. That is my decision. Come, we must get started. I will order some lunch after which we will spend the afternoon putting everything in place."

Monsieur Boesflug turned to Bernard and asked him to cancel his trip to Hawaii.

Still clutching the box under his left arm, Monsieur Boesflug turned and vigorously shook hands with both men, a smile across his face from ear to ear. He bowed to Carrie and he raised Fiona's slightly trembling hand to his lips and kissed it.

"I am very honoured to meet you, Mrs Oliver. You are about to fulfil the legend of the Meng Tuu-Kyi rubies, a task awaited for centuries. Your journey, I am sure, will not be without incident, but you will temporarily possess the Myan power of courage to accomplish your mission. You will be afforded every facility that the modern world can offer you and the rubies themselves will manifest their extraordinary phenomena to ensure your safety in their return."

It seemed to the four people rooted to the spot that he then began to speak very quickly in a strange language. In ordinary circumstances, Alan and Mel would have been so sceptical as to have walked away from the 'nonsense' protruding from this stranger's mouth, but they could not move. They were stuck to the spot like glue, just as Fiona and Carrie were. They talked about it later but no-one could explain why they had all stood motionless while Monsieur Boesflug launched into a language they had never before heard, and couldn't do anything about it. They were completely and utterly helpless to do anything except listen.

They were suddenly following Monsieur Boesflug back through the doorway into the enclosed safety deposit room. He pulled a lever in the wall, and a rectangular piece of marble slid out from the orifice. Two legs electronically protruded from the underside and steadied themselves on the ground before them. Monsieur Boesflug placed the box onto the marble. He pressed another button on the wall and a drawer shot out to its fullest extent with a bang which made them all jump. He lifted out a length of white velvet and laid it on the marble table. He carefully extracted the jewels from their cloth pouch and laid each one on the velvet. The four had never seen the jewels together out of their hiding place and displayed so that each facet could be scrutinised. They were astounded at how many there were.

"I didn't think there were so many", said Fiona. "I remember looking at them in the hotel room."

Monsieur Boesflug looked up at her and smiled. "The rubies possess many strange powers Mrs Oliver."

Alan stifled a loud laugh and Fiona kicked his shin. Bernard suddenly appeared carrying a huge pile of papers, and balancing a small case on top of the pile. He placed these on the glass table at the other end of the room, pulled up a nearby chair, sat down and extracted a pair of headphones from the case. He fished in his inside pocket and a rather ornate pen appeared in his hands. He shuffled papers about on the table and cleared his throat.

Monsieur Boesflug extracted a small device they assumed to be some form of dictating machine from the still protruding drawer, placed it on the desk, and began to speak slowly. He described the first jewel, which was a small single ruby, no chain, no fixing, just a single gem. A totally flawless gem, rich dark red, and perfectly transparent. He turned it every which way, and described every single aspect of it, measuring its length, width and depth. Bernard was busy writing. The four friends stood mesmerised by the ancient way in which the whole process was carried out. They wondered why it hadn't all been done electronically with the fantastic equipment jewellers now had, and a computer for the one writing it all down. But, thought Fiona, if it took this long for one jewel to be itemised, how long would they be there? They were all thinking the same, as they stood, untiring, watching and listening to the whole process. Although they knew it should be lunchtime they felt neither hunger nor thirst. They just stood and quietly witnessed each piece accurately described and Bernard wrote down everything that he heard through the earphones. Both Monsieur Boesflug and Bernard seemed to become excited and agitated over one of the pieces. In fact Monsieur Boesflug almost seemed not to want to touch it at all. When Monsieur Boesflug selected the necklace that Fiona had worn for the Christmas play, Fee thought she felt herself tingling from the ankles up. Not an unpleasant sensation but one she had definitely felt before. She thought she heard voices in her head at the same time but wouldn't succumb and it passed quickly. Nonetheless, her whole body seemed to be evaporating in a stupendous illusion and she felt lightheaded and totally unable to control this curious incident, and began to melt into the sensation. Once Monsieur Boesflug moved on to the next piece her body resumed normality. She wondered if any of the others had sensed the change in her, and couldn't wait until she could speak to Carrie about it.

Monsieur Boesflug continued his fastidious assessment of each individual piece, talking precisely about each and every one. It seemed to them all that the whole process would take days. At an appropriate point in the proceedings, when the larger jewels were the only ones yet unassessed, Monsieur Boesflug asked after their wellbeing, indicating that they would be able to partake of some refreshment in a short time. They each confirmed that they were fine and in no way uncomfortable. Each felt that for that split second someone else had possessed them and answered for them. The larger jewels were now being scrutinised. Fiona and Carrie were captivated and enthralled by their beauty and clarity. It had seemed to them that the longer they stood there, the more brilliant the jewels were becoming. Monsieur Boesflug was relentless in his work and they all marvelled at the knowledge and expertise that he exacted and inwardly celebrated that they could have found nobody more befitting the task, even though extremely archaic. The harmonisation of the two men working tirelessly was like a well-oiled wheel, turning relentlessly, slowly and methodically, towards its destination.

The ultimate piece was about to be assessed when Monsieur Boesflug put down his eye-glass as though some notion had entered his head. He looked toward Bernard, who glancing over to the marble slab had stopped writing. He simultaneously pulled a separate sheet of paper from the pile, this time a creamy coloured parchment. Monsieur Boesflug inclined his head slightly downward and Bernard once again began to write. The last piece took an amazingly long time, and it seemed to the group standing around the marble slab, that the jewel began to light up their dim surroundings. There had only previously been the special light over the table on which Monsieur Boesflug was working so there should be as little artificial light as possible over the proceedings. Both Fiona and Carrie wondered if it was their imagination. The last jewel took much longer than the others, and Bernard was furiously writing away as fast as his fingers could work. Monsieur Boesflug was evidently aware of the necessity to accurately record the details and slowed accordingly. When it was all done, Monsieur Boesflug produced folded sheets of some kind of acetate from the drawer. Each one was unfolded, and one of the pieces of jewellery placed in the centre and the corners folded in, making little parcels. This process was carried out for each piece until the marble slab was devoid of jewellery and all that remained was the white velvet. Monsieur Boesflug folded this carefully and placed it back in the drawer. The little parcels of jewellery were placed back in the cloth bag and put into the safety deposit box. Bernard was summoned. He quickly cleared up his desk, placing all the papers into the case, clasped it shut, slid the chair away from the table and hurried over to the group of people. Monsieur Boesflug indicated that he wished the safety deposit box to be replaced, and the documentation to be completed for Mrs Oliver. Bernard placed the pile of papers and briefcase on the marble slab and hurried away to retrieve the ladders. He then carried the box up the ladder and slid it back into its hole. It slammed shut, making an echoing noise in the room, and he came back down. He handed the key to Monsieur Boesflug. The safety deposit box receipt and a resume of its contents were handed to Fiona together with the key. Monsieur Boesflug suggested that perhaps a safe place of keeping was needed for the key and handed Fee a small pouch with straps containing a clip fastening. He advised that she should pay a visit to the ladies and secure the pouch around her body underneath her clothing.

"When you bathe Mrs Oliver, you should have your companion present, to whom you shall present the pouch until your ablutions are complete."

Carrie couldn't help but smile. "Fiona won't be impressed with that", she thought. Monsieur Boesflug must have caught the smile.

"The companion's task is arduous and varied Mrs Goodwin. You were chosen long before your arrival into this world to complete this assignment. I must speak with you alone."

Carrie remained with Monsieur Boesflug whilst Bernard showed the others the exit. Bernard smiled at Carrie saying, "I will bring you a glass of lemonade and set a place for you for lunch, Mrs Goodwin."

They all supposed he was at least a little mad. Lunchtime must have come and gone hours and hours ago.

When they finally emerged from their enclosure, they were flabbergasted that only an hour had passed since they entered the room. They were all amazed to find how quickly their appetite returned and swallowed the drinks of lemonade they were handed with gusto. They were back in the lounge area, and all three of them settled back into the comfortable sofas, trying to take in all they had witnessed and wondering why Carrie had been asked to remain behind.

The Companion

The second the door closed Carrie felt herself falling. She tried to scream but no noise came. She tried to open her eyes wide to see why she was falling but the feeling continued. She could not open her eyes nor see what she was falling into. She felt sheer panic and thought her heart would burst. She was screaming at the top of her voice but the noise still refused to come. Her consciousness informed her that she should be dead by now. She was still falling. She tried to voice a prayer, but her voice was paralysed. The screams wouldn't come and neither would the prayer. Eventually her body became used to the weightless descent. Perhaps she'd been drugged. 'Yes, that's it, drugged' she thought 'in the lemonade that someone gave me a few minutes before I began to fall.' She was aware enough to know that there had been nowhere to fall to, so it had to be an induced state. She lost consciousness.

Monsieur Boesflug waited until he was certain she was asleep and then picked her up and carried her to a set of lift doors, which opened upon his approach. All the while he muttered apologies to her, explaining that he couldn't depend on face value and that he had to be sure. Inside the lift he shifted closer to the controls and managed to press one of the buttons which took them hurtling down and down into the vaults of the jewellery shop. The lift stopped abruptly knocking him off balance a little. Carrie hung as limp as a rag doll, as he hurried along to another set of doors which once again opened on approach. Had Carrie been awake to see the sight before her it would have taken her breath away. Monsieur Boesflug lay her down on the sumptuous silk covers and hurried away. He must remain invisible until her interrogation was over. Carrie was in a hypnotic state, an art well practised by Monsieur Boesflug, who over the years had witnessed a number of people claiming possession of the Meng Tuu-Kyi rubies in order to acquire more knowledge of them. Monsieur Boesflug knew beyond any reasonable doubt that these were indeed the priceless jewels of which legend foretold. He also had to know beyond any reasonable doubt that Carrie was genuine, rather than allow the jewels to fall into the hands of a perpetrator for her own use. The legend of the Meng Tuu-Kyi rubies was well known in the jewellery world and most dismissed it as poppycock.

Andre Boesflug had suspected from an early age that he possessed unnatural powers. He also knew that his destiny on earth would be fulfilled when the legendary Meng Tuu-Kyi rubies were returned to Mya Palace. The original palace had been ransacked in the 14th century, but a future King had the palace rebuilt three times larger and more ornate than its predecessor. The cabinet in which the rubies were to be displayed had remained almost empty for seven centuries. The only items to be seen from its dull facade were the golden orb which had once adorned the Southern pinnacle of the original palace and one ruby. It was believed that the orb contained powers unknown to humanity, harnessing magic and drawing to it all the fire and passion emanating from the rubies. Ancient inscriptions had been discovered describing the missing jewels and depicting the legend, with prominence being given to the travelling companion of the bearer of the rubies. Two lions walked beside the companion. The human figures wore lotus flowers in their hair. Heading the procession was a white elephant pulling a cart with eight-spoke wheels. The ancient insignia depicted complete harmony between bearer and companion. The companion was of pure heart, strong and courageous in speech and mind. In front of the figures and the symbols between them, lay Mya Palace, its golden orb glistening in sunlight. One ray of sunlight penetrated through the palace rooftop, and down into a glass cabinet. Behind all these symbols was a nondescript figure holding a star out in front of him, with rays of light emanating from the star and lighting the way for the bearer and companion. Andre Boesflug had long suspected he was this figure. His duty was to ensure the jewels were delivered to their resting place and his return to the spiritual world would soon follow. His job was almost done. He must begin his interrogation under the auspices of hypnosis.

Monsieur Boesflug donned the robes of a King. The scene was set. Carrie had been transported back in time seven hundred years. King Meng Tuu-Kyi was in the room with her. The inhabitants of the room could have purveyed all of Burma as the sun was setting. Carrie was still asleep but he knew that she would hear his words. He spoke quietly and told her that the white elephant portrayed power and good fortune. The lotus flowers represented purification of body, speech and mind, wholesome deeds and enlightenment. The lions held a symbolic meaning of

184

courage, dignity, dominion, justice and wisdom and the eight-spoke wheel represented truth.   Carrie opened her eyes and the opulence of the room left her in no doubt that she must be dreaming. She saw a grandly dressed gentleman sitting opposite her, in royal garments. She felt the silken bed covers beneath her hands. She looked across to the window and saw the setting sun delivering its pink rays into the room. Rich colourful wall-hangings adorned the room, opulent rugs lined the floor, and the smell of ancient furniture lingered. She was not restrained in any way and after taking in her surroundings she swung her legs off the bed. Fearlessly she said 'Hello' to the stranger across the room. Monsieur Boesflug walked towards her. His face was familiar. Marvellous silks and velvet bedecked his slim build.

"Hello Carrie", he said gently. "Welcome to Mya Palace."

"Who are you? How did I get here?" Carrie inquired.

"You have been transported to us on a legend from a time far into the future", replied the King.

"I'm fascinated, can you explain?"

"I need to ask you some questions first", said the King and began to inquire into her past.

Carrie imparted the information, apparently unsuspecting anything. Monsieur Boesflug was watching for signs of the hypnosis waning but saw none. He continued to ask questions, satisfying himself that she was speaking the truth. Carrie reiterated all she had told him in the room upstairs. He knew she was the one, waited for down the centuries to escort the bearer of the rubies. The King began to explain to Carrie that he would soon die. He foretold the black reign of his daughter Princess Shariyan and the incarceration of the jewels. He told her of the legend which would bring her to a new palace where there was a place for the jewels to be reunited with their golden orb, and he warned her of the perilous journey upon which she would soon embark. He warned her of men who would attempt to kill her friend to obtain the jewels. He warned her of the scepticism of her partner, who would attempt to dissuade her from completing her journey. He also warned her of prophecies which the legend kept secret. Prophecies from an ancient civilisation. Terrifying words which left doubt in Carrie's mind whether she could fulfil her goal and escort her friend and the jewels back to their rightful place for future generations.

"What are the consequences of success or failure?" Carrie asked the King and requested that he answered truthfully.

"If your friend is successful in bringing the Meng Tuu-Kyi rubies back to Mya, she will enjoy long life and happiness for herself and her family. Mya Palace will once again project its magical powers across the land and fill the hearts of all who rule here. Peace will reign supreme."

"And if we fail?" Carrie whispered.

The King's silence surmounted untold fears inside Carrie's heart. e knew that failure was not an option.

Monsieur Boesflug, sure that Carrie was the

one chosen to be the companion, suggested she have a look at the wonderful sunset. As Carrie crossed the room Monsieur Boesflug kindled his hypnotic powers and Carrie once again felt herself falling. Monsieur Boesflug placed her on the silk bedcovers and hurried to change into his own clothes. Scooping her up he returned her to the room upstairs. Then she was standing firmly back on the spot, he brought her out of hypnosis and asked her a few questions about her past.

"That should do nicely Mrs Goodwin, thank you for your co-operation."

He held her elbow and escorted her to the exit, where the doors opened to reveal her friends relaxing in the lavish luxury of the sofa room.

"That was quick", quipped Fiona. "You all done then? Had your interrogation?"

"Fee, it's weird, I feel like you left me hours ago, but you don't seem to think I've been a long time?"

"No", laughed Fiona. "In fact, we thought you would be a long time, but we only came out about five minutes ago."

The door closed behind Carrie, and she walked across and fell onto the sofa.

"Whew!" she said. "I feel like I've been interrogated, but I only remember him asking me a couple of questions."

"Was he satisfied with your answers?" asked Fiona, eager to know that all was well with her companion.

"Yes, absolutely. He said everything was fine."

"Oh well, we'll just have to see what happens next."

They didn't have to wait long. Carrie gulped her second drink of lemonade, and they were summoned to stand and escorted by Bernard to the dining room, where silver service was the order of the day. They were all famished and quickly took their places at the enormous wooden refectory table. The seat cushions of the chairs were a red striped material and the room was breathtaking. It looked like an old castle dining room, with ancient artefacts lining the walls, but modern up to the minute cutlery and crockery decorated the table. Waitresses poured wine into lead crystal glasses. Candles were lit and beautiful thick napkins rolled up inside silver napkin holders lay at the top of their place settings. Fiona suddenly remembered the pouch around her person, and felt it, to make sure it was still there. It was. She relaxed a little. Carrie watched this movement, and her head began to fill with all sorts of nonsense. Legends and silk bed sheets and escorting rubies and elephants and wheels and sunsets and Kings in lavish robes and she thought she was going to faint.

"What's up", asked Fiona. "You look dreadful, like you're going to faint or something."

Carrie straightened up and said, "No, I just felt a bit funny then. I'll be OK when I've had something to eat."

She sat quietly while the other three were talking. She felt sorry for the men. There had been no sanctimonious comments as she expected and she felt a little guilty that Mel had been subjected to this fantasy. He had been sceptical about the whole thing and probably still was. However, she was delighted that he had shown nothing but utter humility all afternoon and would ensure she thanked him later when they had a chance to talk alone. She would ask him if he'd missed her later as well. She was still not convinced that she'd only been a few minutes behind them in the room with Monsieur Boesflug, and these fantastic notions she was having were making her head swim. She needed to calm down.

The men actually brought some reality to the afternoon. The food that was placed in front of them was fabulous. Carrie and Fiona both knew that the men would be delighted. It was all of their favourite food. Everything edible that delighted their men folk was there at the table.

"How is this possible?" asked Fiona. "All this must have cost a fortune, not to mention how they managed to cook it all at once, and how did they know what we all liked?"

Alan said, "I don't know, and right now, I don't care! It's here, and I for one am going to eat it. It would be rude not to, so let's tuck in, I'm absolutely starving."

For the next hour or so they feasted on their favourite foods. Wine was flowing and to each individual, the wine tasted like the one they loved the most. Even Mel who didn't care for wine tasted something he liked in his glass. They all began to relax a little more, and inevitably, the conversation regained momentum.

"Well, what does happen next?" asked Mel. "We've established that the jewels you found on your doorstep Fiona are something special. Don't know if I believe in all the other stuff about the legends and prophecies, but I guess we have to think seriously about our immediate plans. I mean, if we agree to stay longer, what about the kids? How do we explain it all to them? They'll have to get back for work. We should go home really. We're due back at work. Are we all staying, or just the girls? How do you want to work it?"

"Well, it depends, I suppose on how you two feel about it", said Fiona, "and whether you want to go back and leave us to it, or whether we should all stay and see this thing through."

Alan shook his head in disbelief.

Mel continued, "Well as I see it, the only two that are needed are you Fiona, and Carrie supposedly has to accompany you to wherever they send you.
Does anybody know the legend? I mean he hasn't really told us anything about it, just that there is one?"

"Yes, I do", said Carrie.

"And how do you know?" asked Mel sarcastically.

"I don't know, but I do", snapped Carrie.

"Well come on then, let's all know", said Alan as he finished his main meal and began tucking into dessert.

Carrie swallowed hard. Fiona straightened up, a little alarmed that her friend seemed to be quite upset by this questioning. Carrie began. All the nonsense that came into her head came flooding back, miraculously in some semblance of order. She told them the story of the jewels and their owners, and the inscriptions found and the legend of their return to the Mya Palace. She missed nothing out and told them all that she knew. Mel began to laugh again, uncontrollably like he did when he first heard the story all those weeks ago at home while he was eating his spaghetti bolognaise. His laughter was infectious and soon they were all laughing. Carrie was trying to assure everyone through the laughter that it was all true.

"But how do you know all that stuff?" asked Fiona, concerned about her friend's state of mind.

"I don't know, I just do", said Carrie again. "I'm supposed to be your companion Fee, and it's my job to see to it that you and the jewels arrive at this palace safely."

"I have to say something", said Mel. "I know it's nothing to do with me, I'm really just an onlooker, but is there anything in it for you guys? I mean they rightfully belong to you Fiona. They were given to your father, and your father ultimately gave them to you. That makes them yours, not some bloody legendary make-believe voodoo person or something, that's going to take you and Caz to God only knows where. This could all be a plan to sell you into white slavery or sex trafficking or something. How the hell do we know where this Boesflug fellow's going to take you. I think we better stick around until we know a bit more. I'm not feeling happy about it at all. They're your jewels and as far as I can see, someone wants to take them off you and it's probably for himself. Well that's what I think anyway. I'm not altogether sure I want Carrie to pursue this fiasco."

Mel's outburst left everyone speechless, but if they were all truthful, he was voicing what everyone else was thinking. None of it made sense, except what Mel had just said.

"Well", said Fiona, "I do have the deposit box number, the paperwork and the key. I can go to that room any time I want and extract the contents from the deposit box. Yes, they're mine. And I haven't as yet, been given an exact valuation. So we really don't know what we're playing with. What do you think guys? Shall we take the jewels and run? Take them to another jeweller. See what he'll give us for them, take it and get off back home a bit richer than when we came?"

"We already had them valued. We've been offered ten grand on the spot", Alan reminded them.

"Yes", said Fiona, "but if he was willing to give you that much for them on the spur of the moment, what does that tell you? You said the same yourself at the time. It tells me they're worth a whole lot more than that. Monsieur Boesflug has indicated they're priceless. I'm not doing this for nothing. I want to know more about the actual jewels before we go another step further."

"Here, here", said Mel "that's my girl. Well said."

Carrie hesitated before clearing her throat and speaking. "I don't agree. I believe the jewels are genuine. I believe the story Monsieur Boesflug has told us. I believe there's something in this legend, and I think we should see it through. Otherwise why are we here? Why didn't you take the ten grand back in England? You could have been sunning yourselves in the Caribbean by now and have a stack of change earning you a stack of interest, but you didn't. You chose to pursue the truth. Now that you've found it, you've become unsure again. I don't know why I know this, but I do. Those jewels have to be returned to a place called Mya Palace in Burma. I don't know if there will be some sort of reward. I just know I have to escort Fiona to this place, with the assistance of Monsieur Boesflug. Anyone who doesn't think it's genuine shouldn't be coming with us. You see, you have to believe, and if you don't, we can't pursue this. You either have to sell the jewels Fee and let the next owner of the jewels go through all this stuff or we have to continue on the journey we've started."

"You're right", said Fiona. "They're my responsibility. I have to see this through to the end, no matter what. What do you want to do guys? Are you coming with us, or going back?"

Mel and Alan looked at one another.

"What do you think Mel", asked Alan, looking a bit dejected.

"I've told you what I think", said Mel. "I

think it's a load of baloney and I think we'd be making a big mistake letting the girls go off on their own. I can't afford to take that much time off work and I think you two should collect the damn jewels and head on home. You can do what you want with them when you get back to the UK."

Carrie protested, "But Mel, you knew when we embarked on this journey that it might mean an extended stay."

"Yes", said Mel, "but not to the extent you're talking about now. It could be weeks."

"It's up to you", said Fiona. "I would like to continue. I'm with Carrie, and I think Monsieur Boesflug is genuine. I don't believe we're going to be sold into slavery or sex traffic or anything like that. I would like to see it through. "Is there any way you'll stay?"

Mel was a genuine man, always outspoken, usually right in what he said but always willing to concede the point. He thought for a few moments and turned to Carrie.

"Do you really want to stay Carrie?"

"Yeah, I do. I believe there's something in it. In fact I don't just think, somehow I know. So I'll have to see it through for Fiona's sake, as well as my own."

"OK then, so be it. We'll need to find somewhere to stay."

"No, we don't". said Fiona. "Monsieur Boesflug said all expenses paid."

"So he did", said Mel and grinned.

They ate in silence, each lost in their own thoughts. They raised their glasses to the decision to

194

stay and Mel and Alan would ring home the next day and speak to their respective employers and say they'd been unavoidably delayed in New York and would speak to them again in a few days. They all finished their meal and sat chatting. Bernard came in to ask if they'd had enough.

"Yes thank you", they all shouted in unison.
He smiled at them.

"Monsieur Boesflug will be with you in a moment."

Monsieur Boesflug appeared moments later and asked the quartet if they had hotel accommodation for tonight.

"Yes, thank you", said Fiona. "We are booked into the hotel tonight and tomorrow."

"You may need to cancel tomorrow", said Monsieur Boesflug. "Have you all decided to stay for this journey, or are any of you leaving?"

Alan replied. "We're all staying."

"Very well", replied Monsieur Boesflug. "Your plane leaves Kennedy Airport at nine thirty five tomorrow evening. A taxi will pick you up from your hotel at six o'clock. Please be prompt. I will make arrangements for the package to be waiting for you at airport reception. You will need to call there before you book in. You must put it in your hand luggage Fiona, and you must not let the bag out of your sight for the duration of your journey. Under no circumstances should you put the bag down anywhere. When you need to go to the bathroom, take Carrie along with you. I must warn you, your journey is fraught with danger, but I know you have the capability to overcome anything you might encounter.

I will be close by, although it will not be wise for me to be seen. Just know that I'll be there. Fiona, I have some papers that might explain the legend for you. You should read them and memorise them tonight. Carrie will be your mediator should you get into any difficulties. It's your responsibility to carry the rubies to safe keeping. Carrie is your trusted companion on the journey but her powers are limited."

Fiona's heart leapt. 'What did he mean Carrie's powers? What were they getting into, or already in'.

"That's ok", she said rather sheepishly. "I'll do my best. What happens when we get there? How will I know what to do next? We have no directions to the palace?"

"No you haven't", replied Monsieur Boesflug. "Don't worry about anything. You'll be guided all the way."

"And what's at the end of it all?" enquired Fiona, thinking back to what Mel had said earlier?

"You will have fulfilled our centuries old prophecy," replied Monsieur Boesflug. Fiona and Carrie both felt chills down their spine. He'd said 'our' centuries old prophecy. Oh God, what did that mean, did it mean he was some sort of ghost or something? This was getting scary and the girls were frightened. Monsieur Boesflug smiled at them both, shook their hands and led them out of the dining room, along the corridors, and through a double set of doors right back into the light filled shop at the front of the building that seemed never ending. They turned to wave goodbye to Monsieur Boesflug but he was nowhere to be seen. Carrie fought her way through the shoppers to the doors which would take them out onto the street, and she suddenly turned to Fiona.

"You've still got the key?"

"SSSSHHHHHHHHH" mouthed her friend, then quietly "I know, sshhhhh, we'll talk about it in a minute somewhere quiet."

They hurried back to the coffee bar and talked about the sudden plight they found themselves in.

"How is he going to get the package to the airport, when you have the key strapped around your middle", asked Carrie.

"I don't know. Maybe he's got a master key. If he hasn't, he'll have to find me and I'll have to go back and open it", said Fiona.

They all felt decidedly uncomfortable. Mel suggested they find a cybercafé and look up the rubies on the internet and see if they could find anything about ancient missing jewellery. Alan agreed it was a good idea. They finished their coffees.

The snow was beginning to fall again and it was much colder outside than it had been in their confined spot hours earlier. They were all a bit edgy, and considered every person a threat. Not to mention what they all thought would be waiting in their rooms when they returned to the hotel. Soon, they were all given a reality check. They turned a corner and bumped into Lisa and Graham.

"Where've you been all day", asked Lisa, hugging her Mum and kissing her on both cheeks.

"We've been having a look round, showing Alan and Fiona the sights", replied Carrie quickly. "What have you guys been up to? Did you find anything you were looking for?"

"Yes, we've seen a few things we like", said Lisa "We'd really like you to come back with us to have a look before we buy Mum, please." She turned to Alan and Fiona and said, "Are you happy to join us?"

"Yes, that would be lovely", answered Fiona, knowing full well that she must stay by Carrie. "I'll enjoy looking in all the shop windows".

"Ok love, lead the way", said Carrie.

They followed the youngsters who were excitedly chatting about their finds. Carrie felt a little guilty. She had come on this trip with her daughter to find things for her wedding and hadn't spent nearly as much time with her as she'd hoped. She knew it was going to be difficult to tell Lisa and Graham why they were leaving New York the next evening. She practised how she would break the news to them.

"Oh by the way, love, your Dad and I are going to Myanmar at six o'clock tomorrow evening. See you when we get home."

No. That wouldn't do.

"Dad and I have been thinking about this for some time, but we've actually seen a trip and booked it today while we were out. We're flying out to Myanmar for a couple of days."

No, that wouldn't do either. Lisa would know she hadn't been thinking about it or she would have said so. She had to come up with something good. She asked Mel and he said quite nonchalantly, "You'll think of something Caz!"

Carrie decided not to worry about it any more. She concentrated on her daughter's excitement. As expected, Lisa led them to Bloomingdale's. They spent the next hour looking at all kinds of wedding accessories, but left the store empty handed and headed back to a small shop Lisa had found on 6th Avenue. A wonderful little place tucked away, resembling establishments from the 1930's. Every nook and cranny contained wedding regalia, from hair-pieces to clips for shoes. It looked just like the old fashioned shop Carrie remembered frequenting when Lisa was little. The one with the long rounded wooden counter and walls lined with pigeon holes crammed with goodies. There were glass trays underneath the wooden counter top filled with an array of wedding paraphernalia. Shelved from floor to ceiling all the way round the shop with see-through boxes, you could glimpse the exciting items packed into each one. They were spoilt for choice. The shop keeper emptied a dozen pigeon holes searching for the perfect tiara. She had been extremely helpful and there were dozens of boxes out on the counter for Lisa to have a look through. A myriad of tiaras had been taken out of their boxes. They were strategically placed on a length of material laid across the counter, to avoid scratching the sparkling gems which adorned them. Lisa hadn't been able to make her mind up after narrowing her choice down to two. The clock was ticking and unbeknown to Lisa of course, her mother and father had to prepare for their departure the next day. Carrie was busy looking round the store at garters and hair combs. The array was spectacular and choosing was impossible. She came back to Lisa who was still unable to choose between the two dazzling tiaras. As it was such a special occasion and her choice should be perfect, Carrie suggested that she bought them both and make up her mind in front of her own mirrors at home. Lisa tried them both on again, and paraded in front of a large hand held mirror. Her decision was not forthcoming. She agreed with Carrie's suggestion and asked the lady if she could please take both. She was thrilled beyond belief with her purchases and knew without a doubt it had been an amazing decision to come to New York for her treasure.

While the girls were making their purchases, there had been a commotion outside. Sirens could be heard above the noise inside the shop, and Mel was already looking out of the window to see what was going on in the street. Alan and Fiona had decided to wait outside the shop as Lisa's purchase was very personal. Further to the left and craning his neck to see without spoiling anything in the shop window, Mel could see a black car parked at the side of the road with the passenger door wide open and no-one inside the car. A little to the right and across the road, there was a crowd gathering. Armed police were running about and the little door bell chimed as Mel opened the door and stepped outside. He was horrified to see Alan in the crowd talking to one of the policemen. He raced over, pushing his way through the crowd and saw a policewoman on the floor putting a small pillow underneath Fiona's head.

"Oh my God", he shouted out loud.
Alan heard his voice and turned.
"What the hell's happened", asked Mel.
"This guy suddenly appeared from nowhere and snatched Fiona's bag."

"Where was the bag?" asked Mel.

"Over her shoulder", said Alan, "but he snatched it with such force, the strap broke and he got away with it, pushing Fiona to the ground. Luckily for us there were two police officers just nearby and they heard Fee scream and came to investigate. One of them has run off after the guy who did it, the other one ran the other way."

Mel quickly turned remembering the black car, just in time to see it disappear into a side street.

"Quick", he yelled, "that black car just over the road, quick."

One of the officers, quick on the uptake was already in the squad car following Mel's direction. Mel ran back to the crowd.

"You alright?" he asked, bending down to talk to Fiona.

"I'll be ok. It's just frightened me and I've bumped my head quite badly. Thanks Mel."

Just at that point an ambulance arrived, making the crowd scurry to one side. Meanwhile, Carrie, Lisa and Graham had secured their purchase and were now hurrying over to the commotion. Horrified to find her friend on the ground and asking a million questions in quick succession, Carrie knelt down beside Fiona and stroked her forehead seconds before the paramedics lifted Fiona onto a stretcher.

"Who's coming with her", asked one man in uniform.

"I am. I'm her husband", said Alan.

"Which hospital?" asked Carrie quickly before the ambulance sped off.

The paramedic answered her, and Carrie said "We'll be there shortly."

The ambulance sped off carrying Alan and Fiona to the medical centre nearby. Lisa, clutching her parcel tightly, Graham, Mel and Carrie, jumped into the hailed taxi and minutes later they were entering the medical centre.

Carrie asked Lisa and Graham to wait with Mel at reception. She found Fee in a stable condition having her head bandaged.

She whispered to Fiona, "Do you think it was related or just a one-off?"

"I'd like to think it was a one-off, but I'm laying bets it wasn't. Did you see the black Sedan?"

"I was worried about that", said Carrie. "That's the last time I'll be leaving you alone until this is done."

"Well, I wasn't exactly alone", her friend protested. "We were just stood outside."
Just at that moment, a police officer came into the room, carrying the handbag.

"Did you get him?" asked Fiona.

"No maam", replied the officer in a deep New York accent.

"He ran into an entry, must have been disturbed and pitched the bag. Somebody found it on the floor and had seen me running. They put two and two together. My partner got in his car and sped after someone speeding off in a black car. You are just unlucky maam. This happens a dozen times a day. So long as you're going to be OK, I'll be getting along."

Fiona and the others thanked him profusely for his efforts in returning her bag. As soon as the police officer had left the room, Fiona began to cry. Alan and Carrie tried to comfort her.

"I just can't believe this. What on earth is going on?' she wept.
They both continued to comfort her, until a nurse came in with a cup of coffee for Fiona.
"Wow", said Fiona, "That's what I call treatment! Thank you very much."

One hour later, they were all leaving the hospital. Underneath Fiona's bandaging lurked some swelling reducing ointment. She clutched a little card about head injuries and what to do if….. .

They hailed a taxi, and the six of them were glad to be on their way back to the hotel. They would never forget the day Lisa bought her wedding accessories in New York.

It was blowing quite a blizzard, when they hurried into the hotel foyer. Fiona and Carrie managed to get a few seconds on their own, and it was agreed that Lisa and Graham were told that the four of them had just come across a unique opportunity to travel to Myanmar for a couple of days, and that they were throwing caution to the wind and going. Lisa couldn't believe what her mother was telling her.

"Oh, my God", she exclaimed. "Get you two. What on earth made you do that?"

"We just happened to see the offer", explained Carrie, trying to cross her toes. "We thought if we don't do it now, we'll never do it. We all agreed to find out about it and it was a good deal. There's a taxi picking us up tomorrow evening at six o'clock.

Lisa stood with her mouth open, almost disbelieving, and then said, "You'd better get packing then!"

She smiled at her mum, who turned and hugged her, a big mother-daughter bear hug.

"See you in the foyer in an hour and we'll go and find some dinner", said Mel, also hugging his daughter.

He gave Graham a hefty slap on the back, and Graham grinned. "See you in a bit!" and they disappeared into the lift.

Carrie telephoned the airport and cancelled their flights home. The four adults approached the desk, gave their room numbers and explained the situation about their cancelled flights. Mel and Carrie had been due to depart the next day and asked for their luggage to be stored until the taxi collected them the following evening. Fiona and Alan informed the receptionist that they would be checking out a day early and would be leaving with Mel and Carrie.

The receptionist concluded the paperwork and said to Fiona, "No problem, Mrs Oliver, have a nice evening."

"Oh well, that was painless", said Alan, "Come on Fiona, take me upstairs!" "Oooohhhh", laughed Fiona.

"For a cup of tea!" said Alan and grinned back

at her. She whacked him one, and they all piled into the lift.

"How's your head love?" asked Alan.

"Not too bad. It'd have been better if it hadn't happened, but I'll be alright now." They went to their own rooms and flopped down on their beds, deciding to have forty winks before they showered for dinner. Once inside the haven of their room Carrie asked Mel what he thought now.

"Not sure what to make of it all", he said. "Worried sick about you girls. You don't think that was anything to do with the jewels, do you?"

"Yes I do", answered Carrie. "The black sedan gave the game away really. It's quite scary."

"Yeah, you're not wrong there", replied Mel.

They met up after a short rest and decided it would be nice to dine somewhere close to the Empire State Building so that Lisa and Graham could see it lit up. It was Valentine's Day and their last night together on this trip. There was magic in the air and they spent a wonderful evening together. They all said their goodbyes to Lisa and Graham, wishing the happy couple a safe journey home.

* * * * * *

Myanmar 2005 AD

The airport was unbelievably busy as the four friends wound their way to the reception desk to collect their parcel. The receptionist was a pretty girl in her mid twenties, dark haired and tanned. As she went about her business completing the paperwork for their collection, she asked where they were going and told them she had just come back from Singapore. She chatted nonchalantly about her boyfriend's mum who lived in a luxury apartment overlooking Singapore's famous Orchard Road. Oblivious to the task she was actually doing, and evidently wrapped up in her own thoughts she handed Fiona a ticket and asked her to go to the lost luggage desk for her collection. She had seemed so hairy-fairy Fiona wondered if she had given her the correct ticket at all. Fiona handed in her ticket and thankfully signed on the dotted line. The parcel containing the cloth bag was handed to her. The others stayed close trying to look as inconspicuous as possible while Fiona quickly secreted the bag in her hand luggage. She locked the padlock attached to the zip, and Alan buried the key deep in his pocket. Fiona had the strap of the holdall over her left shoulder and across her chest with the holdall hanging down her right hand side. Alan stayed at the other side of the bag, and together the four of them made their way over to the check-in desk. They were delighted to find themselves at the front of the queue. Their baggage was checked right through to Mandalay, although Carrie was quite excited about seeing Yangon, if only for a couple of hours. Less than half an hour later they were heading for the departure lounge. The boys were looking forward to a big dinner and a couple of beers. The girls just wanted to sit down and relax before the journey of a lifetime. They both felt tingly and silly and adrenalin pumped excitement. Who'd have thought that two schoolgirls, who first met all those years ago, would now be embarking on a voyage across the world, carrying priceless antique jewellery to an ancient palace to fulfil a magical prophecy? Was this real? Or was it some fantastic dream they were both having? No, it was real. They were here, sitting with their husbands in the departure lounge of a foreign airport, waiting to board a plane bound for ancient Burma and a mystical palace.

They didn't know what to expect when they landed and they had no idea how far it was to the palace. Monsieur Boesflug had decided the least they knew the better for their own safety. He hoped their journey would conclude without incident, but he was streetwise enough to know that this would not be likely, and he meant to be on hand should anything go wrong.

Fiona reconsidered what she carried in the bag sitting on her knee. She daydreamed of knights on white horses, and kings and princesses, whilst Carrie almost crushed her hand attempting to reveal the innermost feelings of her soul. She knew she possessed more knowledge than the others, but knew not how. No-one had noticed Monsieur Boesflug. How could they? The man sitting opposite with his family was a small fat man with an enormous belly stuck out in front of him. His wife was tall and thin with a mass of blonde straggly hair. She wore far too much make up and the children were not at all well-behaved. There were a few bald-headed men around, but none matching the description of Monsieur Boesflug. He was quickly forgotten when the air steward called for passengers on flight 823 to make their way to the boarding gate. Boarding the aircraft would take place in five minutes. Carrie was dreading the thirteen and a half hour flight to Yangon and not content with that, they had a connecting flight to Mandalay. Both girls had purchased a number of magazines to keep them occupied. They could not and would not discuss their journey whilst on this flight.

They took their seats. The aircraft seemed unusually luxurious and they were sure they would enjoy the on-board entertainment, and wonderful food. Fiona firmly clutched the strap of the holdall sitting on her lap, with her magazine opened out on top of it. Carrie took off a layer and placed the mohair cardigan on top of the holdall and replaced Fee's magazine on top. She thought the stewardess might make Fiona put the bag in the overhead locker. Her ploy seemed successful. There were lots of vacant seats and although that would normally unnerve her, Carrie tried to remain calm. She had to consider every eventuality. She must ensure that her friend and her valuable cargo arrived unharmed and intact. This, she reminded herself, would be no mean feat. How did she know? How could she know? She just knew.

They all settled into their seats for take off. Carrie clutched Mel's hand so hard it turned white. She tried to sing in her brain. It was one of those takeoffs when the aeroplane seemed to hang motionless above the runway. The surge pushed them back into their seats and Carrie sucked so hard on a boiled sweet, she nearly pulled one of her loose teeth out. It didn't make any difference. She felt they were being pushed into history. When they reached altitude and the plane began its steady passage to Yangon, Carrie was fine again. She relinquished her grip on Mel who grinned and shook his hand vigorously. She focused her attention on her magazine and it was soon time for the first round of refreshments. Carrie noticed the couple who had been opposite them in the airport. The man was small and portly. But she wondered about the tall thin woman who sat beside him, and marvelled at cupid's bizarre match making.

Mel quietly hypothesised. What should they expect? He attempted to emanate Nostradamus and predict their fate. His throat was dry and he doubted his sanity. His exaggerated magnification of their predicament was threatening to turn his brain to mulch and drain his blood. He kept going right back to the beginning to make some sense but to no avail. He adjourned and picked up the in-flight magazine hoping he would gain some inspiration from the glossy advertisements. Fiona was scared stiff, and sat ram-rod upright clutching the bag beneath the mohair cardigan which made her hands itch. Alan sensed her irritability and tried to calm her down by telling jokes. This just annoyed everyone so he closed his eyes and went to sleep. Fiona decided the antidote for paranoia was alcohol. She would have another wine when the next steward brushed passed them. 'No. I might have something stronger. Whisky or perhaps brandy.' That thought in mind, she nudged Carrie and asked her to order one.

"Large please", replied Fiona when the fair haired stewardess asked.

"It'll be just a moment madam", she said in a southern drawl.

Carrie was tempted to reply in her best American accent, but refrained at the last minute.

'Are these the remnants of my life I'm playing with', Carrie thought. 'Am I going to come out of this alive?' She remonstrated as to why she shouldn't die yet. 'Certainly not killed running a mother of mercy mission, even if it is for Fiona. She could have just sold them. Well they were offered ten grand. That's not to be sniffed at.' She imagined the rubies were hers and began to fantasise about the amount of money she'd have if she sold them. As soon as the thought manifested she reproached herself, disbelieving the intensity of sudden pain which racked through her body. 'Oh, oh. Better not stimulate that notion.'

The flight though tedious was uneventful. They were glad to disembark. It was about noon and their connecting flight would leave at fifteen hundred hours. They had a couple of hours before queuing at the boarding gate. They ventured outside. The sun was warm and a delicious breeze kissed their cheeks. Carrie produced some cartons of juice which they drank without tasting. They decided to investigate Yangon and with one eye over their shoulder ran across to a stationary taxi. Alan agreed a round trip price with the driver and handed him some American dollars. They were mesmerised by the scene as they approached the city. There was hustle and bustle everywhere. The smells of the busy open air markets were intoxicating. Street vendors displayed brightly coloured wares from clothing to fruit and vegetables. An elderly monk in traditional robes carried a bag of shopping whilst shielding himself from the midday sun with a rather feminine looking parasol. Carrie watched as he strode out and wondered what his life consisted of. She noticed groups of young monks gathered together having a conference and made a mental note to read up about the monks of Myanmar when she got home. They watched a young girl whom Carrie thought couldn't be more than eight or nine, operating a shoe-shine service. They saw funny little wooden open-air buses crammed with dozens of colourfully clad people hanging out over the sides. They were fascinated by the fabulous smells emanating from the street vendors' food but no-one had the courage to buy and try. The tapering roofs of pagodas in the distance glistened invitingly and Fiona wanted to investigate every nook and cranny.

They had a quick summit meeting and decided not to chance the street vendors or local eating places. It would probably be safer to find something to eat and drink back at the airport. Fiona was suddenly nervous. Was it her imagination or could she feel thousands of eyes upon her. She concluded it was only because they were foreigners and not because of their valuable cargo. No-one could possibly know what was in the holdall still firmly strapped around her shoulder closely flanked by Carrie.

The driver indicated that he would wait for them but instead they asked him to head on back to the airport. They felt sure their taster of Yangon would bring them back one day, but for now they had a plane to catch. Their hopes of a meal at the airport were a disappointment. All they could find was tea or coffee and packaged biscuits and slices of cake. That would have to suffice. Alan and Mel bought extra. They were acutely aware that beyond passport control and baggage collection, they hadn't a clue where to go. Remarkably they were beginning to rely on the knowledge that Monsieur Boesflug was close. They would just wait for him to come forward.

The plane was airborne on time and the flight lasted one hour and fifty minutes. Ahead of schedule they herded off the plane and through customs. Nerves struck. Fiona felt sick and clung onto Alan for dear life. Where was Monsieur Boesflug? Their confidence was waning. They saw their bags move slowly toward them. Alan did his usual stunt and hopped on, picked them up and hopped off again much to the annoyance of all the other passengers. Mel was patient and waited until the bags were exactly parallel with his body and then quickly removed them from their merry-go round and dumped them both down on the ground.

"Right folks, what now?" he asked the others.

Carrie, like Fiona felt nauseas. Every face in the crowd was a potential threat. 'It's a miracle the plane wasn't hi-jacked and diverted', she thought. 'For all we know there could be millions of pounds in that bag. I'm responsible and I haven't a notion where to go or what to do.' Mel interrupted her thoughts.

"Shall we make our way to the terminal exit? There might be someone there with our name on a plaque or something."

"Good thought pal", said Alan.

Just then the fat man pushed past them with his three children in tow, still whining and shouting at one another. The blonde-haired lady brushed past after him and Carrie felt the lady touch her hand as she went past. Slowly so as not to attract attention she brought her hand up into view. There was a tiny round sticker on the back of her hand. Number 82.

"82 what?" whispered Carrie to Mel. "Is it the number of a taxi, a train, a bus? Do they have buses here?"

She looked at Mel, and he pointed to the exit. They stepped outside and drew deep breaths of air into their lungs. Carrie's question was answered immediately when she saw a man standing beside a cab holding up a circular board with the number 82. Carrie headed straight for it. They climbed into the cab. Carrie looked out of the rear window and saw the fat man and the blonde-haired lady climbing into the cab behind them. Their children had disappeared and she knew where Monsieur Boesflug was. She marvelled at the fact she hadn't recognised him before. It was as clear as the nose on her face. She smiled and wondered if the others had cottoned on. She was sure they hadn't. She felt reassured by his close proximity and relaxed a little. She would be glad to soak in a hot bath and fall asleep in crisp white bed linen. She patted Fiona's hand and smiled, assuring her silently that all would be well. But all would not be well. Before morning, Fiona and Carrie would wish they'd never come to Myanmar.

* * * * * *

Journey to Mya Palace

Fiona felt pleasantly woozy after consuming two glasses of wine on the aircraft. This factor probably accounted for why she hadn't noticed the bag on her knee getting hot. When she did realise she thought it was her imagination. Carrie sensed her fidgeting. Fiona tried to lift the bag up but it was extremely heavy and she winced as her wrist wrenched under the weight. Alan asked her what was the matter and she whispered to him that the bag was hot.

"It's very warm in this cab", he said. Fee insisted that the bag was burning her. Alan helped her to place it on the seat between her and Carrie. Carrie looked at her questioningly. Fiona looked down at her knee to investigate the burning sensation. Conditions in the cab were squashed and she decided she was being foolish. Carrie smelt burning. Both girls realised at once. It was too late. The flames caught hold immediately. They screamed at the driver to stop, but he ignored them. They screamed at the boys to open the doors. Carrie's arms flailed about as she tried to douse the flames which threatened to engulf them. Fiona, who still had tightly hold of the strap, clutched onto it and pushed Alan out, leaping out of the burning car after him. They were lucky the terrain over which the car was travelling was unsuitable for speed. The driver seemed oblivious, behaving like a robot. The four of them having flung themselves on to the roadside watched in horror as the taxi careered into the mountainside. There was a huge explosion and the car and its driver became a burning inferno.

Carrie had been thrown into a roll in the leap from the car. The quick succession of battering against the tarmac had doused the flames from her jacket. Her left hand had suffered some slight burns and they were battered and bruised. Fiona clung onto the bag. The taxi which had been travelling behind them at some distance had seen the explosion and telephoned for the police and ambulance. The blonde-haired lady had quietly rung for another taxi. She asked the driver to pull up just behind the scene of the accident and they hurried to administer first aid. The blonde lady managed to have a few words with Carrie.

"Rest assured the driver of the taxi coming to collect you will get you to your destination safely."

"How can you be sure?" asked Carrie.

"Because it's my brother Andre."

Carrie gasped and through her pain, began to laugh.

"I thought you were Monsieur Boesflug. In disguise", she laughed.

"No, he's on his way now", said the blonde-haired lady.

The fat man was certain that no-one had suffered more than minor burns and bruising. Another taxi pulled up alongside with Monsieur Boesflug at the wheel. He beckoned them all to get in and put his foot down hard on the accelerator. He mustered up the fastest speed he could, traversing around potholes and cleverly manoeuvreing the mountain track closely followed by Monsieur Boesflug's sister and the fat man. Fiona's curiosity got the better of her and she touched the bottom of the bag. She looked to Carrie for some sort of explanation. The bag was cold. Monsieur Boesflug spoke to her.

"The rubies detected danger and saved you. Word must have leaked that you were in the country. There are ruthless people who will undoubtedly attempt to kill you. I thought we'd have got a little further before an attempt was made. As I told you the rubies have mystical powers. The fire that burns within them ignited in order to rid you of danger and save your lives. Let's be thankful none of you sustained severe injury."

Half an hour later the two cars drove through a pair of black electric gates. Monsieur Boesflug announced to the four anxious people sat in the car with him, that this would be their refuge for several hours. He invited them to take as much refreshment from the large refrigerator as they would like and urged them to get some sleep.

"I'll return for you at five in the morning. Please be ready, we have a long journey ahead. The earlier we start the better."

Shock and exasperation over their near-death experience had silenced them. They simply took heed of Monsieur Boesflug's advice. They ate slices of cheese and ham with tomatoes, surprised at the typically English food. They tore open cartons of orange juice and drank thirstily. They slept with one eye open and Carrie's mobile alarm sounded at four thirty.

"Come on everyone, time to get ready." yelled Carrie.

No-one had removed any clothing. They had a quick slurp of juice and were stood at the entrance by four fifty-five. There was a thick glass panel in the front entrance and Carrie peered through, eager to see their surroundings. They had been too pre-occupied to pay much attention. Concrete lions flanked either side of the entrance. Carrie turned to attract the others' attention just as Monsieur Boesflug appeared.

"Is everybody ready?" he asked.

"Yes, all present and amounted for", said Carrie.

"Accounted for", corrected Mel and laughed.

"Did you have far to travel last night?' Carrie asked, curious to know how far away he had been.

"No distance at all", smiled Monsieur Boesflug.

With the beautiful building left behind Carrie became aware of its isolation. The mountain road on which they had travelled, gave stunning panoramic views of the landscape and not another building was in sight. She wondered if there had been a small apartment at the back of the building where Monsieur Boesflug had slept. She thought about the events of the previous day. 'How many more psychopaths were lying in wait?' The bandaging on her left hand reminded her of how serious the event had been. Another few moments in that burning car would have been fatal. It had been nothing short of miraculous they'd survived. She thought how quickly Monsieur Boesflug had appeared. 'Why had the ambulance or the police not arrived? What would happen when someone found the burnt out car with a body inside? Would there be an investigation and would they become suspects? How would the police find them? How had it all happened in the first place? Was Monsieur Boesflug speaking the truth? It was all incomprehensible.'

They followed Monsieur Boesflug downhill in front of a small pagoda where they saw a minibus. The driver was Monsieur Boesflug's sister. He asked them to climb inside.

"I will see you later." To Carrie he handed a written set of directions.

"My sister knows the way."

Fiona sat still, grateful that the bag was not hot. She mulled over the events of the previous evening unable to make any sense of it. She wondered what they might encounter today. At present she felt they were in safe hands. Monsieur Boesflug had insisted once again that he could serve them better from a distance. Carrie was able to follow the simple directions. Everybody in and settled they drove off. The landscape was breathtaking. Mist rose up everywhere and pink rays from the early morning sun filtered through the cultivated plains and green groves. As they drove further the horizon was littered with glistening pagodas and stupas. Mesmerised though they were by its magnificence, it was going to be an uncomfortable journey. The large pot holes made it impossible to gain any speed and Carrie ventured the question to their driver.

"Is it a long journey?"

"Mya Palace by road would normally take about twelve hours", she told them. "But because the roads are difficult to manoeuvre and extremely uncomfortable, we will only drive part of the way.

We'll reach our stopover hotel where you can have a good rest and tomorrow morning we'll take you across the river. The remainder of your journey will be by helicopter."

Carrie thanked her and settled into her seat for what she hoped would be an uneventful ride. She was captivated by the scenery passing them by and strengthened her resolve to come back to this fascinating place.

Their time was drawing near. Travelling towards a destiny that belied life as they knew it, wet rainy days at home seemed eons away. Fiona wished she could take out the jewels and enjoy them but was too scared to touch the bag. 'What would happen when they got 'there'? How would it be and who would they see? Where would they put the jewels or who would they give them to? How would they know the people were genuine? How would they know these people would not keep them for themselves? Would there be a reward or should she have kept them for herself and her family and been rich beyond compare?' Fiona mulled it all over a dozen times as did her three travelling companions. 'Were they insane? Was there an invisible force extricating their common sense and bringing them to the other side of the world on a wild goose chase?' Carrie half devised a plan. 'I'll ring a taxi from the hotel and we'll get to hell out of it as soon as possible. We could catch the first available flight back to England. Why are we doing this? Why is Fiona parting with the jewels? Who the hell is this guy Boesflug?' They hadn't seen sight nor sign of him in the past few hours. 'Where is he? His sister's at the wheel of this car but where's he for God's sake?' The more Carrie thought about it the more she thought she must have been mad to agree to this foolishness. Fiona's hand lay on top of the holdall. Carrie put her hand on top of Fiona's. She knew Fee must be thinking exactly the same. She went through her rough knowledge again. 'These rare rubies belonged to a fourteenth century King and his daughter. The palace was ransacked and the jewels went missing.

They turned up again when an old grandmother passed them to her best friend's grandfather, who brought them home from World War Two and gave them to his wife. The jewels became the possession of Fiona's father and lay forgotten for decades. A few weeks before her father's death, Fiona found them in a box in her porch. Why had nobody ever had them valued? The same question kept cropping up. While her thoughts ran riot she began to think about how she and Fiona had come to be friends. All the lovely memories of their childhood together tugged at her heartstrings. She loved Fee and no matter what happened she would always be there for her. She felt a calm descend. Mel was holding her hand and was asleep on her shoulder. She let her eyes close and drifted into a semi conscious state. Her thoughts rolled into a big ball and the ball opened up and swallowed her. She was inside the ball and it was rolling downhill and gathering momentum. She could see through the walls of the ball out onto a road resembling a rainbow. The long straight road incorporated all the colours of the spectrum. It began to roll faster and faster until she could not determine whether they were still on the rainbow road. The clouds that had been spinning blurred until nothing was decipherable and it was all one pastel coloured blur. Suddenly the rolling stopped. A black sedan car was the first thing she saw when she opened her eyes, and in it sat two men in the back seat and a driver. The vision remained for a split second and disappeared. A name came into her head, 'Elliott. Oh, my God, that's Sophie's boyfriend. What would he be doing here.' The thought left her temporarily. Other visions included white elephants, lotus flowers, eight-spoke wheels and a palace with huge golden orbs on top of its towers, shining in the reflection of a wonderful red sunset. Two male lions, with their manes flapping in the breeze walked beside her. Fiona was on the other side. Mel and Alan were behind them. Monsieur Boesflug walked ahead of them all. Her heart was filled with the love of a culture which became extinct centuries ago. She could see rows and rows of rubies and diamonds, other precious gems, necklaces, bracelets, rings, and a beautiful princess. She moved closer to the princess to gaze on her beauty. The Princess leered fiendishly and lurched towards her. The hands turned into black talons and clawed Carrie's face. No sound came when she screamed.

She could see a King in regal clothing who sat gently stroking her forehead while she lay on a bed of silken bed covers. Over the other side of the room was a breathtaking view from the chamber window. She saw a darkened room with hundreds of boxes lining the walls and a set of huge ladders and a drawer pulled out with strands of rubies hanging from it and two men in dark suits standing beneath trying to drag the rubies down from the box. She saw a holdall on fire and a blackened skeleton inside a burnt out car and Uncle Tom dressed in a tweed skirt turning the dials of a safe. She saw her lovely sofa at home and smelt spaghetti bolognaise. She heard herself shouting at Megan to get out of the way. She saw a snow covered lane, and a snow covered 6th Avenue. And now sparkling in all its splendour before her, a palace of gigantic proportions with turrets as high as the clouds, each one topped with a golden orb, all except one. She saw poverty and misery surrounding the palace and she felt sorrow. She walked slowly towards the palace with the lions still flanking her and she felt their strength and wished she had the rubies with her to feel their warmth.

The car suddenly pulled to a halt and jolted Carrie awake. She felt exhausted and out of breath as though she had been working arduously.

"Are you alright?" asked Mel. "Come on hun, we're here, I think we can get something to eat and a proper sleep."

"Where's here?" asked Carrie.

"At the hotel", replied Alan and Fiona simultaneously.

They alighted the vehicle and surveyed the building which towered high above and threatened to engulf them. Its opulence was intoxicating and they could hardly wait to see their rooms. Monsieur Boesflug was striding across the courtyard towards them. Carrie refrained from the inappropriate urge to run and throw herself into his arms. He gave them their room numbers and told them a meal would be served in one hour in the main dining room. He hoped they would relax and enjoy their stay. There would also be an evening meal. They were to make their way to the rear entrance of the hotel by five o'clock the next morning. Having delivered his information, he bowed and turned and the others thought he'd gone back into the hotel, but Carrie could have sworn he just disappeared into thin air. 'I must be overtired.'

The hotel was indeed luxurious and they enjoyed a lovely day in its confines. Carrie's mind was turning somersaults. The vision she was most concerned about was Elliott. 'Why on earth should he have come into my mind? I've only met him a couple of times and who on earth are the other two men?' She hoped that it was just her imagination. It was not. The rubies were extolling their magical attributes and dispensing a premonition of the next trauma they would all endure. She wouldn't have to wait long to see her premonition brought to fruition. It was while they were at dinner that evening.

Fiona had brought the holdall with her to dinner. She had taken her overnight stuff out but it was still extremely uncomfortable. She felt it was actually drawing attention by the mere fact she had it with her. By mutual consent the bag was placed on the floor underneath the table. A mistake they were to bitterly regret.

The four were having a relaxing time, enjoying the wonderful hotel and eating their meal as though it were their first for a week. They had all imbibed a couple of glasses of wine and were engrossed in a raucous conversation. Their table was central in the room, and there were no other guests in that seating area. The light was dim and shadows were cast by a flickering candle on the table. Except for the light behind a bar in the corner, the room was almost in darkness. The waiter was busy attending to his optics and hadn't noticed the man dressed in black drop to his hands and knees in front of the bar and crawl very slowly towards the table of diners. Lurking round the corner of the bar were Sophie's two brothers, Lenny and Bart, believed to have emigrated donkey's years ago. Lenny had his gun poised and aimed right at the back of Fiona's head. Elliott crawled flat on his belly along the floor, slithering like the slimy snake he was, until he saw a gap between the chairs big enough for him to squeeze through. He had been told to take the bag and slide it along the floor without a noise. 'Luckily the background music will drown out the slightest shuffling noises.' he thought. He stretched out his right hand after having come through the gap. He felt around the floor taking care not to touch anyone. He felt the strap on the floor and took a firm hold of it and eased the bag towards him. It wasn't as heavy or as difficult as he was expecting. Elliott kept tugging at the bag. Lenny kept the gun poised while Bart kept a watch on the barman. They were in shadow and it would have been difficult for anyone to detect they were there.

The men were silent as Elliott began to pull the bag through the gap in the chairs, but the bag wouldn't budge. The strap was caught round one of the chair legs. 'Fuck' he almost shouted aloud. "Lucky for me", he thought, "it's a vacant chair." As it was a table for six, it would not be too difficult for him to ease the leg of the chair away from the bag in order to pull it through. He could taste his own sweat. He could also taste the wonderful life he would have with Sophie if he could pull this off. He didn't want bloodshed and had tried to persuade Lenny and Bart to back off with the gun thing, but they insisted if anything went wrong they would need insurance. Elliott had been overruled. The bag was now completely out from underneath the table. All he had to do was slither back in the darkness away from the table with the bag in front of him and hope that nobody else came into the room. If he could manage it they were home and dry. There was a car waiting outside. No-one would ever suspect. He felt giddy with success as he slid along the floor, pushing the bag nearer and nearer to the bar. He was now directly underneath the counter, and only a few feet away from Lenny whom he could now detect quite clearly. Lenny was making no gesticulations to the contrary so Elliott continued. He pushed the bag silently towards Lenny who picked it up and threw it to Bart. Whilst Bart bolted for the door Lenny pointed his gun towards the floor and shot Elliott. He flew outside and into the car beside Bart. Their driver sped away into the darkness.

When the shot rang out, nobody realised at first that it was a gunshot. The music had drowned out some of the impact and it had taken everybody by surprise. No-one really knew what had happened.

The bartender who had been nearest the noise reacted first. He lifted the bar counter up to move towards the group of diners, who by now had stood up to see what the commotion was. He tripped over Elliott's hand and went tumbling to the floor. Alan and Mel raced over to him and saw immediately what had happened. Fiona dived underneath the table to retrieve her bag. She screamed.

"Carrie, my bag's gone. Oh, my God, the bag's gone. What's happening?"

The bartender stood up dazed, his legs covered in the blood that was pouring from Elliott's wound. He telephoned for the emergency services. Moments later, the sirens could be heard out on the patio where most diners had been seated. People ran back into the hotel to find out the cause of the disturbance. It was utter chaos. Fiona was hysterical. Carrie was trying to calm her. Mel and Alan were dashing around looking for the perpetrator. Where had the bag gone? They had detected nothing. They saw no-one come in or leave. They had felt nothing. Had it just vanished into thin air like Monsieur Boesflug?

"This is absolutely crazy." She cried out. "Where are we going to begin? We don't even know where to start looking."

Mel and Alan raced outside but there was no sign of anyone. The car carrying the men and the jewels had gone. There was nothing to give them a clue. The police and ambulance arrived simultaneously and within minutes the dining room was buzzing with uniformed officers asking questions. The area surrounding Elliott's dead body was cordoned off.

Carrie heard one of the ambulance crew talking to the bartender.

"You should have seen the mess we saw coming up the road. We had to ring for another ambulance. One of the local taxis was on fire. One man was completely ablaze and the other man was screaming at the top of his voice."

"Looked like he was trying to drag something from the back of the car", said his partner.

"Feel sorry for the lads who'll have to deal with that one", said the first man.

"Two incidents like this in one night. Must be connected."

Carrie quickly related what she'd heard. They made for the door while everyone else was caught up in the mayhem and headed in the direction the ambulance man had said he'd come. Amidst all the confusion Carrie wondered how on earth she had understood the conversation between the ambulance man and the bartender. It had been spoken in the local language and she was only familiar with a few words.

They ran as fast as they could down the road. They didn't need directions. The flames lit up the night sky like bonfire night. The scene before them was horrific. They saw the body of the driver slumped over the wheel. They assumed the burning heap on the floor was the man the ambulance man had spoken of. They were only interested in the man who had been trying to drag something out of the car. One of the ambulance men shouted what Alan assumed to be 'Do you know what happened?' Alan just shrugged indicating he did not know. They wondered if there

228

was a third person. There was no street lighting to assist them. They heard blood-curdling screams in the distance and raced towards the sound.

The bag lay on the floor with the zip half open. A man was pointing at it and screaming. Mel tried to approach him. He made no attempt to get away. Bart shook uncontrollably and continued screaming. Fiona and Carrie approached the bag while Mel and Alan tried to calm the man down. There appeared to be no reason for him to be in such a frenzied state. Fiona bent down to look inside the bag. All appeared to be in order. The cloth bag looked intact. She closed the zip and placed the strap back round her shoulders. Carrie hugged her and they were both crying. One of the police officers came over to them. When questioned Alan and Mel said they'd been dining at the hotel and come to see if they could help. Nobody mentioned the bag. One of the paramedic team took hold of Bart's arm and began walking him towards the ambulance. Bart made no effort to release himself. Short of breath at the devastating events, the four friends made their way back to the hotel. Nobody had any idea about the theft or retrieval of a bag. Only the bartender noticed that Fiona must have found her bag.

Carrie sensed Monsieur Boesflug's presence but he was nowhere to be seen. She dismissed the idea that he would be lurking round a corner watching without coming forward to help. They could hardly believe what had happened. Someone shot in their dining room, their bag stolen, two men burnt alive and another who appeared to have gone stark raving mad. That they'd come through it all together with the bag intact was something of a miracle. The bartender offered them a drink on the house. He could speak a little English and they sat and conversed, inviting him to have a drink as it was almost closing time. He had discarded the bloodied trousers in favour of a pair of khaki coloured shorts. He too was dumbfounded at the events of the evening. Nothing like this had ever happened in his bar before. The police officers came across to speak to them. The police didn't know anything about the bag having gone missing and ultimately being retrieved. They played it cool and of course the bartender would be a witness that all they had done all night was wine and dine. They all heaved a sigh of relief when the police left. They bade the bartender goodnight and retired to their rooms. Sleep would not come.

"Well, tomorrow's the day", said Fiona to her husband as she lay snuggled in his arms. "I wonder what will become of us tomorrow."

Alan kissed her forehead and murmured quietly, "No matter what, I love you. It'll be alright. We're all here for you. Close your eyes and try to get some sleep."

Fiona did close her eyes, the bag tucked underneath the covers between them.

Carrie and Mel had a longer conversation. Carrie told Mel of all the weird things that had been happening in her head. She told him about the visions and about her uneasy feelings about Monsieur Boesflug.

"I'm really scared Mel?" she said with tears sliding down her face.

"We're all in this together Caz. If we stick together and see this through, it'll turn out okay. Close your eyes and try to get some sleep. I'm right here beside you. Nothing's going to happen to you." Carrie exerted herself enough to kiss him goodnight. Their eyes met.

Mya Palace

At precisely five o'clock, Monsieur Boesflug appeared and led them down a winding path. Sweet scented hedges soared high above them on either side, creating the illusion they were in a maze. They followed downhill in single file and could see a river stretching endlessly out before them. It was a breathtaking sight. They continued on the path, down and down, and found themselves at a little jetty. A small boat was chugging slowly towards them making its approach to the small landing stage. Seconds later they were all seated in the wooden craft and heading out into the river. Monsieur Boesflug sat facing the four of them and began to address them. His words chilled them to the bone.

"Today my friends, is the day you were born for. You will be taken to the edge of the heavens, and experience feelings beyond your wildest imagination. Your integrity will be tested to the boundaries of life itself. If you fail you will suffer inexplicable self doubt and live eternally in the fire of the rubies. If you are true to yourselves, you will emerge from your mission victorious in the knowledge that you have restored balance to our provinces. You will have conquered centuries of evil and have more riches than you ever dreamed of."

"Wow this sounds serious. What exactly do I have to do?" asked Fiona.

` "You must replace the mystical ruby into the golden orb of Mya Palace." replied Monsieur

Boesflug. He began the ancient story.

"King Meng Tuu-Kyi reigned over these provinces for many years. His loyal subjects held him in great esteem and affection. His Queen bore a daughter, the Princess Shariyan. It was said that the devil himself possessed her. Even as a small child, evil emanated from her. One look could reduce a man to a babbling imbecile. The legend told of demons cowering in her presence. The King was a man of great wealth and owned all the ruby and diamond mines. His realm was prosperous, the land plentiful and his people happy. Until the birth of Shariyan, King Meng Tuu-Kyi's wealth was never contested and he shared it with his people. In times of drought, he apportioned his fortune and became renowned as the greatest King of ancient Burma. While Princess Shariyan was maturing, the land darkened. People felt inhibited and threatened. They feared for their lives in her proximity. Her eyes burnt into people's souls and made them feel anxious and troubled. It was prophesied that when Princess Shariyan was twelve moons into her eighteenth year she would betray the King. Marauding warriors would burn his palace and murder him. Upon his death, Shariyan would inherit his wealth and become Queen and ruler. The King removed the precious rubies from the golden orb of Mya Palace and kept them with his private collection. As prophesied, twelve moons into Shariyan's eighteenth year, the King took one of the mystical rubies and placed it under his skin, believing its powers could save him from death. Shariyan's evil conquered the frail old man and the King perished at the hand of one of his own warriors. His Palace was burnt to the ground. Shariyan found one of the mystical rubies beside his body. She placed it in an amulet round her neck. Shariyan possessed a beauty which engaged men to gaze upon her. But those who looked cowered and shrank in fear. Lovers who clung to a shred of life told terrifying tales of a demon that threatened to devour them. She spent her life searching for the King's private collection of jewels. But success eluded her. Every inch of the Kingdom was ransacked by her armies. Each failure brought torture for her warriors. Her venomous hate following unsuccessful attempts to recover the rubies distorted her features. She became abhorrent even unto herself and ultimately relinquished the search by aborting her own reign. She swallowed the ruby together with a phial of poison. The ruby that was found in her decayed bones was placed in a nearby palace. The precious Meng Tuu-Kyi Rubies would be lost for centuries. They would re-appear in time and enter into a new palace built by a fresh royal bloodline. One orb was ominously omitted from its turret. The people believed that one day, far into the future, the second mystical ruby and the Meng Tuu-Kyi Rubies would be found and returned to Mya Palace. The prophecy concluded that an act of kindness would begin the journey that would bring them home. The ancient inscriptions found, showed a number of symbolic figures and through translation indicated there would be a trusted companion accompanying the bearer of the rubies. Once the Meng Tuu-Kyi Rubies were returned, the land would prosper and once again become a supreme sovereignty. The person returning the jewels would enjoy riches beyond their comprehension in this life and into eternity."

They listened in utter disbelief hardly daring to breathe. Fiona's scepticism broke through:

"And the people have waited seven hundred years for me to come along to return the jewels? What about all the others who must have handled the rubies. Why did they not return them? Did they not know about the prophecy? What about the old grandmother who gave them to my father. Why did she not return them to the Palace?"

Monsieur Boesflug continued.

"Yes, Fiona, there have been many people throughout the years who have handled the rubies. They were contained in a chest which was buried beneath the old palace and were unearthed during the excavation and rebuilding of the new palace and subsequently belonged to a wonderful Princess whose wealth was beyond compare. Although she loved the jewels she loved her friend even more. The jewels were in her royal possession but she did not believe in the prophecy and never replaced the ruby in the golden orb. She gave the jewels to her best friend, who was the old grandmother who gave them to your grandfather. The time is now right for the rubies to be returned to their place in history, and to end the poverty that engulfs this land. Today, Mrs Oliver, this is what you must do."

Fiona took a deep breath.

"I'll do my best, but what do I actually have to do. Can I not just take the rubies into the palace and leave them there? Will that not do?"

Monsieur Boesflug shook his head indicating that it most certainly would not do. They disembarked the boat and made the short walk to the helipad.

It was chilly waiting for their ride but they soon heard the distinctive sound of the helicopter blades rotating and moments later they were soaring into the air high above the Myanmar landscape. The sun had risen and its golden rays cast a luxuriant glow on the world below them. They sat in silence with their headphones on. A majestic structure materialised on the horizon and they instinctively knew this was where their destiny had brought them. Fiona felt dizzy. Carrie felt an indescribable feeling rise in her throat. Both the men remained sceptical, intent on detecting would-be attackers. Monsieur Boesflug spoke again. He addressed Alan and Mel.

"You can go no further my friends. Your wives are in good hands and no harm will come to them from this world. You will see them again shortly. Please trust me."

"What's that supposed to mean, I'm not happy about this", said Alan.

Mel thought he would explode. He considered everything that had happened so far. He would not be intimidated by the dogmatic Monsieur Boesflug, who, sensing Mel's anger, knew what to do.

The grounds around the palace extended for dozens of square miles. The helicopter landed close to a small pagoda constructed within the colossal palace ramparts. Monsieur Boesflug ushered them inside and reluctantly exercised his hypnotic powers. Completely unaware of the phenomenon that had befallen them, Mel and Alan instantly fell into a deep sleep. He turned towards the girls.

"I must leave you now. You have already proved you are strong in mind and deed. You have carried the precious Meng Tuu-Kyi rubies and shown no fear. With no thought for your own safety, you have overcome numerous evil attempts to prevent their restoration. The prophecy is about to be fulfilled. Fiona, please take the rubies out of the holdall."

Reticently, Fiona followed Monsieur Boesflug's instructions. She took out the cloth bag and laid it on her lap. Monsieur Boesflug handed her a large amulet. She placed the rubies inside and secured the amulet around her waist. He asked them both to walk over to him. Both the girls were more than a little apprehensive. Monsieur Boesflug stood the girls back to back and asked them to lock arms. They were stood on a stone circle which without warning began to rotate. Slowly at first it became so fast they had to shut their eyes. It seemed to be spinning them into oblivion. When the spinning topped, they opened their eyes to find themselves in exactly the same spot they had started. Yet somehow it felt different. The boys were not there.

They stepped outside the pagoda.

"What's happened?" asked Fiona, beginning to cry a little.

"Don't worry. We're still together. Come on I can see the palace over there. Let's go and have a look" replied Carrie.

The palace was much further away than either of them had thought.

Fiona clutched Carrie in abject fear. They stopped dead in their tracks and froze.

"Keep perfectly still." said Carrie. "Don't move a single muscle."

Fiona, terrified by the sight before her did exactly as she was told. Two large male lions were walking slowly towards them.

"Don't run, don't do anything", said Carrie.

The magnificent animals walked up to them, and without lifting their heads at all, they slowly turned so they were standing slightly in front of them facing the same way, one either side of the girls. They then lifted up their heads, manes blowing in the gentle breeze and began to walk forward.

"Go with it Fiona. Pretend this isn't real and just go with it."

The girls began to follow the lions. They hadn't been walking too long before they saw an old cart lumbering along on top of four eight-spoke wheels. The lions stopped beside the cart.

"I think we're supposed to get in", said Carrie.

Fiona was paralysed with fear, but managed to climb up and into the cart. Carrie followed. The lions walked to the front of the cart and the wheels began turning again.

"Don't ask", said Carrie. "Just don't ask.

"I think there's someone up front, but I can't see who", said Fiona.

"Like I said, don't ask. Someone or something has to be pulling this thing."

The strange group moved forward. Unnervingly, it seemed to be moving away from the palace. Slowly forward they moved and Carrie thought she saw an elephant in the distance, decorated as though for a regatta. When the group became level with the huge beast, it turned and faced the same way, leading the group. Carrie noticed two white hair combs with lotus flowers attached lying on the seat beside them.

"I think we should put these in our hair" said Carrie, sounding like she was actually demanding this action.

Both girls pushed a comb into their hair.

"Now what?" asked Fiona.

"I think this is going to be the ride of our lives", quipped back Carrie. "Settle back into your seat and make yourself comfortable!"

The small convoy moved gradually forward. The girls began to feel timorous and strangely transitional. They saw hundreds of people all around them and were horrified to note at close range they were undernourished, their clothing tattered and torn. People lay dying on the streets and the stench of death was in the air. Nobody stopped to stare at their strange entourage. They were invisible. The stench worsened as the convoy moved forward. Children lay wretched and abandoned in the gutters, desolation, anguish and misery etched on their faces. Some were barely alive and others lifeless. They could see soldiers with great clanging armoury on enormous horses, slaughtering at will. Ear-piercing screams could be heard in the blood-soaked land around them. They saw an imperial jewel-studded chariot ahead, transporting a figure dressed in opulent white clothing. As they drew closer, they saw a woman of boundless beauty from whom they could not avert their eyes. As her chariot moved closer towards them, they felt threatened by her fiercely menacing smile. The smile transformed into a ghastly leer bearing down on them. The girls screamed and tried to jump from the cart, but were immobilised. The diabolical apparition moved over the cart and disappeared behind them. They felt inconsolable melancholy and despaired at the horrors humanity was suffering. There had been no escape from witnessing death and destruction. Their hearts were heavy, their eyes red and sore from the tears they had shed, and they felt breathless and anxious. As they continued to move forward the scenery around them began to change. The people were dressed in different attire. Still unable to tear their eyes from the horrors, they moved through the centuries watching extermination of life until they appeared to be in their own time zone. The people were in dire poverty. Clothing was dirty and tattered. Women and children sat with empty bowls held out in front of them. Young men and women lay prostrate with hypodermic syringes beside them. Through filthy windows they could decipher young emaciated children slaving in degrading conditions. Fiona and Carrie were humbled and cried uncontrollably.

The original Mya Palace stood resplendent before them. External appearance suggested it might be unoccupied. The wheels of the cart no longer rolled along the ground. However bizarre it seemed, they were hovering. They drifted through the outer walls of the palace and into the courtyard. They marvelled at the superb architecture and gazed in awe of its magnificent opulence. They entered the palace gliding in and out of the rooms, the huge animals still in front leading the way. The cart stopped in a room which Carrie instantly recognised.

"I've been in this room before", said Carrie. "Oh, my God, I've been here."

"Don't be daft. How could you possibly ever have been here? You keep telling me this isn't real."

Carrie quickly scrambled the pieces together in her mind and knew that this was the King's chamber where it had all begun and she felt complete humility. Although she didn't know why, Fiona felt the same. Carrie tried to explain and her friend listened intently.

"Fee, the rubies and jewels that your father left on your doorstop, belonged to King Meng Tuu-Kyi who owned this palace and the rooms we are now in were his private chambers. Instead of the land continuing to grow in wealth and happiness, Princess Shariyan's dark reign of terror embittered it. The rubies have remained hidden for centuries. Then they were found and retained for a while until an act of kindness by your father brought them into your possession. You can now restore the balance and the land will begin to prosper again. Perhaps some of their wealth will be used to end some of the poverty. Maybe they will bring peace and happiness for the people."

Fiona was overwhelmed.

"Why me Carrie? I'm nothing. Why me?"

Carrie hugged her friend.

"I'll tell you why Fee. You're a wonderful warm, caring human being. You care intensely about others and you never want anything for yourself. You constantly look after everyone else with no thought for your own needs and desires. I think that's 'why you'. I can't think of anyone more suited for this than you."

When they emerged from their embrace, Fiona spoke.

"Carrie, you've been my best friend all my life. I can't think of anyone I'd rather have with me than you. You are my strength, my courage and my mentor. Come on, let's do it".

The moment Fiona finished speaking the cart began twirling round on the spot. The girls felt dizzy and cried out. When the spinning stopped, they found themselves stood at the entrance to the new Mya Palace. They walked up the five hundred steps to the huge gold doors. There was a small door ajar at the foot of one of the giant doors and they stepped through, gasping at the sight before them. A gigantic space of dazzling radiance engulfed them. Rising up from the solid gold floor were fifty foot golden pillars like warriors guarding the room. After the initial shock they hesitantly inched forward. An invisible force propelled them towards a set of stone steps. They climbed the steps and through an archway into a smaller space which was shrinking. Fiona panicked. She inadvertently touched the large amulet tied around her waist, and the space seemed to open up again. Carrie was right beside her and Fiona grabbed her hand.

"Look Carrie, straight ahead."

The massive glass cabinet loomed, dull and lack lustre and completely contrary to their surroundings. They could see quite clearly a golden ball sitting on the top shelf of the cabinet as they approached.

"There it is" said Fiona. "I think I have to put the large ruby into that orb and the rest of the jewels into the cabinet."

Fiona wondered how on earth she would reach the top shelf, let alone lift the orb down to insert the ruby. She glanced around for something to stand on. There was nothing. She walked around the cabinet to the other side. It seemed to be on a flight of stairs. She climbed up and round the back of the cabinet, where she could see the back was open. 'If we stand on the top stair I can reach the top shelf.' she said to Carrie right beside her. With extreme care Fiona untied the strap of the amulet and handed it to Carrie. She stood on her tiptoes and tried to dislodge the orb. It was immediately evident that it was much too heavy. 'Probably solid gold', she thought. "What am I supposed to do? The mystical ruby must be inserted into this object."

As she was feeling for some leverage to roll it nearer to her, the golden sphere opened. "I must have touched a lever or something." she whispered. In the centre was a beautiful velvet case. On one side was a ruby as big as a golf ball. She gulped. The space next to it was the same size.

"But our ruby is not nearly as big as that, how am I going to secure it in place?"

Fiona undid the amulet which Carrie held for her. She felt for the ruby and lifted it out still in its acetate paper. As she extracted the ruby she touched every facet. From their vantage point they looked across at the doorway. They were pleasantly surprised to see Monsieur Boesflug. He was not alone. Fiona drew in her breath. "It couldn't be the King could it Carrie?"

"Yes Fee, it's King Meng Tuu-Kyi."

Both men were flanked by the lions and the elephant.

The girls were about to wave but their blood ran cold. They watched motionless, believing their eyes deceived them as a pair of gold sandals materialised in front of the King. As the sandals began to move towards the girls the lower half of a clothed female body became visible. Abject horror paralysed them as they watched the whole apparition manifest itself. It continued to glide through the air coming closer. There was a citrus sweet aroma in the air. Their eyes transfixed on the face in awe of its intense beauty yet each was acutely aware of a sharp pain searing through them.

"Shariyan" was the name on both girls' lips but their voices died instantly as a terrifying sound emanated from the mouth of the exquisite form hovering ten feet above the ground. In a split second, as the chimera began to draw near, Fiona found her legs again. In sheer terror she reached out for Carrie's hand and both girls ran like the wind. Down the flight of stairs away from the cabinet, hoping to reach the doorway where Monsieur Boesflug and the King had stood.

"Don't look back" Carrie screamed. "Just keep running."

Fiona's grip tightened on the ruby. "I shouldn't have run" she thought. "I should have placed the ruby. I know I should. This creature would lose its power I'm sure." But she could not risk losing the ruby to the evil Shariyan. The girls tried to run faster but their legs had turned to lead. The more they tried, the heavier they became. Monsieur Boesflug and the King were no longer in the doorway. The petrified girls were aware that Shariyan had undergone her metamorphosis and as they continued trying to run, they saw a reflection of their tormentor in a gold pillar. Carrie screamed at Fiona.

"Make for the archway. It won't go through that."

Carrie was banking on Monsieur Boesflug assisting them in some way. She remembered his words to the boys. "Trust me", he had said. She suddenly knew what to do. She believed he would not let them down. She screamed out again to Fiona.

"Keep tight hold of the ruby."

Fiona's eyes were focused on the archway and had not seen the thick black talons clawing the air close to her right shoulder, getting ever nearer to the ruby in her right hand. The creature was within inches of its target when they arrived at the archway. Carrie yelled to Fiona.

"Believe Fee. Believe in the ruby's powers. Energise the power in your hand and paralyse the creature while we get back to the cabinet"

"How do I do that?" screamed Fiona.

"Believe Fee. Tell the ruby."

Fiona squeezed the stone in her hand.

"It's not working"

"Yes, it is. Look"

Monsieur Boesflug and the King suddenly appeared again in the doorway beckoning them into the cart.

"Where is that … thing?" cried Fiona, her heart thumping.

King Meng Tuu-Kyi spoke.

"Fiona, keep the stone tight in your hand and continue believing. Shariyan is paralysed, but it will only last while you believe."

The curious group in the cart made their way across the cavernous gap between the archway and the glass cabinet. They passed Shariyan on the way. Whilst Fiona gasped at the grotesque creature, her clammy hand relinquished its grip on the stone slightly and the spell broke. Shariyan circled and resumed her chase.

"Believe." yelled everyone in the cart as loud as they could. Fiona was hysterical. The group were approaching the steps to the glass cabinet. The girls still had to dismount their primitive carriage. Carrie leapt out first, grabbing hold of Fiona's left hand and pulling her out on to the penultimate stair.

"Fiona, believe in the ruby."

Fiona tripped up the last step and tried to grab something to steady herself. In so doing she released the ruby, which rolled down the stairs. She screamed. The creature's talons opened wide enough to scoop up the precious stone and a loud blood-curdling noise echoed in the hollow expanse. With no thought for her own safety, Carrie sprinted down the stairs, ducking underneath Shariyan's body but the creature was too close. Fiona stood motionless, closed her eyes tight and willed the ruby to paralyse the creature. She still had her eyes closed when Carrie pressed the stone into her hands.

"Thanks Fee, now go and do it. Now. Quickly."

Fiona made her final leap of faith. As she was about to place the ruby in its space, Shariyan shook off her paralysis, reared up and made straight for the cabinet. The diabolical sound echoed in everyone's ears. King Meng Tuu-Kyi aimed the cart in the creature's direction but he'd had no need to intercept. As Fiona placed the mystical ruby in the empty space they saw the glass cabinet take on a glistening luminosity. The light emitted from the cabinet formed a huge completely shaped six-ray star. The needle-like points of the star began rotating until the point of one of the needles touched Shariyan. The creature shrieked and withdrew. The star continued rotating until its second needle touched her. This rendered it half monster, half princess. The sight was indescribable. When the sixth and last ray of the mystical ruby touched Shariyan, the evil left her and for a split second, she took on the appearance of King Meng Tuu-Kyi's daughter again. The moment was brief and Shariyan's body evaporated.

Hugely relieved they were no longer being chased and eager to complete her task Fiona dropped down a step. She removed the pieces from the amulet one by one, placing them on the cabinet shelves.

"This feels like I'm having an out-of-body experience. The strangest thing is that the ruby fitted perfectly into its space. How was that possible?" she said.

She placed the amulet on the bottom shelf.

"Is that it? Is it over?"

Carrie smiled and the room began to spin.

The girls were back in the pagoda talking to the boys who had just woken up. It was obvious they didn't know the girls had been missing. Bernard appeared, seemingly out of thin air with a tray of refreshments. They didn't need an invitation to partake of the beverages and light snacks. They were far too busy nurturing their human needs to notice the King enter the pagoda with the lions and the elephant. Mel choked on his biscuit when he turned and saw them approaching. A scream tried to leave Alan's throat. The odd quartet made their way over to the group and stopped a few feet away. The animals stood perfectly still and the King spoke.

"I am King Meng Tuu-Kyi and you have this day restored order to my province. We have waited seven hundred years to put an end to the misery left by my daughter Shariyan. Your trust and love of humanity, your genuineness, your humility and your strength of character will bring about the necessary changes to this land. I can never thank you enough for your endurance for the good of humanity. Your lives will be filled with health and happiness. Your wealth is in the nature of your hearts and your families. We thank you from the bottom of our hearts. Shariyan will perish in the depths of Hades and all the suffering of the centuries will bear on her for eternity. Fiona and Carrie, Alan and Mel, you will return to your normal lives but once back in your own country, the memories of your mission here will elude you. I must leave you now. Monsieur Boesflug will be with you shortly to direct you back to the airport for your flights home. Thank you. You will be remembered for all time. Because of you our land will prosper. There will be an end to poverty and balance will be restored to my people."

The King and the animals turned and headed for the exit and vanished into thin air.

* * * * * *

The Trip Home

Fiona didn't know if she felt relieved or sad that she no longer had the amulet containing the jewels and she felt positively naked without the holdall strapped to her. 'Had it all really happened? Had she just been listening to a ghost from seven hundred years ago? How could she bear it if she could never remember? She was a little disappointed. She had just parted with ancient jewellery that was in all probability worth an absolute fortune and would have given her family a life beyond compare. The lives of her descendents would have been changed forever. Instead, she had travelled half way round the world, suffered countless attempts on her life, been buffeted from pillar to post, seen people burnt alive, killed on her account and now this seven hundred-year old spectre had told her she would remember nothing. She was not best suited. How on earth could she return to a normal life? Then again, if she never remembered it, would it make any difference? The King had said 'once you get back to your own country'.

Carrie mulling over everything that had happened had also picked up on the King's words and planned to write everything down. She had long aspired to be a writer. Teachers at primary school had read out her essays. She was always top of the class in English and knew that good writing came from the heart. She had written bits of poetry which had been published and a number of short stories.

'What a story this would make', she thought.

'If I can just get everything written down before we get home. I'll start straight away. As soon as we're back at the hotel I'll fish out my pad and pen.'

Monsieur Boesflug arrived. He shook hands vigorously with each of them, thanking them profusely for their part in bringing balance back to the people of the land.

"We will meet again briefly in the not too distant future, but there will soon be no need for me in this world. I have been the keeper of the legend waiting for the rubies to be returned. The orb will now be placed back atop Mya Palace for eternity. While the rubies lie in the orb there will be peace and prosperity. I can go to my own rest, my work is now done. Your helicopter will collect you in five minutes. Your tickets home are at the reception desk in your hotel. I have taken the liberty of booking you all right through to the UK and I wish you all a very good journey and farewell."

The sight they saw next made them gasp. Monsieur Boesflug dissolved in front of them. Carrie almost fainted.
"I can't believe we've just seen that. The King and Shariyan were bad enough but not Monsieur Boesflug."
"What do you mean", asked Mel and Alan in unison.
"We'll explain later", said the girls and smiled.

Mel thought he heard the helicopter overhead.

"Come on guys, we've got a ride waiting outside."

They all ran out into the warm sunshine, and sure enough the helicopter was on the pad. They dashed over and climbed aboard. Seconds later they were harnessed and soaring over the top of Mya Palace and the modern day lives of an ancient civilisation. They wondered if the fulfilled prophecy really meant this land would change forever. The golden orb, they were surprised to see, was already back atop the palace turret and gleaming in the sunlight. They settled into their seats. The journey and the events of the past few days took its toll and they fell asleep.

They checked in at reception. Carrie raced up to her room, pulled out her pad and pen and began to write. She tried to remember every single thing and simply jotted down every memory she had. 'It's imperative to write down everything I can remember. I'll write the story later.' She scribbled furiously while the others collected all their belongings. They hurried back to the helicopter. The receptionist had informed them their flight would return them directly to Yangon Airport. They were thrilled. Nobody felt like being subjected to the road journey.

Sitting in the departure lounge Alan and Mel downed a few beers while Carrie wrote. Carrie was very excited about seeing Lisa. 'What would she tell her about their journey to Myanmar? The King said their memories would elude them. Was that just about the jewels and the palace, or everything else too? She would have to wait and see.'

Carrie spent the entire journey writing and when the Boeing 747 from Yangon to Heathrow levelled after take-off, Carrie wrote. She ate and drank what was put in front of her and wrote. Whilst the others slept for a little while she wrote. Her brain worked overtime and she wrote. She had written down everything she remembered from first arriving in New York until they got on the plane to come home from Burma. She folded all the sheets of paper in half and unzipped the top of her hand luggage. She put the papers into a zipped compartment in the back of the bag, zipped it all back up again and settled to have a snooze before their journey ended. Monsieur Boesflug had booked them a connecting flight back to the North of England and they caught the shuttle to their northern airport. Carrie was tired and the entire journey had drained her. When they arrived at the airport nothing seemed real. 'Why were they waiting in the middle of the night for a taxi at the airport when they hadn't booked one? How weird.' A young bloke with a moustache held up a board with Oliver written on it. The journey home in the taxi was odd. As always when holidays were over, a dark cloud of despondency descended because nobody wanted to go back to work. They chatted about New York and about their impulsive purchase of tickets to Burma and about the fabulous pagodas and that it had been the trip of a lifetime and they were all so glad that they'd done it, even though they would now have to suffer the consequences at work. They decided to tell their own truth about the extended trip. They had seen a deal too good to miss and went for it. They had no regrets and would work hard to make up for their extra few days.

The taxi dropped them off at their respective homes. There were tears when they parted.

"I'll ring you in the week" said Carrie to Fiona. "Thanks for a fabulous time. It was lovely that you could join us." Fiona hugged Carrie again.

"It was amazing, I'm just so glad we decided to do it, and the trip to Myanmar was just a wonderful experience, a trip of a lifetime for us. Hope to see you later in the week. Bye for now. Thanks guys."

And they were gone. Now it was just Carrie and Mel in the taxi home. Carrie linked her hand into Mel's and he smiled down at her and kissed her head.

"Not long now love, and you can have a lovely long soak in the bath and we can climb into our own bed."

Carrie didn't hear him, she was asleep.

They were about to climb into bed when the telephone rang. It was Fiona.

"Carrie", she whispered, "The strangest thing has happened."

"What is it Fee, are you alright?"

"Yes, but I was just getting ready for a bath. When I got undressed I found a little pouch round my waist. When I looked inside there was a key. How the dickens has it got there and what on earth is the key for?"

Carrie felt an unexplainable sensation surge through her. She replied firmly but sympathetically.

"Just put the key back in the pouch and leave it somewhere safe until morning."

"But how the hell did it get here in the first place, and why didn't I feel it before now? It's bizarre. Oh well, I am tired, I won't need much rocking. Ok then, see you soon. I'll speak to you tomorrow. Bye."

"Ok. Bye".

Mel asked who'd rung and Carrie related Fiona's dilemma. She told Mel she'd had a peculiar feeling when Fiona had told her. Like she should know something about it but didn't.

"You're over-reacting Carrie. We've had a hectic few days and we haven't had time to wind down. Fiona probably did it for a bet or a dare for one of the kids or something and it's been there that long she's forgotten it."

"But I'm presuming she's had it on all the time she's been away", said Carrie "In which case, she should have known it was there. I know she's had showers while we've been away. Oh well, no point worrying about it, I'll speak to her again tomorrow and see if she can shed any light on it by then."

They both climbed into bed.

"Night night, God Bless."

"Night, God Bless."

Carrie turned out the light.

The next morning she spoke to Lisa who was thrilled about her stay in New York and desperately wanted to know about Carrie's trip to Myanmar. They arranged to have coffee together that afternoon.

Lisa's Version

"Right Mum, come on, spill the beans, what did Dad buy you in that jewellery shop?" laughed Lisa.

Carrie almost choked on her cappuccino.
"What jewellery shop?"
"The one you four were in such an all-fired hurry to get to. You'd all been acting rather strangely. I'm sorry mum but we were curious and followed you. We saw you go in but must have missed you coming out. We were just a bit worried about you."
"Lisa, as true as I'm sat here drinking coffee and talking to you I have absolutely no idea what you're talking about. But as it happens something else odd has happened."

She told Lisa of her conversation with Fiona the night before.
"Something weird is happening here, and I don't know what or why." Carrie added.
"Why did Alan and Fiona go with us to New York Mum? I mean, it was lovely that they were able to come, but they knew you were coming on the trip with us for our wedding."
Carrie felt decidedly uncomfortable.
"I can't remember love, I can't remember much about anything at the moment. It's quite disconcerting."
Enigmas like this were just up Lisa's street. She loved trying to solve mysteries and it looked like she might have to take this one on board.

The day they had followed their parents to the jewellery shop in Midtown East Manhattan would linger in Lisa's memory for ever. She had some real issues with this whole thing with Fee and Alan. Short of being rude to her mother which of course she wouldn't dream of, she would have to make some subtle enquiries herself. 'Maybe I should visit Fiona myself and ask her a few questions. We need to put this amnesia mum has developed to rest.'

She had thought there was something more than met the eye from the moment she bumped into Alan and Fiona in the foyer of the hotel. Her mother hadn't even mentioned to her they were coming to New York, never mind staying in the same hotel. Alarm bells had started ringing and thankfully she and Graham had been just in time to see the four friends disappearing out of the hotel that morning. Now it seemed her mother didn't remember going to the place or worse, for some obscure reason, didn't want to tell her. She had supposed it could have been a surprise for her wedding. But her mother had no recollection of going. 'How could mum possibly forget such an awful building? She's behaving most strangely.'

The shop they had visited was the most unlikely place you would expect to see in New York City. Lisa had thought it looked like something out of an old fairy story, except it looked dark and dirty. There were no lights on inside and it looked like the place was closed down. They had watched their parents approach the shop. They had turned away and gone into a coffee bar nearby. They had watched them leave the coffee bar and go back to the shop and seen them go inside. Once Lisa and Graham thought the four of them were well inside the shop, they approached the shop front but it had looked exactly the same as before, dirty, in darkness and closed. They had waited a short while for them to emerge but they didn't. Lisa and Graham had both believed something very odd had been happening and of course were delighted to find them all safe and sound later that day. Her mother didn't mention anything about the funny old jeweller's shop and that in itself was strange because Carrie usually told Lisa everything. She could always be relied upon to turn every event into a story. Lisa couldn't understand for the life of her why her mum hadn't even broached the topic when she'd seen her later that day. That convinced her that something dodgy was going on. She would have to keep her eye out for more clues.

Lisa took another sip of her coffee and began questioning Carrie.

"Do you remember leaving the hotel in the snow with Dad and Alan and Fiona? You walked down the avenue until you reached that funny little back street with the old dirty looking jeweller's shop? The one with the funny windows? You didn't come upon it by chance, you were obviously making straight for it. How can you possibly not remember which shop I mean? Mum, this is crazy. This is me you're talking to."

Carrie racked her brains and just couldn't bring it to mind.

"Did we all go in?" she asked Lisa.

"Yes mum, all four of you, but the weird thing is it wasn't open. You arrived, looked at it, went in a coffee bar further down the road and then went back. It was still closed but you all went in. We waited half an hour or so but you didn't come back out. In the end, Graham and I decided you must be alright as you hadn't rung to say there was anything wrong. We went to do some shopping and left you to it."

"Well why would you have thought there was anything wrong?"

"Because of the kind of place it was. Seconds after you all disappeared inside, we approached it and it was closed. Don't you think that's a bit funny?"

"Well, yes I do. I'd have been worried about me too", laughed Carrie. "I wonder what all that was about then. Maybe we should ask Fiona if she remembers."

"Or Dad when he comes home. He'll remember. He's got a memory like an elephant. He never forgets."

"It isn't that I've forgotten love. I have absolutely no recollection of the incident you're describing."

They weren't getting anywhere so Lisa just enjoyed her coffee and Danish. She would begin another tactic later. 'I will find out what's going on. From this moment on it's my duty' she thought.

Lisa remembered the shop across the road. It was called 'Barden's Spectacles'. She remembered it distinctly. Whereas the jewellery shop didn't seem to have a name at all and had just said 'Jewellery', the spectacle shop did. Lisa decided to look on the Internet for Barden's Spectacles, find a telephone number and ring and ask them if the jeweller's across the road was open today. Later on that afternoon, when she'd left her mother and gone to pick up Graham from work, she stopped at Fiona's under the pretences of having a cuppa and a slice of Fiona's delicious Christmas cake. She always had some left over way into the year and Fiona knew that Lisa loved her Christmas cake. When Lisa broached the topic of the jewellery shop, Fiona looked even more confused than her mother and swore they had never been to a jeweller's whilst they'd been in New York. Lisa now knew that something was going on. 'What are they trying to hide from me? I wonder if it's something they've bought for my birthday or the wedding and they want to keep it a secret?' She decided this was not the case. 'Mmmmmm', she thought. 'I'll have to really think this one through. What on earth can it be? Mother can't remember ever going to this particular jeweller's. Fiona doesn't remember going to a jeweller's at all, yet Graham and I watched them all walk in.'

She thanked Fiona for the tea and cake and made her journey home. She found the number for the spectacle shop and scribbled it down. 'What time is it?' she thought. 'I'll have to remember the time difference. I think they're five hours behind us. They should still be open.' She dialled the number and waited with baited breath. There was an evident time delay on the line, but she was thrilled when someone answered.

"Good afternoon. Barden's Spectacles. Rosie speaking. How may I help you today?"

Lisa bade Rosie a good afternoon and explained she was telephoning from the UK and wondered if she could possibly tell her if the jeweller's across the road was open. Lisa added, "You know, the one that looks ancient and a bit scruffy and no name, just says jewellery."

"Yes maam, I know the exact one you mean. Real spooky shop that. Frightens me a bit. It's been closed down two years now. I don't like walking past it. I really wish someone would take it over. So, no, sorry maam, it's not open. Is there anything else I can help you with?"

"No thank you", replied Lisa. "You've been very helpful indeed, thank you again for your time."

She replaced the receiver and shivers ran up and down her spine. 'What's going on? Why did mum and dad go into a jewellery shop that wasn't open with Alan and Fiona? Why does mum say she doesn't remember? Even more improbable, neither does Fiona.'

Whatever was wrong she had to find out. She rang her father and asked him what he'd bought for her in the jewellers. She wished she hadn't. She got the same reply from him too. He had no recollection of any jewellery shop.

"And anyway, what were you doing following us?" he asked.

Lisa knew that she could say anything to her father. No subject was taboo. She related her version of events that day, adding that no-one was owning up to it. That meant it was either a secret or something

261

was obviously wrong. They chatted a while about other events and concluded their conversation.

'How utterly peculiar', thought Lisa. 'More importantly, how am I ever going to find out what's going on? I'll have to quiz mum further. Maybe about her conversation with Fiona last night. Let's start there', she thought. 'Maybe if I keep pressing, somebody will remember something.'

When Lisa and Carrie met later that day, they went over the conversation Carrie had had with Fiona the night before. How could Fiona have possibly not known that she had a pouch tied round her waist which contained a key? Worse than that, how could she not know how it got there? Then there were a myriad of questions. What did the key open?

"Did Fiona say what kind of key it was?" asked Lisa, searching her mother's face for some vestige of truth or lie.

"No she didn't. She just said she'd found the pouch when she got undressed and that there was a key inside it."

"How could she possibly not know it was there mum? Could she not feel it? Who put it there if not herself? Something odd is going on mum. Are you not concerned?"

"Yes, I am. Of course I am. There are lots of strange things happening, but I
can't just put my finger on what it might be."

"I wonder if we should make an appointment for you or Fiona to go and see someone. Maybe a doctor or a psychiatrist?"

"Hey, steady on", laughed Carrie, "We're not that bad!"

"I wasn't suggesting ….but hey, something just touched a trigger. What about a hypnotist? Maybe they could take you or Fiona back in time and stretch the thought waves back to New York. 'Regression' I think they call it. I mean whatever's happened, it must have been while you were in New York."

"Or Myanmar."

"Well, yeah. That too."

Carrie was digging deep into her memory for something. She went back over and over everything. It was patchy and odd. They decided to go with the hypnotist idea. Lisa searched through the local paper.

"I think we should ring Fiona and bring her in on this." laughed Lisa. "She's the one with the pouch round her waist. She's the one who doesn't remember how it got there and we don't know if she'll agree to go to anyone do we?"

"OK, I'll give her a call."

Carrie rang Fiona who answered immediately in a bit of a state.

"Well", she began in answer to Carrie's concern. "I'm scared Carrie. I can't quite believe the chain of events. I know I was going to New York and why I was going. Uncle Tom and all of that stuff and now he's dead. Nellie rang me yesterday. Apparently Sophie has been contacted by the police in Myanmar. They want her to go over and identify two bodies. They think they're her brothers. I'm scared. What does all this mean, and why can't I remember anything. And where are the jewels I took to New

York? I haven't got them. I just have this stupid key and nothing to unlock."

She was on loud speaker. Lisa jumped up and started pacing the room. Fiona had said she took jewels to New York. Why hadn't her mother told her that when she told her she'd seen them going into a jewellers? This was all getting a bit out of hand.

Carrie tried to calm Fiona down.

"If you're not busy Fee, Lisa and I will come over. Have the kettle on."

The two distraught women wanted to reach Fiona before she forgot anything again. The three of them pooled all their knowledge about the last few days, and wrote it all down. The findings were utterly amazing. They had to find answers. It was now their mission to find some.

"So, Fee, you remember taking some jewels to New York?"

"Yes" said Fiona rather sheepishly.

"Whose jewels were they? Who did they belong to?"

"My father gave them to me a few weeks before he died. He left them on my doorstep in a cardboard box. His father had them given to him during World War II for helping to save an old lady and her grandchildren. He gave them to my grandmother when he came home, but she didn't much care for them and when Gran died, he gave the jewels to my father. They stayed in his possession after his divorce. Then he just brought them one day. For all I know, he may not have even known they were in the box. Alan took them to have them valued and the jeweller said he thought they were worth a lot of money. Alan thought they might be worth a whole lot more, and we were advised to seek out a man they call The Expert who resides in New York. That's why we co-ordinated our trip with your mum and dad. It's a little more involved than that, but that's basically it."

"Did you find this 'expert'?" quizzed Lisa.

"Well, this is what's so peculiar. My memory seems to fade after that and I can't for the life of me remember what happened. I remember Uncle Tom chasing us. He must have found out somehow that the jewels had come to light. He was always a bad lot but I didn't expect him to die trying to get his hands on them. But now this business with Nellie and Sophie. I'm terrified that somehow I'm involved, but I can't remember why or how."

"We need to devise a strategy." said Lisa. "We need to tell Dad and Alan about all this, and try to fathom it. My guess is that we need to do it sooner rather than later."

A plan was formulated that afternoon. The written findings were quite astounding to the three women pouring over the astonishing facts they'd discovered that afternoon. It seemed to Lisa there were still quite a lot of missing pieces. The boys were aghast when Lisa began to explain their findings.

"What the hell does it all mean?"
 Alan was making more of a statement, than asking a question.

"I don't know, but we're sure as hell gonna try'n find out" said Fiona, beginning to feel more and more edgy.

Lisa told Fiona about the idea to visit a

hypnotist. Fiona remembered recently seeing a flier put through the letterbox advertising hypnosis. She didn't know why she hadn't remembered it earlier. She immediately rose from her chair.

"What a coincidence. I remember seeing a flier advertising hypnosis when we arrived back from New York."

Fiona believed she'd never been hypnotised before and was initially terrified at the prospect. Little did they know the consequences that flier would bring for its author.

Number twenty one Voresay Court was quite a building. A long-disused but recently renovated warehouse with a mirrored frontage, overlooking nearby dockland. When they entered the front door they were faced with a long corridor. Gorgeous red deep-pile carpet beneath their feet led them to an ascending staircase, up which they had to climb two floors. They could have taken the lift, but curiosity begged the climb. The walls were dominated by photographs of properties within the building which were for sale.

"Wouldn't mind living in one of these!" said Carrie.
"Yeah, they're something else aren't they", answered Mel. "Wouldn't fancy carrying the shopping up though if the lift was broken."

They were almost at the top and just to their left they could see a big white sturdy looking door with black studs at intermittent levels and a large black polished handle. On the door was a highly polished brass plaque displaying the name of the hypnotist 'Marianne Montrose'.

"I'm getting a bit scared now I'm here' said Fiona.

"You'll be fine hun. We're all here with you."

"I know. That's what worries me." laughed Fiona.

Alan pressed the bell-push. The door opened immediately and a young lady in a white uniform ushered them into a clinical looking room. The white décor was broken up by an extra large square cut glass vase containing an exquisite Japanese flower arrangement in vivid orange. Two orange cushions lay scattered on the white leather sofa. It was breathtaking. 'Oh my goodness', thought Fee, 'this is going to cost an absolute fortune.'

She whispered to Carrie, "Did you check the price out sweetheart? I think perhaps we'd better say we're in the wrong place and leave before it's too late."

Carrie smiled.

"You know I did. You agreed it was a very good price if it was going to reveal a lead."

The young lady beckoned to them to be seated and asked if they would like a drink of water.

Fiona responded with a mighty "Yes please."

Her mouth was as dry as a board and she

needed some lubrication. The iced water was brought promptly in an expensive looking glass with the customary slices of lemon and lime. 'Very refreshing', she thought and gulped the water down. Meanwhile the others were craning their necks looking out of the window over the dock where a massive container ship was sailing up the estuary.

"How fabulous to be able to see all this from your workplace window", said Carrie. She directed her statement to the young lady, but the telephone rang. It must have been Marianne Montrose, for seconds later, they were asked to step inside Marianne's consulting rooms. The waiting room was comfortable with lots of glossy magazines lying on various sized glass tables. A splash of colour was lent to the all-white environment courtesy of a giant orange gerbera. The morning sunshine caught and reflected the colour casting an orangey glow in the room. 'Very nice', thought Fiona.

"Miss Montrose will be with you in a few moments", said the young girl and disappeared back into the reception area.

Marianne Montrose was stunning. Alan's mouth drooped and his eyes were popping out of his head. Fiona had to restrain him from flirting with her. Even the girls had to agree she was beautiful. Tall and slim with long blonde hair and beautiful big blue eyes. Her healthy looking tanned skin implied she may have recently been on an exotic holiday. Marianne was very perceptive.

"Yes, I only got back yesterday. Barbados.

Smiling at Fiona she said "Would you like to come this way Mrs …" She looked at her clipboard …. "Oh yes … Mrs Oliver."

Fiona followed her and Marianne Montrose closed the door behind them.

* * * * * *

Marianne Montrose

Marianne Montrose had been to see her bank manager before she went on holiday. He advised her to advertise her business to boost profits by delivering a new spate of fliers. She had done this immediately, completely unaware of the coincidences and consequences her actions would have. When she returned from Barbados, she heard from Molly her youngest sister about the shenanigans in New York and Myanmar concerning Sophie's boyfriend and brothers. She couldn't believe her ears when her secretary told her that Mrs Oliver would be paying her a visit. This was the lady who was in possession of the precious jewels. Her sister's acquaintances had been chasing them half way round the world. Of course she hadn't the remotest idea why Mrs Oliver would come and visit her, but she had been hoping to meet a rich client for a long time. It had been a long shot to push fliers through the local neighbourhood doors and she had no idea that it might pay dividends as bountiful as this. She could not believe her luck and immediately began her preparations.

She knew just what questions to ask, in what order and the answers she would expect to receive. She suspected she would be able to gauge Mrs Oliver's opinion of her before she left. Everything would be perfect. Her secretary would never suspect in a million years she was using this consultation to her own ends. Marianne Montrose. She had chosen the name herself. Her legal surname had been Kelly and she had been baptised Stella. She was the daughter of a dead beat father and a drunken mother, living on the fourth floor of a tenement block of flats in the city centre. She considered her assets in life had been her looks, her ability to mimic and the gift. Her burning ambition from as young as she could remember was to abandon her childhood, leave every vestige of her former life behind and make it big in the world. She had been the second oldest of six girls who were cramped into a space some people called a broom cupboard. They had no beds. Their sleeping place had been a pile of their own washing. Whether clean or dirty it was where they had to lay their head each night. The oldest one had looked after the younger one right down the line. The youngest whom they all adored was little Molly and once old enough was at their beck and call. Molly soon learned she must have a forte in life other than the one her destiny had provided her with. She joined a team of Marionettes at the local convent, cleaning and polishing and looking after the old nuns. She helped to feed them and took them their morning drink. She was paid a few pence a week for her chores. It kept her out of the grasp of her older siblings and her dreaded parents, and provided her with the opportunity to steal whatever food she could and deliver her from the pangs of hunger. Little Molly's life was mapped out. She inevitably became a much sought after criminal. A clever one, dodging the authorities and slipping out of their hands like a bar of soap. Most of her contacts had been slipping the police net for many years and included unsavoury characters Elliott, Lenny and Bart. She was a young up and coming protégé and was much admired in the circles within which she moved. She became Stella

Kelly's ticket to a better life. Molly's boyfriend, however, was Stella's worst nightmare. She had despised him from the moment they met, when in front of Molly, he had ogled her and forced his foul-smelling breath onto her face whilst trying to kiss her. She never forgave him and vowed she would have revenge on her sister's behalf, a vow that she had recently learnt she could never fulfil. She heard a few days ago that he'd been killed in a freak accident somewhere abroad. Molly had scuttled off to find out what had happened to her boyfriend. The stories emerging were frightening. Stella wondered if her sister was somehow involved in the incidents but couldn't protest too loudly. It was Molly who had procured this business and wonderful premises for her and Molly's ill-gotten gains had put 'Marianne Montrose' on the map. Now here, under her nose, was her ticket to total freedom and she was going to use every fibre of her being to ensure her success.

"Mrs Oliver", Marianne began sweetly. "I'm very pleased to meet you. I'm Marianne. I'm here to help you in whatever way I can. Do you want to begin by telling me why you seek the services of a hypnotist and how you think I can help you? Whatever you say within these walls remains completely confidential and you have my promise we'll do all we possibly can for you."

Fiona was taken in by Marianne's easy manner and relaxed.

"Would you like to just sit back in your chair and pop your feet up. We'll just have a little chat."

Marianne Montrose was spellbinding. Fiona

was unable to take her eyes off her hypnotist. Marianne knew this hypnotherapy session would be an easy one to conduct. The next thirty minutes however, were difficult for Fiona as she was taken into the depths of her soul to try and recall the happenings of the past few weeks. Marianne Montrose couldn't understand why the task was so difficult for Fiona. Recent events in Myanmar had been muted at in the papers and yet this lady seemed unable to remember the basics of the tabloid stories. Marianne continued questioning, waiting for one small thing to indicate there was any truth in the story she'd heard. And 'Bingo', here it was. A key.

Fiona described how she found the pouch with a key inside tied round her waist. Marianne used every method at her disposal to find the missing jigsaw piece that would buy her the life she longed for with Emmeline. She and Emmeline had made enquiries in Barbados about a property. She was just a couple of hundred thousand dollars short of her goal and Mrs Oliver could change all that for her. She would have to play this carefully. After thirty minutes of extracting all the information she could Marianne spent the next fifteen minutes doing her job. Her skill and expertise induced Fiona into a complete trance-like state of relaxation. She marvelled at the gift she had inherited from a long lost ancestor. Although common practice in this field may have been to use a sleep inducing drug, Marianne believed firmly that she didn't need to use artificial means. She thought of the early charlatans denounced from her profession some centuries ago for possessing the same gift.

When Fiona returned to complete awareness, she clung to the thought that she must write down anything and everything which popped into her head for the next week regarding the pouch. She was to keep a pen and paper with her at all times. Twice a day she would find herself relaxing in a comfy chair thinking about what had happened to her in the past few months. She was to write it all down. Marianne Montrose had tactfully tried to extract information surrounding the mystery key without shedding one shred of doubt on her integrity. She asked Fiona to make an appointment for one week hence and suggested she should undertake the hypnotic influence at least once a week. Fiona agreed. When she left the room she felt a little woozy and put it down to her state of relaxation. She headed for reception to make her appointments. Carrie leapt up and hugged her when she reappeared in the waiting room.

"What was it like?" asked Carrie. "Did it work? Was she able to tell you anything? "
"No. Not this time." answered Fiona, sounding a little dejected. "I have to come every week for six weeks."

Carrie thought Fiona looked drained and decided to take them all for a coffee. The others quizzed her to find out what sort of questions Marianne had asked. After five minutes or so it was evident she'd had enough questioning for one day.

Carrie made a mental note to accompany Fiona each time she went to the hypnotist. She didn't know why but she felt uneasy. She said nothing but wondered if this was a prelude to some sort of trouble. 'I'm becoming paranoid', she thought. 'Why should I think there's anything wrong? Why am I thinking these weird thoughts? What possible motive could a hypnotist have to use the information for her own benefit?' She thought again about the flier which had been delivered to Fiona's house and pursued her train of thought. She was going to stick by her guns and each time Fiona went to see Marianne Montrose, Carrie would go along.

Marianne was on the phone seconds after Fiona left her consulting room. She chatted excitedly to Emmeline. Moving into their dream home in Barbados might only be a few short weeks away.

Emmeline asked, "How come?"

"Do you remember Lenny, Sophie's brother?"

"How could I forget", replied Emmeline sarcastically, remembering that Marianne had had an affair with Lenny's girlfriend, Pamela.

"Well, Fiona Oliver has just been in."

"No", whispered Emmeline disbelievingly. "What did she want you for?"

"Tell you later sweetheart. Book us our usual table at Ronaldo's tonight. Order a bottle of pink champagne. Eight thirty will do. Wear your best stuff and we'll party later. Bye for now."

Marianne buzzed for her secretary.

"Lucy, how many appointments do I have this afternoon?"

"Mr Fisher, Mrs Porter and I think Miss Cooper's your last one at four o'clock", rattled off

Lucy in her efficient fashion.

"Please ring and cancel the last two Lucy. Something's come up and I have to leave in an hour."

"Your next appointment will be here shortly", said Lucy.

"I know. I'll see Mr Fisher, although I'll have to cut his appointment short, but if you could cancel the other two. "

"Ok", said Lucy and went to her desk.
Marianne lifted out her mobile phone and quickly made a call to her ex lover.

"Can we meet at half past three for a drink?" was all she said.

She saw Mr Fisher and although he wasn't very pleased at having his appointment curtailed, she sounded so plausible he couldn't object. She left the office at half past one and hurried to her apartment to prepare herself for her date. She rang the estate agent to ascertain the property in Barbados was still available. It was. Her heart fluttered and she knew this was her destiny. She had to play it just right and make no mistakes to ensure her cut in the Oliver fortune which she was certain lay in waiting for her. She must also ensure she didn't say too much elsewhere. Emmeline was the only one she would confide in. She would tell her only what she needed to know. Of course she could be struck from practising, but she was going to quit anyway. She started making plans to transfer her patients to another practice. She would ask Lucy to start writing letters in a couple of weeks. She would make Lucy redundant and give her a thousand pounds to tide her over until she got another position. She would put the offices up for sale. 'They may take a little while to sell', she thought. She would put her plans into operation straightaway, but right now she had an appointment for sex with Pamela Faulkes.

Marianne Montrose emerged from her apartment and took the taxi driver's breath away. Her beauty was bountiful even without materialistic trimmings. With her masterful appliance of make-up she was exquisite. She had on a pair of black pearlescent cut-offs, below which, hugging her calves were a pair of four inch stiletto black patent leather pointed boots. Her breasts were perfectly formed and made their statement perfectly in the white cotton blouse with baggy sleeves, puffy at the shoulders and wrists. This was tucked inside the trousers and between the two sat a three inch wide patent belt with imitation diamond studding. A diamond pendant clung to her throat complemented by matching stud earrings from which hung white pearlescent threads with tiny diamonds. She had on her left wrist a huge chunky black and pearlescent bracelet, and on her right wrist she wore the white leather diamond studded watch Emmeline had bought her last Christmas. A black and grey silk scarf tied loosely round her neck completed the look. The curling tongues had invoked just the right amount of curl, the ends sitting just above her belt, and her make-up was impeccable. Her plump lips pouted in a deep pink translucent gloss, and her large brown eyes lit up her face. She emerged from the taxi at their rendezvous at exactly twenty-eight minutes past three. Just enough time to make her way to the table she had booked for what she was hoping would only be thirty minutes. She couldn't wait to show off her impeccable sexy lingerie and would enjoy a physical liaison whilst generating enough knowledge to make her next move.

Pamela Faulkes was sat on a high barstool, legs crossed, twirling her left foot. Her newly painted toenails peeped out from a delicate saffron stiletto sandal. She too was a very attractive woman and was the reason Marianne Montrose had tasted her first lesbian relationship. The afternoon went exactly according to plan. Pamela unwittingly divulged names and places whilst being driven to sexual ecstasy by the manipulative Miss Montrose. By the time Marianne met Emmeline for their champagne dinner at eight thirty that evening she had everything in place for the two of them to celebrate their forthcoming move to Barbados. There was just the small matter of how to extract the funds from her client. 'Nothing too much to worry about', she thought. She was a great believer in fate and firmly of the opinion her fascination with Pamela had led her to discover the story of some ancient rubies. She commemorated determination to succeed. She paid no attention to how devious and merciless she had become in her quest and felt her success was preordained. The proximity to her goal only served to heighten her resolve and endorse her lifelong endeavour. Her present optimism and preoccupation with securing their future, revealed a slightly less endearing side to her nature. Emmeline wondered if giving up her job to live with Marianne Montrose in Barbados was an option, even if it would be in the lap of luxury. She knew she wasn't privy to the nitty-gritty of this latest development but had a feeling the master plan included some unmitigated plundering. She quickly reproached herself for that thought. It was probably some innocuous stroke of luck her inimitable partner had inadvertently stumbled upon and she was therefore happy to succumb to her prescribed future.

The Key

When Fiona Oliver emerged from her second hypnotherapy session Carrie was waiting. She had sensed from the beginning that something was amiss but couldn't put her finger on it. Now she knew. Intuition told her Fiona should not visit Miss Montrose again. She voiced her concerns over a coffee. The two women sat opposite one another at a small window table in a tiny French café. The waitress brought two mugs of hot chocolate, dripping with cream and marshmallows. A little green foil covered mint sat at the side of each one.

"Fee, we've got to talk", Carrie began. "Something's wrong. I know you know it too but we've both been keeping wraps on it. I think it's time we unwrapped it. I know you have to do what you think is right but I'm smelling a rat, a very large devious one and I think it's name is Marianne Montrose."

For a moment Fiona didn't answer. She just held her mug in both hands and slurped the cream off the top of the chocolate. She looked up at Carrie over the top of the mug as though searching her friend's face for solace. Big tears poured down her face and dripped off into her drink. Carrie fished in her handbag and found a tissue. Fiona blew her nose fiercely, sniffed hard, and stuffed the tissue up her sleeve.

"What am I going to do Carrie?"
"Are the sessions working or not?" quizzed

Carrie willing her friend to give her a clue what had transpired behind closed doors.

"It's really weird", answered Fiona. "I know these sessions are supposed to help me remember how I got the key. Miss Montrose tells me she will use regression to help me remember. But when I come out I seem to remember less than when I went in. I can't help wondering why I'm not feeling more positive about it."

"Fiona", said Carrie, "Something is occurring here. After your first session Mel and I were uneasy about something and couldn't fathom it. I mentioned it to Lisa and she's done a bit of delving. It seems your Mother in Law …."

"You mean Nellie?" interrupted Fiona.

" … had two sons and a daughter to a previous marriage".

"Yes", said Fee "I know that of course. What are you getting at? I don't understand."

"Well", continued Carrie, "Lenny, her youngest son had a girlfriend called Pamela Faulkes and Marianne Montrose had an affair with both of them while they were still going out together. Lisa said that Marianne Montrose was seen yesterday with Pamela Faulkes. Lenny was killed recently in Burma and I can't help feeling there's a connection. Marianne Montrose could have known about the jewels before you went to see her or worse. She could have lured you to her?"

"You're getting paranoid", laughed Fiona, but conceded the point Marianne may be using information gained from the sessions to her own ends.

"You do still have the pouch with the key

Fee?"

"Yes."

"Then you have to stop these sessions and we have to find another way to retrieve your memory."

Fiona made the telephone call that afternoon. She told Marianne's secretary something had come up and she had to go abroad and wouldn't be taking any more sessions.

Marianne was initially hysterical when she heard the news that Mrs Oliver had cancelled all her appointments. Her state of mind denied her forgiveness for a failed attempt to unethically locate the lock which Mrs Oliver's key would open. Her hysteria turned into a violent mania. She had been so close to securing her future. Marianne Montrose's hypnotherapy parlour closed down one week later. It was rumoured she had attempted to take her own life. Her partner Emmeline Fitzsimons had found and saved her. She deposited Marianne at a private hospital and emigrated. Marianne Montrose was incarcerated indefinitely.

Carrie felt a sudden sharp pain. The feeling passed as soon as it came.

"Fee, please can I see the key?"

"Yes, of course, when would you like to see it?"

"Well, do you have it on you now?"

"No, it's at home."

"Do you think that's wise, Fee, after all you've been through in recent weeks?"

"Well, I got sick and tired of having it

attached to me. I don't know what the hell it's for. I don't know how it got there. I don't know what it opens, so I took it off. Maybe it's as well, if we both now think there's something dodgy about the only person we thought might be able to help. Anyway, it's buried in a drawer somewhere at home. You're welcome to come and have a look."

They made arrangements for that evening. Both girls felt they were living in a dream. Life had seemed surreal since they came back from Myanmar. They both knew the reason for Fiona's visit to New York. They both remembered that she was taking a parcel of jewellery for a valuation. Neither of them could remember if or where that valuation took place. They remembered a trip to Myanmar which had been on special offer, but had no recollection of anything that happened there. The only remnant of their journey that shed doubt on the whole trip was the key that Fiona found when she took a bath the night they returned. She had no knowledge of how it got there, or what it might open. Carrie knew there were answers somewhere close by and it was aggravating her beyond comprehension that she couldn't fathom it. The intense frustration highlighted her own inability to remember any of the events either, and it was this fact that Lisa picked up on.

'Mum, can I ask you a question? Why can't you remember much about your trip either? It's a bit weird that neither of you can remember anything about the jewels that you took into a jeweller's shop in New York. The whole thing is absurd. You can't remember. Dad can't. Alan and Fiona can't. There must be something you can remember between you to shed some light on it. If someone can hypnotise you to help you remember, maybe someone already did it to make you forget."

Lisa's words struck a chord. Carrie sat upright.

"That's right Leece, why haven't we thought about that before?"

"Maybe we've been so close to it but looking in all the wrong places. Can you remember anything Mum?"

They sat again all afternoon going over and over, trying to jolt some memory, but to no avail. Lisa's words remained with Carrie and she racked her brains to establish a thought pattern along those lines.

"Why can't I remember either?" She felt another searing pain, worse than the one she felt earlier. She suffered from acute attacks of pain whenever the subject was broached. It doubled her resolve to interpret this clue.

* * * * * *

The Answer

On Wednesday morning all the newspapers reported that Elliott Jones had been shot in a bar in Myanmar. His girlfriend's two brothers had also suffered a tragedy. One of them had burnt to death in a car accident, and the other one had been detained in an asylum. Neither Carrie nor Fiona normally read newspapers, but this particular morning, Mel had bought one and Carrie was glancing through it while she ate her breakfast cereal. She raced to the phone to call Fiona.

"I'm on my way over, are you in for a while?"

"Yes" said Fiona.

"There's an article in the paper I think you should see. Get that pouch and key out, something is happening in my little brain box."

"See you in a mo", laughed Fiona, completely unaware of Carrie's brainstorm. Once again, Carrie drove to Fiona's at breakneck speed. She jerked the car to a halt in their drive and ran to the front door which was open. She threw the open paper onto the breakfast bar.

"What do think of this?" Fiona handed her a cup of coffee and sat down on one of the stainless steel bar stools, put her glasses on and read out: 'Local Lad Shot Dead in Bar in Myanmar'. Fiona continued to read the story and the harsh reality of it had a profound effect on her.

"My Uncle Tom died trying to steal my jewellery. Two members of my family die in tragic accidents, another is in a lunatic asylum. All incidents took place where we've just been and while

285

we were there. I have no jewels, just a damn key with nothing to unlock. Carrie what does it all mean?"

"I don't know Fee. Have you got a piece of paper and a pen?"

Fiona produced the requested items and Carrie began to write. I'm going to write down everything you and I can both remember."

"We've already done that a dozen times", griped Fiona.

"Yes, but we've been playing at it", returned Carrie. "Now, we seem to have something more to go at. What time is it?"

As she looked up at the cuckoo clock on the wall behind Fiona's kitchen table, her eye glanced at the decorative wagon wheel hung on the wall beside the clock and she felt a sharp pain in her head. As she put the pen on the paper to write, a strange sensation coursed right through her.

"I've already done this Fee. I've just had an overwhelming sense of déjà vu. I looked at your clock and saw the wheel on the wall and felt a sharp pain. When I put the pen on the paper to start writing, I felt something. As if I've already written everything down. The answers to the questions I was going to start writing are already written somewhere. I know it. I'm going home to search through my bags."

"Well, at least it's something to do instead of just sitting here", sighed Fiona.

"You coming with me?"

"Yeah course I am."

A new sense of urgency and decisiveness engulfed them. As they walked into Carrie's hallway, Fiona caught sight of the wooden lion, one of Carrie's African collection and felt a twinge in her neck. The pain made her cry out.

"What's the matter?" asked Carrie.

"I don't know", replied Fiona. I glanced at the wooden lion in the hall and felt a sharp pain."

"Come on, let's find these bags."

Carrie's house was upside down as so much had been happening lately. She couldn't remember where she'd put her bags. They rummaged around in Carrie's bedroom. Carrie found her suitcase under Mel's side of the bed, dragged it out and opened it. It was empty except for the bag which she'd taken as hand luggage. She unzipped the handbag and found a few receipts in the bottom, a couple of hairclips and a lipstick.

"Not much in here", she said. "Wait a minute, there might be something in the little compartment here. Feels like there's something. Probably a packet of tissues."

She opened it and extracted a wad of papers.

"Bingo", she snapped. "Fee, I think we've got all the answers written down here. My déjà vu earlier was absolutely bang to rights. Look at this." Fee was desperately trying to see what was contained in the papers Carrie was clutching. They ran through to the kitchen.

"Sit down Fee and I'll read it out to you."

They were completely stunned. Everything was there in black and white, the whole tale. The trip to New York, the visit to the jewellers, the trip to Burma. Uncle Tom, Elliott, Lenny and Bart, the Palace. They were flabbergasted and terrified.

"What do we do with this information now though?" asked Fiona, quite overcome by the significance of it all.

The only bit of information that wasn't there was the piece of the puzzle they'd begun to look for. Where had the pouch and key come from? Of course Carrie wrote all this down while she could still remember it all. But they didn't know anything about the pouch and key until after they arrived home. The revelation revitalised their energy and they rang their husbands. Carrie rang Lisa. They agreed to have dinner and discuss their next move.

* * * * * *

The Operating Theatre

On the way to the shop to get the milk, Carrie had brought the car that she and Fiona were travelling in to a halt at the white give way line. It was early evening and there was still a fair amount of rush hour traffic in both directions. Two hundred yards to the left were traffic lights and they were about to turn red. An articulated vehicle was hurtling its way towards the lights at a terrific speed.

Colin had a deadline for his flammable cargo. He'd had a really bad day. Nothing had gone right. He'd been pulled by the ministry earlier in the day, and although everything had been in order, it had delayed him. There had been the usual standstill traffic on the motorway delaying him even further. He still had twenty five miles to go. He would lose his job if he was late again. He was stressed. He lit a cigarette, took a few puffs and threw it out of the window but the wind blew it back in. It had landed on his bunk and lay smouldering. By the time he realised there was a fire it had got a good hold. He saw the lights up ahead and aimed to get through them to the lay-by at the other side so he could douse the fire.

Carrie assumed correctly that he was trying to outrun the lights. Both women commented on the speed he was travelling.

"Yes", Carrie had said, "I'm not going to argue with him. I'll wait."

At that precise moment, a black sedan

ploughed into the back of Carrie's car, pushing her vehicle into the path of the speeding lorry. Everything had gone black.

There had been blood everywhere and the scene had been total carnage. The tanker driver had jammed on his brakes, standing on them willing his twenty-two stone bulk to bring his vehicle to a halt, but to no avail. The girls didn't stand a chance. When the paramedics got to him, he was burnt beyond recognition. He had turned the wheel and after careering into Carrie's car his vehicle had come to a halt buried in the wall of the house on the corner of the main road. Carrie's car had spun around and around and had finished up smashing into the bollard in the middle of the road with two frail broken bodies inside it. The driver and passenger in the black sedan had been hurtled through the windscreen and lay dead on the road. A shard of glass from one of the vehicles had pierced the forehead of the driver of the black sedan, giving the appearance of a bullet wound. Carrie and Fiona were the only survivors and had been in such a weak state, they weren't expected to live. Witnesses to the accident had stopped to do what they could while they waited for the ambulance to arrive. The road had been closed off in both directions. All the emergency services had been in attendance and the girls had been whisked off in the ambulance. The intermittent noise of the ambulance siren had pierced the early evening sky and the blue lights flashed.

Mel and Alan went over and over the fateful evening's events. Carrie had hurriedly gobbled her tea to get to Fiona's because Fiona had rung her and asked her to go back for, what was at the time, an unknown reason. Alan had informed Mel of the content of that visit. As Carrie had been leaving to go home, Fiona had asked for a lift to the shop to buy some milk. Carrie had offered to bring her home again but Fiona had declined saying that the short walk back would be good exercise. Both the girls had left but neither of them arrived home.

And so their families sat in the hospital and continued to wait for news.

The Miracle

Both surgeons agreed it would be nothing short of a miracle if either of the girls survived. They had informed the two families of the worst scenario. Going into the operation armed with the knowledge that they may lose their patients was no easy task for either of the men who were considered the best in their field. They were not in the habit of having patients die in their care, even ones in the diabolical state of their current responsibilities. The medical teams in both theatres were dedicated young men and women with distinguished records of service in their profession. Carrie and Fiona couldn't have had a more accomplished team of medics to help save their lives. They had suffered horrific head injuries. One of the dangers, the surgeons had told the families, was that in addition to their shattered bones and crushed chests, their brains could have been irreversibly damaged.

The operations had been concluded and their families were allowed by their bedsides two at a time. All any of them could do was pray to their God and watch. They kept a vigil night and day watching for any sign of improvement. There was none. Two or three times, staff had raced to Carrie's side as her vital signs deteriorated. Each time they left the bedside the machines still indicated life. For four nights and three days, the girls lay in total reliance on their destiny. Their families prayed and willed for their swift recovery. Each day brought diminishing hope and taut nerves.

On the morning of the fourth day, Mel's hand was resting on top of Carrie's. He was talking to her. Over and over he spoke about the wonderful times they'd had together. He wasn't expecting replies. He was just simply talking, hoping that his voice would bring some spark to his wife's limp body. He thought he felt one of her fingers move beneath his and immediately called a nurse. The nurse came running and he explained what had happened. The nurse looked at the machine above Carrie's bed. She smiled and crossed the room to where the graph was emerging.

"This is very good Mr Goodwin, very good indeed."

Two days later, Carrie Goodwin opened her eyes for the first time since her accident. She felt she had metamorphosised both physically and mentally. When she was able to speak she asked about the whereabouts of her friend. Fiona had suffered similar injuries but due to an operation some years ago, had incurred further complications. She would be moved to another hospital when she was able to cope with the journey. There were tubes and wires protruding from various parts of Carrie's body but Mel and Lisa knew she was agitated about something else. Mel kept stroking her forehead and telling her not to think or worry. She was just to lie there and rest. Carrie was still very weak and did not need telling twice. She asked if she could see Fiona before she was moved. The following day Carrie was wheeled in to see Fiona. They gingerly smiled at one another and with every ounce of strength they could muster they squeezed one another's hands. Fiona was being transferred to a hospital which specialised in neurological disorders. Two days later Alan was told his wife was a very lucky woman to have pulled through.

"If you believe in a God sir, I'd thank him for performing a miracle. Your wife's going to be fine."

Return of the Rubies

A few weeks later, both girls were back home and gaining strength each day. There had been a few get-togethers to discuss their memories of the fateful evening.

"Oh, my God, Caz, how could that have happened to us? By all the laws in the universe we should be dead."

"I know", said Carrie quietly. She looked at her friend and smiled.

"I had a few peculiar dreams while I was out of it."

"Yes, so did I", grinned Fiona. "Shall we confer?"

Their recuperation was aided by recollections of the incident and their unconscious state. Was it utter coincidence that two stories were identical? From the black sedan to the hypnotist, it was all there. From the expert's room to the tragic deaths in Myanmar. Uncle Tom's death to the demise of Marianne Montrose. Fantasy, distress, trepidation, tragedy and absolute consternation as to how this was possible touched both women as they sat and recalled it all. They had been discussing what to do about the beautiful gem stones that Fiona's dad had left in a cardboard box on her front porch. Hadn't they been valued? Didn't Alan take them to a jeweller and as Fiona recalled, he'd been offered ten thousand pounds for them there and then. And hadn't they left the jewels in a safety deposit box at the bank? And then, ah yes, it was all coming back to them now. Alan and

Fiona had decided to have them valued by an expert in America.

"Yes, and that's when Alan and I decided to make a joint trip with you and Mel."

"But we never got there", said Carrie. "And yet everything I must have dreamt was so real. You've had virtually the same dream. You'd just never believe it in a million years."

"It must be because we're so close", said Fiona.

"I know Fee, but it's still odd. What are you going to do? Are you going to make another appointment?"

"Yes, as soon as we have the dates for the trip, but I think the first thing I want to do when I can get about on my own properly, is go to the safety deposit box and bring the jewels home and have another look at them."

"Do you think that's wise?" asked Carrie, remembering some of the horrific parts of her dream.

"I want to see them again properly. I didn't really do that before."

"Will Alan go with you? Or do you want some company?"

"Well, according to legend …..", began Fiona, sarcastically.

"I am the companion", continued Carrie.

The two girls sat in silence, each thinking their own thoughts, and all the far-fetched, crazy, improbable things they had dreamt suddenly demanded more attention.

The following weeks saw their lives return to normal. Alan and Fiona, Mel and Carrie and Graham and Lisa booked another trip to New York. Their holiday insurances more than covered their financial loss of the last trip. Fiona and Alan, armed with the precious key opened their safety deposit box and retrieved their precious jewels.

In June the Boeing 747 left Manchester Airport bound for New York. They were all excited for different reasons. Lisa and Graham chatted excitedly about their shopping trip. Mel and Carrie excited on one count and apprehensive on the other. Carrie and Fiona were a little tired from their traumatic near death ordeal and slept for most of the flight. Their minds were held in the grip of expectancy and they abandoned themselves to a dream. The rubies sat in the cloth bag inside a zipped compartment in a locked suitcase in the hold of the aeroplane. Current airport legalities were emotive and they didn't want to inflame curiosity and interest, so had decided to pack them. The rubies were becoming warm.

A hot summer's day greeted them in New York and as they travelled across the Hudson River, Carrie and Fiona cried. Only in their dreams had they seen anything like it. Carrie felt like an emissary, protector of the jewels. Fiona was passionate about her quest and Lisa was simply in love. They settled into their hotel and felt a sense of unexplained familiarity with their surroundings. Fiona was convinced she had been there before in colder weather conditions. Alan reminded her they had never been to New York. Carrie smiled and shivered remembering the falling snow.

Their appointment with the expert was to be the next day in the late afternoon. They planned an early breakfast so they could see as much as possible before the appointment. Lisa and Graham would have the afternoon to look for Lisa's tiara, and the others would go together to the jewellery shop. The inconsequential likelihood that they would recognise the shop momentarily crossed the girls' minds. They both did and knew instinctively this was the place they had journeyed half way across the world to visit. In they went. It was precisely as portrayed in their dreams. The boys marvelled at the way in which the girls navigated the crowds once inside the shop, as if they knew exactly where they were going. The name plaque on the door read 'Monsieur Boesflug'. Both girls felt a cold tremor run up and down their spine. They knocked and were invited to enter. A small man, immaculately dressed, came forward to greet them. He sported a Van Dyke beard, a pair of dark glasses and smelt of expensive perfume. He smiled at them, a gold tooth gleaming amongst the row of otherwise perfectly white teeth, and introduced himself as Monsieur Boesflug's assistant, Bernard. He led them over to a table and asked them all to sign and date the guestbook. They all complied. Carrie and Fiona were trembling with fear yet trying to appear unconcerned as another gentleman entered the room, revealing the precise description. Exactly as the girls remembered, Monsieur Boesflug examined the stones.

"Mrs Oliver", he began, "I should very much like to tell you that you have in your possession the legendary Meng Tuu-Kyi rubies. We must begin the procedures which accompany a find of this nature. Congratulations. People have searched for many centuries, hoping to find these ancient gems. You will, of course, be pleased to know that the Museum will offer you a substantial reward. You should also feel rewarded in the knowledge that an ancient prophecy will have been fulfilled and that finally the Meng Tuu-Kyi Ruby collection will be complete and therefore according to ancient Myan legend, their land will be restored to prosperity." He smiled at them all and added, "If you believe in all that stuff!"

Fiona and Carrie felt quite chilled. Monsieur Boesflug invited them to follow him and led them into another room where there were some comfy sofas and offered them some refreshment. He left them alone for a few moments and returned with some forms and asked Fiona to complete them. He served their refreshments and leaned back against one of the cream and black chenille cushions.

"We would like you to donate your findings to the museum local to the place where legend indicates the rubies originate. There is a section of Myan Rubies at the museum and there are spaces reserved for those which have been missing. We always expected them to be found. The Myan people have waited for centuries. It is said that the fire of the rubies themselves will burn for eternity and the stones will never be lost. The legend of the Meng Tuu-Kyi rubies demands that when the stones are recovered, a companion must accompany the person returning them."

He continued to tell the four young adults in front of him the story he thought he would never tell. Carrie and Fiona both knew the story and filled in the blanks before he had chance to voice the words. It was incredulous. He smiled at Fiona.

"The prophecy concludes, 'the person returning the jewels will enjoy riches beyond his comprehension in this life and into eternity. May I ask you to accompany me to Myanmar? Of course all your expenses to date will be refunded in full."

Without hesitation the four agreed. They returned the following morning at the appointed time and Monsieur Boesflug produced tickets for their flight.

Upon their arrival at the museum, Monsieur Boesflug turned to Alan and Mel and asked them to wait in an ante-room, complying with the rules of the legend that only the bearer and companion could carry out the final task. The girls followed Monsieur Boesflug. They wound their way around the slate floors of the museum until they saw a huge archway over which was a plaque indicating that the Meng Tuu-Kyi rubies lay beyond.

"Fiona, please take out the rubies."

Fiona did as she was told and took the cloth bag out of the holdall. She laid it on her lap.

Monsieur Boesflug handed her a large amulet, into which he asked her to put the rubies. He asked her to fasten the amulet around her waist. She secured it as instructed and he asked them both to walk over to him. The girls were apprehensive, remembering the amulet from their dream. Monsieur Boesflug stood the girls back to back and asked them to lock arms. They seemed to be stood in a circle of some kind. He begged them not to be frightened, that no harm would come to them. He asked them to turn slowly and face one another and then to look straight ahead. There before them was a miniature Mya Palace, flanked at the front entrance by two lions. On the opposite corner of the entrance was a white elephant and just to the left of the model palace was a miniature cart with eight-spoke wheels. The girls remembered every minute detail. Monsieur Boesflug handed each of the girls a comb with a fresh lotus flower and asked them to slide them onto their hair. They had anticipated this and complied without question. The palace was quite incredible. Resembling a modern-day model village. Everything an exact miniature replica of the scene it represented. Monsieur Boesflug led them to an area labelled the King's Chamber. He explained to Fiona that she must place the largest of the rubies into the golden orb and the rest of the jewellery into the glass cabinet lining the staircase. Fiona untied the strap of the amulet from around her waist and handed it to Carrie, exactly as she had done in her dream. She instinctively knew what to do and opened up the back of the golden orb. Inside she knew she would find a beautiful velvet case embedded into the centre. She undid the bag that Carrie held for her, and put her hand inside. She lifted the large ruby out. She felt every facet of the ruby as she went to place it into its resting place. As she did so, she saw the glass cabinet take on a glistening luminosity. She dropped down a step and placed all the stones on the cabinet shelves.

"They're all in the cabinet Monsieur Boesflug", she said.

"The amulet please Fiona", he beckoned to her.

Fiona placed the amulet in his hand.

"Is that it? Is it all over now?" asked Carrie.

Monsieur Boesflug turned to Carrie and grasped her hands.

"Mrs Goodwin, the Myanmar authorities will be eternally grateful. Not only have you executed your duty, you have done it with grace, love and humility. In today's modern world these are qualities seldom found and you will not go unrewarded. I have instructions to thank you now, and assure you that you'll be invited to attend Mya Palace itself for the tribute which will surely take place before the end of the summer. The people of Myanmar have waited a long time for this moment and they will want you all to be present for the rituals. Please permit me to tell them you will attend?"

Carrie thought she should perhaps curtsy, but simply said in a squeaky voice, "Yes. Thank you."

The two girls turned to look at one another and slowly embraced. They followed Monsieur

Boesflug who was now striding back through the museum. Their journey was almost over. They collected the men and returned to the airport where Monsieur Boesflug informed them a private jet would fly them back to their local airport. There would be a few other carefully vetted passengers aboard and there would be one stop en route for fuel. They bade him goodbye and crossed the tarmac to their waiting plane. As Fiona shook his hand, he pressed a small beige coloured amulet into her hand and suggested that she store it in a safe place. Fiona knew she had to tie the amulet around her waist.

Carrie kept thinking about Lisa and the imminent wedding. Their shopping trip had been curtailed. Lisa had been understanding and Carrie was sure she'd be longing to share her purchases with her.

'I wonder what he meant when he said I would not go unrewarded', thought Carrie. 'Oh well. Have to wait and see', she mused. She leaned against Mel and closed her eyes.

The plane lurched and seemed to drop a couple of hundred feet. Carrie was nearly sick. Fiona screamed and the boys held their breath.
"Oh my God, what was that?"
Their hearts were racing. It was taking them all their time to catch their breath from the shock of dropping so suddenly. The pilot's voice was heard over the tannoy.
"Nothing to worry about, we just hit a bit of turbulence, please don't be alarmed. Unfortunately,

we'll have to land at an alternative refuelling airport. You may feel a little more turbulence. Please remain seated until the aeroplane has landed."

Alarm bells were ringing and without speaking, they all knew intuitively that this turn of events could spell trouble even though they no longer had possession of the rubies. They might be landing in the middle of nowhere. What hope had they got of fending off any would-be attackers? The boys had no knowledge that Fiona carried an amulet around her waist. Neither did Carrie. Fiona decided to remove the amulet and hide it somewhere else before they landed. She squeezed past Alan and out onto the aisle, when suddenly the plane seemed to drop again. She fell to her knees clinging onto Alan's leg. He grabbed her hands and told her to stay put. The plane levelled off again. Fiona stayed on her hands and knees and crawled to the back of the plane. Once inside the toilet cubicle she looked round trying to find a suitable hiding place for the amulet. She had not looked inside it, nor did she dare. The others didn't know of its existence. Perhaps it would be better all round if she had no knowledge of its contents. There was nowhere to store the bag. Nowhere that anyone could look and not find what was hidden. She panicked. Alan was worried about her and went to see if she was alright. He knocked on the toilet door.

Fiona whispered, "Is that you Caz?"
"No, it's me, let me in."

With two of them inside the tiny space, they were squashed against the sides. Fiona briefly told Alan her plight. He asked if she had looked inside.

They agreed to look. Their eyes lit up when they saw the largest of the rubies there in Fiona's hand.

"But I put that ruby in the golden orb in the palace at the museum", winced Fiona. "This isn't possible."

"Maybe it's another one", said Alan, getting anxious about the space and the heat the pair of them were generating.

"Are you thinking what I am?" asked Alan.

"Yes love, we're going to be searched for this", she said squeezing the gem into her hand. It was at this point the crazy notion entered her head.

"I think I know what to do. Please will you go and get Carrie for me. Now. Hurry, before this thing lands. And ask her to bring her handbag with her."

Alan was wise enough to do as he was bid and alerted Carrie that Fiona needed her help in the ladies. Carrie quickly walked down the aisle trying not to draw attention to herself. Fiona had no idea where this crazy notion had come from, but she knew it could work. She asked Carrie to ask the air stewardess for a first aid kit and a pair of scissors.

"Tell her I've got an in-growing toe nail that is paining me and I'm going to try to cut the nail and then bandage my toe."

Carrie did as she was told. The stewardess seemed a bit dopey and it took her a few minutes to actually find a first-aid kit, but did manage to produce both the scissors and the kit. Carrie hurried back to the loo and squashed herself back into the compartment.

"What are you going to do Fiona?"

"I'm not Carrie, I'm very much afraid it'll have to be you. Please don't ask too many questions. It's going to hurt and there'll be a lot of blood. I hope you've got those baby wipes with you."

"Yes, in my bag."

"I was banking on it!"

"I don't understand Fee, please tell me."

"I'm sorry Caz, but it's either this, or I think we might be killed."

"Do you mean like in our dreams when we were chased for the jewels?"

"That's exactly what I mean Caz. This is not a game, it's for real. I have one of the Meng Tuu-Kyi Rubies here in this amulet. There's nowhere to hide it. I can't be the one to do it. They'll search every inch of me, but I doubt they'll suspect you. You're the companion and I think it has to be you. Not because I don't want to do it to myself, but because I think it'll save our lives if we perform the ritual on you."

"I don't know how I know, but I know what you're going to do Fee. How will we stop the blood?"

"There's a few toilet rolls here in this bit of a cupboard to mop with and if you've got the baby wipes, the ruby will do the healing. We can use one of these bandages to secure all the packing and it'll be ok. I promise."

"Just get on with it then Fee. Hurry."

The plane lurched again and both girls banged

into the side of the compartment. The operation was performed by first rubbing the fattest part of Carrie's arm with the baby wipe. She stifled a scream as Fiona gripped her skin tight and made a small incision creating a flap of skin. She inserted the ruby and closed the flap of skin across it. Blood dripped. Carrie held her arm over the toilet and the blood still dripped. They held wads of baby wipes over the incision and then Fiona wound an entire toilet roll round and using a bandage from the first aid kit, pulled it as tight as possible to stem the flow of blood. She screwed the small amulet up into as tight a ball as she could, dropped it down the toilet, cleaned the blood up from round the bowl, and flushed the toilet, hoping that the amulet would disappear. Their luck was in. All they had to do was wait for the blood to stop. Carrie would have to hold the bandaging tightly, pressing hard down on the cut, which was extremely painful, as the large ruby was underneath. Carrie hoped that the sleeve of her black cardigan would cover all it needed to. Fiona had told her that she must believe in the ruby. Eventually the flow of blood subsided and the girls were glad to get out of the confined space and back into the aisle of the plane.

They were descending. The girls went back to their seats. Carrie was nearly passing out with pain and Fiona was frightened that Carrie would become infected. They had come this far. Surely nothing more could happen to jeopardise their lives. The plane landed with a hefty bump and was soon taxiing round to the refuelling station. But instead of turning along the runway that would take them to the fuel lines, the plane carried on and came to a halt on an isolated square of tarmac some two miles from their preferred destination. The other passengers were quite distressed.

"Why are we stopping here?" said one man in a demanding tone. Sitting on the opposite side of the aircraft two or three rows behind them, a man left his seat, climbing over his partner's legs and straightening up, his legs and back obviously stiff from the cramped seating. He was their Achilles heel. It didn't take Fiona long to realise Uncle Tom had surfaced to claim what he believed was rightfully his.

"Why did you have to go to all this trouble with an aeroplane? Why didn't you just steal the jewellery from my house like you've probably tried before?"

Alan felt the skin on the back of his neck start to prickle.

'Why was Fiona behaving this way? Surely it would be better not to antagonise Uncle Tom?'

"You're too late Tom", screamed Fiona. "The jewels are in a Burmese museum where you can't get your hands on them."

Carrie prayed, winced, and prayed again.

"Nice try Fiona."

Fiona ventured to ask, "How did you get your filthy butt on this flight anyway? It's a private plane?"

"Not that it's any of your business, but the pilot owed Lenny a favour."

"Well, you're wasting your time and everyone

else's. The jewels have gone back to where they belong. There's nothing here Tom."

"Well we'll see about that now won't we. Get out into aisle Fiona."

Fiona, angry and frightened did as she was told. Alan right by her side was trying to fathom how he could overcome Tom and take control of the situation. Mel was on the same wavelength. He kept turning round and looking over his shoulder as best he could, whilst still clutching Carrie's hand, and trying to see if there was a stewardess at the back of the plane who could have tried to knock Tom to the floor. This was the tack he would try and was confident he could pull it off if the stewardess had an ounce of go in her. Then he saw the gun.

'Oh, my god this guy's a complete lunatic', thought Mel. He patted Carrie's arm and she winced.

"What happened then?" he whispered.

"Nothing", she answered, terrified in case Mel pursued this train of questioning. He didn't. Something else had caught his eye. Another passenger sitting on the opposite side of the plane, and shielding his female partner from the swinging arm with the gun, saw the opportunity too. Both men knew instantly that they had to take control. Tom would never suspect there was anybody thinking remotely along these lines. He was standing in the aisle confronting Fiona who was in the aisle facing him. He took a few steps towards her, pointing the gun straight at her. He told her to take off her shoes. She looked to her right as if getting confirmation from Alan that she should do it. She caught Mel's glance across the plane and knew instinctively that something was occurring. She took her cue and took off her right shoe and pushed it with her toes as far into the leg space where Alan was seated as she could. Tom ordered her to take off the other one and this time to push it towards him. In that split second, everyone knew exactly what to do. Tom was not the brightest and Alan and Mel knew he was going to examine every piece of clothing and footwear that Fiona had on. Goodness only knew what he would try after that, but they had been given the perfect opportunity to do something. Mel slowly eased his arm down towards the floor to retrieve the sturdy shoe that Fiona had kicked towards them. He glanced over his shoulder and saw that the man across the aisle was ready. As Tom bent down to collect Fiona's shoe, the man across the plane, who was a couple of rows behind Tom, quickly grabbed the seat with both hands and raised up his body, straightened his legs out in front of him and pushed Tom as hard as he could.

Fiona jumped backwards to avoid being knocked over by Tom, and Mel threw the shoe as hard as he could hitting Tom squarely on the head. While Tom was stunned, the man across the plane had leapt out of his seat and had his foot ready to stand on Tom's right arm, rendering his shooting arm useless. The stewardess had radioed in to the terminal and soon four police cars, two ambulances and a fire engine were alongside the plane. Tom was roughly escorted from the plane, and Alan informed the police that the pilot had been bribed to take Tom on board. The pilot was escorted from the plane. Elliott, Lenny and Bart would be located and arrested for their part in the conspiracy. The stewardess informed the passengers that they should remain seated and she would serve refreshments. A new captain was already on the way. There was a round of applause. Meanwhile Fiona had collapsed back onto her seat and was crying hysterically.

"That's it baby, all over now", whispered Alan. "It's all over now."

Home Sweet Home

The aeroplane landed on a private strip at seven o'clock on a rainy English morning. The puddles were enormous denoting it had been heavy. Carrie was in agony. Fiona told the men in muted whispers what had happened, and they were all eager to have the ruby extracted and her arm tended to. Carrie and Fiona dashed to the ladies as soon as they disembarked, leaving the men to collect the suitcases. Carrie removed the black cardigan to reveal a blood soaked arm. Fiona stripped the bandage, toilet roll and wipes from the wound, to see that it had in fact stopped bleeding. They removed the ruby which forced the wound to start bleeding again. They bandaged her arm back up as best they could and Fiona wrapped the gem in bundles of toilet paper and placed the ruby in her trouser side pocket and fastened the zip, making it bulge somewhat.

"Well, I guess that's it Caz. We need to take this to a jeweller."

The two of them fell about laughing. Even with her wounded arm Carrie laughed until she cried. On a more serious note they needed to seek medical attention for Carrie. They sat in silence in the taxi. Their experience had rendered them speechless. The only thing they wanted was an English cup of tea and normality. The events of the past few weeks had taken their toll. Fiona had the precious ruby in her possession. She guessed it would sell for a tidy sum of money, but had no idea just how much. Carrie was still wondering how her reward would come about.

Perhaps Monsieur Boesflug had been fabricating the truth a little. Perhaps there would be nothing for her. Perhaps the legend about the companion was all a load of codswallop. Maybe her reward was the adventure which she would remember for the rest of her life. She had thought about writing a book. 'Perhaps it's time to think about it seriously and write my recent adventure for the world to see. It would sell in fourteen different languages and make a fortune.'

For now she was content to rest with her eyes closed and let the movement of the travelling car lull her into a short content sleep. It didn't seem two seconds until Mel was shaking her awake.

When Carrie was asked by the hospital staff the nature of her injury, there was an abject silence. What should she say? That she was a self harmer? She couldn't expect the A & E receptionist to believe a word of anything she said, so she tried to say as little as possible and feigned stupidity, as did Fiona. They sat for almost an hour until eventually a nurse shouted Carrie's name and the two weary women trooped through to the doctor. He looked at it, looked at the girls, looked at the notes, checked Carrie's temperature, wrote out a prescription and asked his nurse to patch her up. The girls both knew what he was thinking. He had also had a good look for 'other' signs. When he found none, he decided not to pursue the questioning. He just did his job to get them out and make way for the next patient who may or may not have caused their own injuries.

Relieved when it was all over, they headed home for their longed for cup of tea. They both had an unprecedented feeling of contentment, of inner happiness and couldn't wait to run inside the house and fall into the arms of their respective spouses. Carrie's house was a buzz of activity. Lisa and Graham were there. Megan was running about excitedly sniffing every single inch of Mel and Carrie, then twizzing round and round in circles. Then she looked at them both and ran off into a corner where there was a bone 'buried' and starting pushing it further into the corner with her nose. Alan had made a large pot of tea. Everyone was talking excitedly. Graham walked in with two cold bottles of champagne and half a dozen glasses in a box. He placed them all on the table, poured the champagne, and invited everyone to raise a glass. The champagne immediately went to Fiona's head and she felt instantly drunk. Her behaviour changed just ever so slightly which made everyone laugh.

Amongst all the hilarity, no-one heard the postman come. It lay on the mat in the hallway, a small parcel about six inches by ten inches. Graham had left the front door ajar, and the postman had placed it inside the house. He had smiled to himself when he heard all the laughter and thought 'now there's a happy household.' The parcel lay there quietly defying anybody to pick it up. No-one noticed it except Megan. She heard the postman and trotted into the hall to investigate. She sniffed the parcel. There was nothing tasty about it and she left it alone. But curiosity got the better of her and she pushed the parcel under the sideboard with her nose and considered it 'buried'.

"Well, I think it's time we got back. We must let these people get some rest", said Alan to Fiona.

"Yes, I know. It's going to pretty dull around here after all this."

"When are you going to take the ruby?" asked Carrie.

"I'll take it down to London tomorrow", replied Alan "And we'll see what they say. I don't know if they'll give me anything for it or whether they'll suggest the big auction houses. It'll probably attract a great deal of interest whatever happens." They all hugged and said their goodbyes. Fiona was overwhelmed with emotion and thanked them both for their endurance on her behalf. Alan and Fiona loaded Mel's car with their luggage and Mel drove them home.

'Yes', he thought as he was driving back home. "It is going to be dull around here. But it won't be dull in their household for long, when they realise what they have in their possession. It'll never be dull again.'

He still couldn't believe that all of this had happened. He wanted a quiet five minutes with his wife to just sit and talk about everything that had happened. He would have to wait until much later for that. Carrie was on the telephone when he got home. She was obviously talking to Fiona.

"Good heavens, you've been with her for days. What can you possibly find to talk about so soon?"

When Carrie came off the telephone, she told Mel there had been an envelope waiting for Fiona when she arrived home. She'd opened it and inside was an invitation to the Ceremony of Rubies at the Palace in Myanmar in two week's time. Also enclosed was a cheque for £3,000 to cover their expenses for the trip.

"Where's ours?" griped Mel.

"We didn't get one. Well, not yet anyway. Maybe we won't. Maybe our bit is done. Maybe it was all a load of pocus about the companion."

"But, if Fiona's received an invitation, it's not pocus, is it?"

"Maybe ours will come tomorrow."

Carrie was vacuuming the hallway the following morning.

"Good Lord, my house looks like a bomb's hit", said Carrie out loud.

There had been no time for cleaning. First the accident and then the trip. Mel had gone back to work and Megan, as usual was running round in circles at the sound of the vacuum cleaner. She began sniffing underneath the sideboard. She lay down and tried to get her whole body underneath.

"What's the matter Megan? What's under there? One of your bones?"

She knelt down, gave her a hug and put her

316

hand underneath the sideboard. Her fingers felt something, and she stretched herself a little further and pulled out the envelope. She screeched and raced for the phone.

"I think we've got our invitation", she said excitedly when he picked up.

"Oh, wonderful", said Mel, beginning to get excited. "The postman came early didn't he?"

"The postman hasn't been this morning. I was vacuuming and Megan was chasing her tail. Then she tried to get underneath the sideboard. She must have buried it there yesterday."

"Have you opened it yet?"

"No, I thought I'd ring you first."

"Well open it Caz, go on I'll wait."

Carrie threw the telephone down and undid the flap. Sure enough it contained the same as Fiona's. Now they were excited. She rang Lisa and they arranged to go for coffee at Fiona's. Life had suddenly taken on a new meaning for Mel and Carrie with this extraordinary chain of events.

The Ceremony of the Meng Tuu-Kyi Rubies

When they entered Mya Palace two weeks later it was as though they had been transported back to a time long forgotten. They had travelled first class and been treated like royalty. Two trishaws had transported them from the airport to their hotel. Carrie and Fiona were thrilled. The seats resembled thrones, ornately carved around the top, with back padding in vibrant colours. There was a huge canopy covering the entire vehicle, and this was adorned with scented fresh flowers and green foliage which hung down slightly off the canopy. This provided a further screen from the scorching sun. The seating was covered in thick sumptuous silk, exquisitely embroidered with birds and flowers. Underneath the handlebars at the front of the trishaw were cone-shaped containers filled to capacity with beautiful exotic flower arrangements. It was a surprisingly easy ride, evenly riding out all the bumps. They left the hustle and bustle far behind and the skilled driver gave them a running commentary on the surrounding area. The scenery was breathtaking. They passed awe-inspiring pagodas, temples and monuments, but nothing could have prepared them for the sight now before them. It seemed to be hidden from the road and only when the driver turned into a wide entrance, did they realise this was their journey's end. When they pulled up in front of the hotel they gasped in amazement. It was nothing short of majestic. A magnificent pagoda set in stunning landscaped gardens. The building itself was infused with ancient and modern influences, and towered high above them as they alighted the trishaw. They thanked their driver who was busily attending to the luggage brought by a third and much plainer mode of transport. The recreational facilities at their hotel included an Olympic-size outdoor swimming pool. They could just see the water glistening. Carrie and Fiona couldn't wait to put on their costumes. The hotel oozed a tranquil ambience and excitement was building to a crescendo. The thought hardly daring to escape from each of them, 'If this is the hotel, what's the palace going to be like?' They held onto that thought as they climbed the steps leading to the foyer of the hotel and stepped inside. They were greeted by a number of hotel staff. The porter took their luggage, another offered them seating, another brought a large tray of refreshments and one who sat down beside them on the luxurious sofa and introduced himself. He was concerned for their immediate welfare and enquired about their journey and what they would like to alleviate the strain of travel. Satisfied he had offered every facility, they were escorted to their rooms, the like of which none of them could have imagined. The gentleman informed them that everything in the large fridge was complimentary. Room service was offered as a token of gratitude from the Myanmar authorities who had instructed the hotel staff to make their stay as comfortable as possible. They were to be treated with the same calibre of attention as any visiting VIP.

There were festivals galore in the city. Along the river banks were signs that festivals were either being prepared for or winding down. Their courier told them that the Ceremony of the Meng Tuu-Kyi rubies would be the most celebrated of all the festivals. They would be considered saviours after centuries of waiting and would feature in Myanmar history forever. Tourism brochures would be rewritten to include the celebrations of the return of the Meng Tuu-Kyi rubies. Although they longed to sink into the warm waters of the bathing facilities and pamper themselves with the potions provided in their bathrooms, they were loving this undivided attention.

'This is what it must be like for royalty and celebrities', they each thought. They had an amazing time. The hotel facilities were second to none. Everything they could possibly dream of was there. They were given the services of an interpreter, a travel courier, escorts and bodyguards. They enjoyed tasting cuisine completely alien to them. The unadulterated luxury in their hotel suites was beyond compare. They were measured for the robes they would wear for the ceremony. The ritual would predominantly feature Fiona and Carrie, but the boys would also play a small part.

The day of the ceremony dawned. A beautiful sunny morning and an entourage of bodies appeared in both hotel rooms, and escorted each of them to their preparation lounge. When they emerged they were unrecognisable. They wore long exquisite robes. Stage make-up had been applied to enhance their features for distant onlookers. The girls wore wigs in the fashion of the ancient Burmese people, and one could be forgiven for believing they were natives. Their carriage arrived to take them to Mya Palace. They had been briefed on what they must do. The performance at the Museum had prepared Fiona and

Carrie well for their role in the ceremony and had been the reason it had been conducted. The whole ceremonial ritual was a resounding success. They were constantly flanked by countless professionals, who showed great expertise in suggestion and example and the girls carried out their role as though they were born for it. The cheers from the estimated three hundred thousand strong crowd in and around the palace were deafening. They all loved every minute of the attention they attracted. Fiona placed the rubies exactly as instructed at the museum, only this time they were exaggerated fake ones for the purposes of show. The real ones were secure in the museum and would remain there forever. This festival of the return of the Meng Tuu-Kyi rubies would become an annual event. Carrie and Fiona would not be expected to perform every year, but were invited to attend the ceremony for the rest of their natural lives as guests of the Myanmar authorities. Their descendants too, would be considered part of the new Myanmar culture. Carrie just couldn't get over the whole thing. All her life she had struggled to put a meal on the table for her family. Nothing had come easy for them. Yet here she was, in a fabulous foreign country, with her husband and lifelong friend enjoying luxury beyond imagination, with the promise of a repeated trip every single year for the rest of her life, and for the lives of her offspring and their descendants. What opportunities could that induce for her family? She was sipping some champagne with one hand, and holding Mel's hand when their courier indicated they had one more task. The men were asked to remain seated and the girls

321

were escorted over to a podium in front of a massive archway. The archway was decorated in flowers and beneath the arch was a human arch of small children dressed in white gowns. They each carried something. The two children flanking the outside of the arch brought two large baskets and placed them either side of Fiona and Carrie. The narrator was explaining to the crowds that the ancient Meng Tuu-Kyi rubies had now been returned to their final resting place. New rubies had been mined and one by one each child filed past and dropped a red stone into their baskets. Each ruby represented a token of gratitude from each of the provinces of ancient Burma. The two girls tried to suppress the threatening flow of tears as the full recognition of the event struck them. Their smiles reflected the joy of their audience and their elation was manifested in their persona. They played their part exquisitely. Alan and Mel swallowed hard as they watched the strange festivities. Their wives were being paid the highest honour. Collected upon the rays of sunshine, the ancients bestowed their gestures of sincerity, overjoyed that the precious Meng Tuu-Kyi rubies were home at last.

Four people had been through so much to ensure the safe return of the land's most prized treasure. The crowd were cheering so loud it drowned out the sound when Fiona and Carrie could suppress their cries no longer. The fulfilment of a prophecy made centuries before a peace-loving King died trying to preserve prosperity for his people. The legend that had emerged foretold of peace, tranquillity and hope. Fiona and her faithful friend would be inscribed in the history books forever. The gratitude of the people offered them a life of happiness and contentment.

Their couriers indicated they should pick up the baskets containing the rubies and hold them in front of them. Each child now came forward with a lotus flower and placed it on top of the rubies. The narrator continued.

"The lotus flower is considered one of the most ancient and deepest symbols of our planet and is said to symbolise the purity of the heart and the mind and to represent long life, health, honour, enlightenment and good luck."

Experiencing total euphoria the girls were led back to their changing spaces. The men were led to greet them, and one of the couriers produced a bottle of vintage champagne and some glasses. They rested on the luxurious sofas and sipped the sparkling intoxicating liquid.

The festival was set to go on for a further four days. Fiona and Carrie were not expected to stay. They had completed their mission and were free to go. They removed their robes and laid them across the table, re-dressed and waited for their next instruction. They gasped when Monsieur Boesflug came striding across to them. Carrie couldn't help herself and ran to him, throwing her arms around his neck and hugging him. He surprised himself and hugged her back. Fiona hugged him and both men shook his hand vigorously. The baskets were lying beside them on the sofas, the lotus flowers still lying across the rubies. Monsieur Boesflug gently moved aside the flowers, to enable him to see the contents of the basket.

"You did well, my friends. You were amazing. This day will be remembered forever. Your good fortune does not end here. You are free to take your precious stones to any jeweller of your choice for a valuation. News of this calibre will only serve to increase the value of the gemstones. By the time you reach home, their price will have doubled. We have a jeweller in the hotel who will create masterpieces for you if you so wish. You and your descendants will be given the freedom of Myanmar. There are many lost and ancient cities of old Burma. Your names will be translated into our language and one of the cities will be renamed in your honour. Upon the site of your choice, there is to be built a new hotel, representing new blood from old, good emerging from evil. There will be a penthouse suite of rooms for your exclusive use when you visit Myanmar. We would be highly honoured if you and your families would consider relocation."

Overwhelmed with this latest news, one question sat unspoken on their lips. Why was Monsieur Boesflug suddenly talking as if Myanmar was his own land? Carrie decided to ask him. She put it as tactfully as she could and he smiled and began to explain.

"My great great grandmother married a Burmese native. Though they lived in France the

Burmese influence remained strong. Centuries of war has moved people on. Wealth has been lost, some regained, some not. It was discovered that King Meng Tuu-Kyi was a direct ancestor. I inherited his love of rubies and believe my destiny was preordained. I became passionate about the ancient legend." He added, "And I waited for you!"

"So the King who owned the mines was an ancestor of yours?" exclaimed Fiona.

"Yes. One can never predict or escape one's destiny. And so, my dears we have arranged a special dinner in your honour tonight and we hope that you will also join us tomorrow on a tour of the Meng Tuu-Kyi mines."

They all nodded in silent agreement.

* * * * * *

The Wedding

A bright Saturday morning saw huge excitement in the Goodwin household, as they prepared for Lisa and Graham's wedding. The ceremony was to be held in the nearby village church and the bell-ringers were ready and waiting. They had been practising for a few weeks now and believed they were sound perfect. In stunning gold silk and taffeta dresses, with matching shoes and wraps were four bridesmaids. Their hair was secured in place with a small diamond tiara and they each carried a Dorothy bag studded with tiny diamonds. To complete their ensemble, they carried a simple bunch of cream roses and foliage wrapped with taffeta and silk bows. Mel looked handsome in his top hat and tails with diamond studded cufflinks. Carrie wore a full length skirt which hugged her size twelve body perfectly. A kick pleat at the hem moved gracefully when she walked. A bustier was decorated with three roses in the arch of her back and a designer jacket complemented the coffee and cream colours. A huge silk hat with a cream rose sat on top of her ringlets.

For Lisa it was her dream come true. The vintage open-topped 1930's tourer in cream and brown waited outside for her. She emerged from the main bedroom looking like a princess in her white fairytale wedding gown. She clutched the exquisitely embroidered eight foot train and trailing waterfall bouquet. The ceremony was beautiful, the readings poignant, the priest's sermon soul-searching and the bell ringing heavenly. The choir of schoolchildren sang like angels in perfect harmony. The huge displays of flowers were breathtaking. The smells of candle wax, incense, beeswax and perfume were intoxicating. The rustling of gowns was evocative of centuries gone by and the serenity of the bride instilled her parents with pride. When they were all poised for photographs outside the church, guests began to point at the wall opposite. Some were laughing; some were craning their necks to see what others were laughing at. All that could be seen was a chimney sweep's brush moving along on the other side of the wall. The 'brush' eventually emerged through a gateway, carried by the lucky chimney sweep hired by Mel and Carrie to add a touch of magic to the day. He came and stood beside the bride and groom, grinning from ear to ear. His face was camouflaged by fake soot and he carried the customary wooden gift. The sweep's face, although discoloured with thick sooty deposits seemed familiar. That was impossible. He'd been hired from a town a considerable distance away. The chimney sweep leaned towards Lisa pretending to peck her on the cheek and the snap was taken. All provided a day that would never be forgotten. Lisa and Graham were escorted to their car which would carry them through the countryside to the reception. Lisa was helped into the back of the car, looking stunning with the ruffles of her dress billowing up around her, creating a halo of taffeta and silk. She was handed a glass of pink champagne which she chinked with Graham's glass. The car photograph was taken and they were soon on their way, amidst shouts and cries and hoorays and confetti and tin cans trailing along behind them. When they had finished their drinks, they settled back into the comfortable seats and Graham took Lisa's hand. Their hands rested on her lap, and Graham felt the little wooden box.

"Hey Mrs Boswick, are we going to open the box?"

Lisa laughed, and took the smooth wooden lid off the top.

"Oh my goodness, this looks interesting. Wonder what it is?"

"I think, traditionally, they're little hand made wooden gifts", said Graham.

"I don't think this is wooden. It's wrapped in a kind of acetate."

Lisa carefully removed the acetate, and sparkling in the bright sunlight was the most beautiful ruby Lisa had ever seen in her life. The words "Oh, my God" escaped in a whisper from her lips and they both just stared.

"I wonder if the chimney sweep was Monsieur Boesflug?"

Graham was totally overcome and tightened his grip on Lisa's hand.

"What a fantastic day!", was all he could say.

The bride and groom were to spend a few days in New York, and would then fly out to the Maldives, which had been their chosen honeymoon venue. A letter had arrived a couple of weeks earlier, to say that the hotel in Myanmar was complete and a suite of rooms was ready for occupation. Lisa and Graham had been screaming with excitement and of course, as Lisa had said, it would be rude not to accept. Unprecedented pampering would be bestowed upon the bride and groom. Well, that's what honeymoons were for!

Mel and Carrie took their rubies to a jeweller recommended by Monsieur Boesflug. Their collection netted five million pounds. They would never struggle to find another meal. Carrie would never wonder if she could afford steak instead of mince and all they'd ever dreamed of would be theirs. Their new house was perfect. Carrie cried when she saw it. They had a garden with trees and flowers and robins, and Megan had enough bones to bury forever.

* * * * * * *

www.ingramcontent.com/pod-product-compliance
Lightning Source LLC
Chambersburg PA
CBHW061326170626
46817CB00001B/337